FINALLY HOME

GRAND SLAM LOVE
BOOK 1

HOLLY CRAWFORD

THE GRAND SLAM LOVE SERIES

SEATTLE, WA | CHARLESTON, SC

CONTENTS

Content Warnings	ix
Playlist	xi
Dedication	xiii
Prologue	1
Prologue Cont.	15
1. Wren	19
2. Wren	29
3. Rhodes	38
4. Wren	47
5. Rhodes	59
6. Wren	67
7. Rhodes	71
8. Wren	77
9. Rhodes	84
10. Wren	89
11. Rhodes	96
12. Wren	106
Rhodes	111
13. Wren	113
14. Rhodes	119
15. Wren	124
16. Rhodes	135
17. Wren	142
18. Rhodes	148
19. Wren	156
20. Rhodes	165
21. Rhodes	172
22. Wren	179
23. Rhodes	184
24. Wren	188

25. Rhodes	194
26. Wren	201
27. Wren	207
28. Rhodes	216
29. Wren	223
30. Wren	229
31. Rhodes	235
32. Wren	241
33. Wren	247
34. Rhodes	253
35. Wren	262
36. Wren	271
37. Wren	277
38. Rhodes	286
39. Rhodes	296
Epilogue	304
Epilogue Cont.	307
Acknowledgments	311
Character Guide	313
About the Author	315

Copyright © 2024 by Holly Crawford

All rights reserved.

No part of this book may be reproduced in any form or by any electronic or mechanical means, including information storage and retrieval systems, without written permission from the author, except for the use of brief quotations in a book review.

This novel is entirely a work of fiction. The names, characters and incidents portrayed in it are the work of the author's imagination. Any resemblance to actual persons, living or dead, events or localities is entirely coincidental. First edition.

Edited by Two Girls, One Book

Cover by Chelsea Kemp

Chapter Art by Disturbed Valkyrie Designs

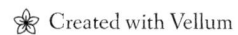

❦ Created with Vellum

CONTENT WARNINGS

Content warnings include but are not limited to:

Domestic violence (off page)
Cheating (NOT between the main characters)
Revenge porn
Mentions of child abandonment
Mentions of drug use and rehab

This isn't a dark book by any means, but there are some darker themes discussed. Your mental health means more than a story so if one or more of these is a trigger for you, read with caution.

PLAYLIST

"Shivers" by Ed Sheeran
"Somebody To You" by The Vamps, Demi Lovato
"Speak Now" by Taylor Swift (Taylor's Version)
"Crazier Best Friend" by Andi
"Love Letter" by Knox
"happier than ever" by Loveless
"Still into You" by Paramore
"Power Over Me" by Dermot Kennedy
"Take Me to Church" by Hozier
"Put You Through Me" by Arrows in Action
"Sparks Fly" by Taylor Swift
"break my heart" by Matt Hansen
"Bucket List" by Mitchell Tenpenny
"I GUESS I'M IN LOVE" by Clinton Kane
"Finally Home" by Alex Roe, Abby Ryder Fortson

DEDICATION

For every person that made 18 memorable,
this one's for you.

PROLOGUE

Rhodes
Freshman Year - Memorial Stadium

I'M SO DAMNED LATE.

I sprint down the tunnel inside the stadium and check my watch again. If I haul ass, I can make it in the next two minutes and avoid getting reamed out by Coach later when he finds out I was late on *day one*.

I'm honestly not sure why he has such a stick up his ass about his players being on time to orientation when we've already been living on campus for three weeks for training camp, but I'm not about to piss off the guy who controls my life for the next four years—less, if I manage to get drafted my junior year.

I manage to sneak past the door guard and up the stands right as the dean calls attention to himself and let out a sigh of relief as I drop into a random seat. While I pull deep breaths of the hot South Carolina air into my lungs, I hear a quiet giggle next to me. It's the kind of laugh that you wouldn't mind hearing all the time, soft and musical.

Letting a cocky smirk slip onto my face, I turn in my seat only to be blinded by what must be an actual angel-come-to-earth. This girl is *stunning*.

The angel in question has incredible ocean-blue eyes that I don't think I've ever seen on a person in real life before. They're the same color as the water in all those travel shows Mom likes to watch when Dad's away for work. She has an adorable little nose and short blonde hair that looks so soft my fingers actually twitch with the need to touch it.

My gaze leaves her face and briefly runs over her toned body clad in a cute yellow tank—thing—with buttons on it that expose smooth shoulders, and light-blue jean shorts. She's sitting, so it's hard to tell how tall she is, but her long, tan legs look like they go on for miles.

She's a freaking goddess.

The realization that I've been acting like a total perv hits me, so I quickly pick my jaw off the floor and snap my eyes up to hers, seeing amusement there. She bites her plump bottom lip, and *God* I wish I was the one biting it instead.

Her nose crinkles as she smiles at me, and she darts a quick glance to the podium. Seemingly satisfied she won't get in trouble; she holds out her hand to shake.

"Hi." She has a slight twang to her words. Her eyes glitter, a wide grin showcasing perfect white teeth. "My name's Wren. Did you get lost on the way here? I did, too. I swear, my daddy always says I couldn't find my way out of a wet paper bag in the midday sun," she rambles, still holding her hand out, and it might be the cutest thing I've ever heard.

I take her hand and suck in a breath at the spark that zings up my arm, making the hairs on the back of my neck stand on end. Wren jolts slightly, and I'd like to think she felt it too, whatever *it* was.

"My name's Rhodes. And unfortunately, I don't have an excuse as good as getting lost. I'm just chronically late," I whisper with a grimace. People have been on my case about time management for pretty much my entire life. My parents gave up years ago, instead choosing to run on what they like to call "Rhodes Standard Time," or RST for short. God, I miss them so much already.

Wren squeezes my hand with a soft look that immediately wipes away the sadness that was threatening to take over. "Well, Rhodes. It's nice to meet you. And don't feel bad about bein' late. You were actually right on time. Sorry about all the chatter." Her eyebrows knit together. "I've been told I talk a lot when I'm nervous, and you would think practically growing up on this campus would make things easier, but it really doesn't."

My curiosity is at an all-time high, but it's my turn to smile reassuringly at her. "I'm assuming you grew up local then, if you spent a lot of time on campus." I trail off with the hope she'll share more.

Her face flushes pink as she nods, which brings my attention to the freckles on her cheeks and nose that I didn't notice earlier.

"I did." Her voice twangs again on 'did', making it sound kind of like 'dee-id.' I roll my lips to hold back the chuckle that threatens to escape.

She's so goddamn cute.

With a discreet glance around us, she looks back at me and leans in, whispering, "I know we just met, but can you keep a secret?"

My heart races as I realize this goddess is choosing to trust *me*, a near perfect stranger, with something important to her. I hold out my pinky and give her a serious face. "I promise, Wren, you can trust me with anything. I'm a vault." I use my other hand to mime zipping my lips, locking them, and throwing away the key.

She giggles and rolls her eyes but still takes my pinky, holding it with hers rather than letting it go right away. "Okay, well," she whispers again, "my dad is a professor here on campus. So, I haven't told anybody my last name just in case they connect the dots. I spent most of my time here after..." Her face falls. "Well, anyway," she says with a grimace. "I spent pretty much my entire childhood on campus with Daddy. I was barely knee-high to a grasshopper when I would sit in on lectures and play hide-and-seek with whatever students would pay me any attention." Her voice is timid, and I hold back another chuckle at the borderline-mortified look on her face and the expression she used to describe herself.

Instead of answering right away, I lean forward and kiss my thumb, waggling my eyebrows as hers lift with shock or confusion, or maybe both. "My mom taught me you always seal a pinky promise like this. You kiss your thumbs and then press them together." She looks hesitant, so I press on. I know I'm laying it on thick, but I honestly can't help it.

"Listen, we *bonded* here in seats..." I turn around, and one glance at the seat numbers has me beaming when I see what they are. "Ten and eleven. I mean, your seat is literally my lucky number! If that isn't fate, then I don't know what is. You and me, Wren? We're gonna be best friends for life after this pinky promise. I don't know about you, but I'm not about to mess with fate," I say casually, shrugging my shoulders like I'm not desperate to know this girl—to be in her presence as often as I can, even if it's just as her friend.

Her face reveals zero emotions as she gives me an assessing look. "I just have one question, *Rhodes*," she says seriously.

I'm a little anxious, but I refuse to show it, so I slap an easy grin on my face and raise an eyebrow at her. "Oh yeah, *Wren*? What's that?" I make sure to emphasize her name like she did mine.

Her face finally cracks as a quiet giggle slips free. "What's your middle name?"

I bark out a laugh and quickly force a cough to cover it up, glancing around to make sure nobody heard me. The last thing I need is coach to hear from another professor that I was fucking around in the middle of the dean's opening speech.

When I get my laughter under control, I lean in close to whisper in her ear, taking a deep inhale of her sweet apple-and-honey smell. "I'll do you one better, Little Bird. My full name is Rhodes Colter Gray. Now I wanna know yours."

"I'll tell you, but you can't make fun of me or tell anybody else, okay?" She actually looks anxious, and I feel an uncomfortable ache in my chest. I don't even know this girl, but the *need* to have her trust me is an incessant thrum under the surface of my skin.

I nod, hoping she can see how touched I am that she trusts me with whatever she has to say. "Of course, Wren. We pinky promised, remember? Best friends don't share each other's secrets, *especially* not full names."

She blushes bright as she bites her lip. "My full name is Wren Andromeda Reid," she whispers. "My dad is the astronomy professor here, and he's been obsessed with stars my whole life. I'm sure if you ever take his class, he'll tell y'all all about the story of Andromeda."

A sly look crosses my face, and she groans. "You're signed up for his class already, aren't you?"

"Every Tuesday and Thursday at 10 a.m," I say with a smirk that earns me an eye roll. Her lashes are so long they nearly touch her eyebrows when she does that.

"Well, I have good news for you then, Rho. You're stuck with me at least for the semester since I'm in that class too."

My chest expands with genuine happiness, and I feel like an overexcited puppy knowing we'll have a class together. "See what I mean about fate? You and me, blondie. We're destined to be best friends forever. And now I get a cute study buddy too. So, what do you say? Friends?" I ask with a tap of my thumb to the back of her hand since we're still holding pinkies.

Her smile nearly blinds me as she kisses her own thumb and gently presses it against mine.

"You've got yourself a deal, Rhodes."

Three years later, draft day

My knees bounce as we stare at the TV, impatiently waiting for the announcer. Wren, her dad Archie, my parents, and Derrick, my old roommate and Wren's boyfriend, sit around us at Archie's house, as anxious for the news as we are. Wren is holding my hand while her idiot boyfriend plays on his phone.

Derrick and I are up for the draft today and that's the *only* reason he's here. To say I was pissed when he went after Wren late last year is an understatement. True to our pact, she and I have been best friends since the first day we met three years ago, and unfortunately, I want her even more now than I did back then. She's everything to me, but she's only ever seen me as a friend, and as much as that sucks, I'd rather have her as a friend than nothing at all.

What makes it even worse is that I can't seem to hold an attraction for anyone else. I've been on plenty of dates and kissed girls and guys both but never felt so much as a spark. And I've sure as hell never felt anything even close to what I feel any time I'm around Wren. Being in sports doesn't make it easy either. I have to pretend I'm sexually active just so the guys on the team stay off my ass about finding a hot girl to hook up with at every party.

Google eventually led me to a bunch of forums, and I feel pretty comfortable admitting I'm demisexual, which basically means I only feel sexual attraction if I've formed a close emotional bond with someone. The only people I'm comfortable telling are Wren and my parents, but for obvious reasons I can't tell Wren that I'm literally only attracted to her.

I'm not ready to blow up our friendship with that bomb, so I sit back and watch the girl of my dreams fawn over my sleazy ex-roommate, knowing I'll likely never have a chance to be with her.

She's been dating Derrick for more than six months, but the other night I overheard him talk about how many girls he's going to have 'throwing themselves at him pussy first' when he's drafted, and how Wren is just a way to fill the time during his last year here. I almost beat the shit out of him right then, but we were at a party, and I didn't want him or anyone else to spin it so that I'd look guilty. I plan to tell her tonight, hopefully *after* we find out Douchey D is getting drafted to a West Coast team.

"And for the second pick of the 2018 MLB Draft, the Charleston Raptors select... Rhodes Gray of Ridgeview University!"

"Holy shit," I murmur as my mom screams and the dads hug each other.

Wren wraps me a tight embrace, whispering that she's proud and happy I'll be close to home. I squeeze her back even tighter, fighting the happy tears that try to spill over.

When she pulls back, she's crying, too, before my mom pulls us both into a hard hug.

"Dominic!" my mom, Kaci, shouts. "Call the realtor and put in the offer. If our baby is going to live in Charleston, so are we!"

I pull back, gaping at her even as Archie and my dad grin knowingly at each other before Dad leaves the room, typing on his phone.

"I'm sorry, you're *what*?" I ask incredulously.

She and Wren have equally bright looks on their faces as they hold hands and stare at me. Their bond is one of my favorite things to watch. Mom took Wren in and treated her like her own daughter, and I know how much it means to them to have that kind of relationship in their lives. "You heard me. You think I won't be in the stands cheering at every single one of your games, Rhodes Gray? Your dad and I have been looking at places for months all over the country until we started hearing rumors Charleston was eager to pick you up."

There's no holding back the tears now as I throw myself at my mom like a little boy. I haven't admitted it to anybody but Wren, but the thought of being alone in a new city is scary as hell, not to mention how much I've missed my parents the last three years at university. I saw them on breaks and holidays, sure, but they stayed in my childhood home in Oregon after I moved to South Carolina.

"Are you fucking *kidding* me?" Derrick shouts, startling us all.

I pull back from my mom with a discreet wipe of my eyes, and I glance up to find Derrick looks furious. He's glaring at the screen like he wants to beat it with his ridiculously expensive bat. If smoke could come out of a person's ears, it would be happening right now.

Wren turns back to the TV with wide eyes, whispering, "Oh, no."

When I turn to see what the issue is, I get a sick sense of satisfaction when I realize that Derrick wasn't drafted today, which means he has to wait another year and enter the 2019 draft as a free agent unless somebody fucks up and he gets picked up to fill out a roster.

Which also means he'll be alone with Wren for an entire year...and I'll be two hours away.

Shit.

Wren is on her feet trying to console him, but he shoves her off and storms out of the house, muttering under his breath. We're not quite twenty-one but based on his attitude I have no doubt he'll be hungover in a frat basement come morning.

Watching my girl deflate as Derrick leaves has me seeing red, but as I hop up to chase him, my mom wraps a hand around my wrist and tugs sharply. When I look up at her, she shakes her head and tilts it toward Wren.

Wren's slumped on the couch with the most pitiful

look on her face, her watery eyes trained on the front door. One of the reasons I love her so much is because she has a huge fucking heart and wants everybody around her to be happy, but it's also one of the things that annoys me most. Her mom left when she was just a baby, so now she feels a compulsion to make sure the people she loves don't leave, too.

I've encouraged her to see a therapist several times but none of those times ended well for me, so I stopped trying. I can't make decisions for her as much as I want to.

Even though it's frustrating that she doesn't want to see a professional, I can't help the twitch to my lips as I think about the last time I tried. Wren was so mad at me she didn't speak to me for a week, but because it was finals week and we were both stressed out, she still came over every night to hang out and study. *In complete silence.*

Dropping down next to her, I pull her into my arms and breathe out a sigh of relief when she melts against my chest just like she always does. I bury my face in her hair and suck in a deep inhale of her apple shampoo. Hearing her quiet sniffles breaks my heart, so I drop a kiss to the top of her head and run my hand along her back soothingly.

"He'll be okay, Starling. He's upset he wasn't drafted right now, but he has another shot next year," I whisper around the lump in my throat. Comforting her over another guy has always made me feel sick, but I'd do anything to take away her pain.

With one last sigh, my tender-hearted best friend sits up and wipes her eyes with the back of her hand. "I know. And I know it's not my fault he's upset. It just sucks when he's angry, you know? I'm gonna end up on frat row later when he inevitably calls me to drag him out of some basement..." She trails off as our dads come back in the room.

Archie's brows furrow as he takes in Wren's tear-stained cheeks, and I see the banked anger in his eyes that match hers perfectly. He's never liked Derrick, especially after all the stories he's heard from my year of horror living with the guy. We shared a cramped twelve-by-twenty-foot room that he made sure was a disaster and always smelled like the inside of a gym bag.

Archie shoots a curious glance my way, silently asking if it was Derrick who made her cry again. I'm not surprised he figured it out since this is a regular occurrence. Giving him the slightest incline of my head, he rolls his eyes before putting on a big smile as he approaches the couch. He holds his hand out to me, and I take it, expecting a shake, but he shocks me when he pulls me in for a hug instead. "My family felt complete the first time I saw my baby girl, but I hope you know you've become as much a part of my family as she is, Rhodes. I'm so incredibly proud of you, and I'm here if you ever need anything. And I do mean *anything*. You hear me?" he squeezes me tightly once before letting go and levels me with a serious look.

A little confused, but a lot happy, I nod at him. "Thanks, Archie. I'll keep that in mind." Then I smirk. "And yes, you'll have season tickets with my parents."

He lets out a loud guffaw with his hand against his chest. "You got me, son. I've been angling for season tickets for three years. Letting you around my baby twenty-four-seven, feeding you, picking you up from cornfields when y'all were three sheets to the wind, cleaning barf out of the bed of my truck... multiple times." He gives me a side-eye, and I turn a sheepish grin to my mom, who's got her arms crossed and eyebrows raised. "None of that was because I love you like my own, or just out of the goodness of my heart. I just knew your sarcastic ass would be drafted and get me a decent seat with my friends."

With a wide grin, I clap my hand on his shoulder. "Well then, you're welcome, old man. Glad I could be of service."

His comment about my sarcasm is completely true, and I have zero shame about it until Mom smacks me upside the head. "Ouch," I whine, rubbing my head. "Starling, Mom hit me!"

Wren gets up and moves to stand by my mom, offering her a high five. "Good goin', Mama K." She snickers, turns to me, and cocks her hip. The stance steals my focus as I try not to drool over her like a lovesick weirdo. "Roly-Coly-Oly," she sing-songs, her eyes lighting up when she says the ridiculous nickname she gave me three years ago.

I mash my lips together to hide my amusement and give her an annoyed look. "Yes, Dodo?" I switch to the bird's name that annoys her most, earning a cute glare.

"Be nice to your mama," she chides. I gasp in mock outrage. Rolling her eyes, she continues on what I'm sure is about to be a very southern soapbox. "You were bein' smart, and Mama K was just remindin' you to mind your manners and respect your elders."

Archie turns a playful glare at Wren for her 'elder' comment, but he can't hold it for more than a few seconds. The way he tells it, Wren has been his entire world since the day the stick showed two lines, but when her mom ran out on them when she was only a few months old, she became his sole reason for living. That girl has him wrapped around her little finger, and he doesn't even realize it.

Me too, Archie.

My dad comes up behind me and ruffles my hair, bringing a scowl to my face. "We should head out. Big man on campus over here has an important exam in the morning and a contract to review with our lawyer," he says, grinning widely at me.

I sigh and nod. I have to ace that exam in order to graduate early. Pulling Wren into my arms for one last hug, I kiss her on the cheek. "See you tomorrow for coffee, Starling?"

She nods and holds me tight. "I'm so incredibly proud of you, Rho. Don't forget about little old me now that you've made it big, okay?"

My chest aches. "Not in a million years, Wren. You'll always remind me where home is when my head gets too big."

Keeping my feelings from her is borderline painful, but now is definitely not the right time to let them out. Between Derrick's tantrum, the excitement of the draft, and me moving to Charleston soon, she's not ready to hear what I really feel.

But one day she'll finally know that she doesn't just remind me where home is.

She is my home.

Wren

Six months after the draft - wedding day

"Are you absolutely sure about this?" Rhodes asks dejectedly. "There's still time to run, Starling."

I roll my eyes and set down my mascara to look at him. "I'm sure, Rho. It was just a little fight. Besides, we're already living together across the country; it just makes sense."

A mix of anger and something I can't name crosses his face before he masks it. "*Just a little fight?* Wren, the night before your fucking *wedding* he went out with his buddies, cut all contact, and ignored you for hours. Then he has the audacity to show up this morning so hungover he had to stop outside the church and puke in the bushes."

I can feel my face getting hot as my eyes widen slightly, and Rhodes nods his head. Unfortunately, he's able to read me as well as he always has, so he can see the embarrassment I wish I could hide.

Rhodes sighs and places a warm hand on my shoulder. "His best man is doing what he can to clean him up right now, but he made a damned fool out of himself in front of an impressive number of guests."

This isn't the first time Derrick has gotten too drunk and thrown up somewhere wildly inappropriate, but I thought he'd at least rein it in on our wedding day.

Six months ago, on the night of the draft, I had to pick him up from somebody's basement at four in the morning because he was so drunk he couldn't walk, and then he proceeded to puke all over the hood of my car, the floor mat, *and* in his bed. He proposed less than a month later, and if I'm completely honest with myself, I think I only said yes because he asked.

Now here we are on what should be the best day of our lives, and I don't even know if he'll make it through the ceremony without passing out. I keep my gaze down as I talk to Rhodes. "He's just nervous, Roly-Coly-Oly. Trust me to make my own decisions, please?"

He sighs and hugs me gently. "I know, Starling, and I do. I just love you, and I want what's best for you. I've never thought Derrick was that. And now you're going to be across the country in Seattle with him? I'm just anxious."

My heart races at his touch, but I shove the feeling down. Rhodes Gray is gorgeous. Standing ridiculously tall at six foot four, he has gorgeous hazel eyes and wavy brown hair that I know is as soft as it looks. I had a major crush on him when we first met, but then he mentioned wanting us to be friends and it stuck. Rho and I have spent every holiday, vacation, and spare minute together since the day we met. I've gone to every game, every event, everything with him, and living away from him is going to be hell.

"I'm anxious too, Rhodes. I'll miss you so dang much, but this job is too incredible to pass up. You know that," I say gently.

Seattle's professional baseball team, the Sirens, offered me a full-time position in their public relations department last week, so Derrick and I will be moving after graduation next month. He was also picked up by the Sirens in December to fill out their roster.

"Alright, well, you ready then?" he asks. "It's just about time."

Rhodes is my Man of Honor to Derrick's irritation,

but he's my best friend in the entire world, and it's a very small ceremony, so I put my foot down and told him it was that, or I wouldn't be getting married.

I take a deep breath and send up a prayer I don't pull a Derrick and throw up all over my dress. Slipping my arm in his, I silently count to three. "Okay, let's go."

CHAPTER 1
WREN

Present day

THE VIDEO on my screen has been playing on a loop for several minutes as Ella and I look on in horror. There, in high definition, is Derrick.

Normally, that wouldn't be anything out of the ordinary since tips and media coverage of the players are emailed to me every day. Kind of comes with the territory when you're the Director of Public Relations for Seattle's major league baseball team. The problem is the bench third baseman, who also happens to be my husband of four years, is on my monitor with his dick in some woman's mouth in an alley. And that woman is *not me*.

"*Wow*," I whisper, my hands shaking where they rest on my keyboard. "It's already been picked up by a couple of news outlets *and* Bleacher Report."

My words snap my coworker and friend out of her stunned trance, and she slams my laptop closed. "*Fuck him*," Ella curses. "After all you've done for that selfish prick, he has the audacity to cheat on you with some damn cleat chaser in *public*?!" Her words are whisper-yelled, but they're still loud enough to bring our boss out of his large, glass-walled office.

Jeremy Cross is the team's manager, and an absolute beast of a man. He stands at over six and a half feet tall and nearly three hundred pounds, which means he looks more like a linebacker than one of the best pitchers in the country. He played for Seattle professionally for a long time before he finally retired and took the job as head coach, then eventually he was hired on as the general manager.

He's perpetually calm and has never had a single negative word to say about anyone since I was hired four years ago, save the few asshole players who got traded after their first season for causing problems. And it's because of his normally even keel that I'm so startled when he storms into my office looking madder than a raccoon the day after trash pickup. He stops less than six inches from me and lifts his giant arms to envelop me in a bear hug.

"Want me to kill him?" His gruff question startles a laugh out of me that quickly devolves into a choked sniffle.

I return the hug and lean my head against his chest, shaking it back and forth. "What am I gonna do, Jer? I can't face him right now. And what about my job? God, I can't come to work every day and be the team joke," I whine miserably, my words nearly inaudible because my mouth is blocked by Jeremy's large chest.

He strokes my hair gently, shushing me. "None of that now, Cupcake. You know as well as I do that nearly every single player on this team will take your side. As for your job, we'll figure it out. You're so much more valuable to this organization than that jackass.".

I smile at the nickname. On my very first day of work, I wanted to make a good impression, so I stayed up way too late baking cupcakes for everyone in the office. I was so intimidated when my larger-than-life new boss grunted and left the room without a word, only to catch him sneaking *six of them* back to his office an hour later. He swore me to secrecy and ever since then he's called me Cupcake.

I feel a hand on my shoulder and turn teary eyes to my only real girlfriend.

Ella smiles at me sadly. "Why don't you go home for a while?" I shake my head, but she powers on. "No, I'm serious here, Wren. You've never taken a vacation in four years, *and* we're in pre-season so you can work remotely. Let's go to your apartment, pack your shit, and get you on the team's jet to Charleston."

Jeremy is nodding his head when I peek up at him through blurry eyes. "Ella is right, Cupcake. You have my blessing to work remotely for as long as you'd like *after* you take four weeks paid vacation to recuperate and see your family. My only stipulation is that you call my lawyer the second you get on that plane and file for divorce. You *are* gonna divorce the bastard, right?"

His single raised eyebrow makes me giggle, and I agree before he even finishes his speech. "Of course, I am. Thank God he made me sign a prenup and let me keep my name."

That had been a huge point of contention between us in the month before our wedding because I naïvely thought people who were in love didn't need a prenup. I thank every deity I can that he forced the issue and insisted on separate bank accounts so I wouldn't "take advantage of his salary."

Wanting to keep my last name was another issue for him. I had already started my career using my maiden name, and in a field dominated by men, I didn't want to ride in on the coattails of my new husband's status as a player. Keeping my name ensured my independence, especially with this being my first job out of college. I didn't want to be known only as 'Derrick Monroe's wife'.

Looking back, I can see the red flags, but I was young and in love and desperate to be wanted. I ignored everyone who told me marrying Derrick was a bad idea, including Rhodes.

Butterflies take flight in my stomach as I smile thinking of Rhodes. I haven't seen him in person in two years, so even though we text often, I still miss him like crazy.

Jeremy smirks and finally releases me from the cage of his arms. "Good thing, indeed, since you make more than he does," he says with a wink. He grabs his cell and starts arranging my transportation. He's just getting off the phone with his lawyer a few minutes later when three hulking figures burst through my office door.

When I joined the Siren team four years ago, something I didn't realize was that my only-child status would literally be changed overnight. Nearly all the guys adopted me as their little sister and have treated me that way ever since. The most overbearing members of the team are currently breathing like they sprinted here from the suburbs. These guys are my closest friends in the world outside of Rhodes, and we literally don't go more than a few hours without talking in our group chat.

I raise my brows and put my hands on my hips. "Should y'all be so breathless from running up a single flight of stairs? What the hell do you do during the off-season that you're this out of shape?"

They flip me off simultaneously, making me do what they like to call my "sunshine laugh" since, according to them, it lights up whatever room I'm in. I think it's stupid, but I stopped arguing with them about it years ago.

Jamison Reed, starting pitcher for the Sirens, grabs my shoulders and bends down so he's level with my face. "Did you see it?" he asks gently.

My face falls as the events from this morning hit me again full force. Tears well in my eyes, and Jamie looks panicked before he pulls me into his arms, nearly smothering me.

"Group hug!" comes a voice from behind us. Suddenly, two more sets of arms surround me tightly, and the tears fall faster down my cheeks, soaking Jamie's shirt even as a hiccuped giggle escapes.

"It'll be okay, Baby Reid." The booming voice belongs to our catcher, Asher Linwood.

"Yeah," Wes says, ruffling my hair. "We never liked the bastard anyway. You deserve so much better."

Wesley Black is our resident golden boy shortstop and arguably the closest friend I've had since I graduated college. He knows every detail of my life and never hesitates to tell me what I need to hear, even if I don't necessarily *want* to hear it.

I scoff at the Baby Reid comment. "Y'all do know I'm not actually related to Jamie, right?" My words are muffled by the three incredibly muscular chests currently restricting my air.

I pull back and catch Jamie rolling his blue eyes, which are eerily similar to mine. "My sweet, naïve little Wren, we have the same hair, eye, *and* skin color, and we share the same birthday one year apart. I'm telling you, we're long-lost siblings," he says seriously. "After all, I'm adopted so it's definitely possible."

The day I started with the team is the day I met Jamison, and it took him one minute to decide we must be long-lost family and five minutes to decide we were *actually* long-lost siblings. He's been bugging me for a DNA test for years, but I'm pretty sure if I had a brother I would know about it.

Rolling my eyes, I extricate myself from the idiot sandwich. "Okay but you're a year younger than me, so *me* being Baby Reid doesn't even make sense."

Jamie ruffles my hair with a sly grin. "It's because you're cute and shorter than all of us."

I smack his hand away with a scowl. "Five foot eight is *not* short. But you can ask my dad if he knows about our secret sibling status when you come visit me in South Carolina in two weeks. But I think you forget that even though our last names *sound* the same, they're spelled differently."

Their eyes widen at my words.

"Wren, you're leaving?" Wes looks at me like somebody crushed his ice cream cone, and that, combined with his pitiful tone, makes my eyes water *again* knowing I have an incredible support system here. I haven't cried this much since I was a kid and broke my arm learning to ride a bike.

I rush forward and hug him tight. "It's not forever,

Wes. I just need some time away to get my head on straight and get things rolling with a divorce." My voice breaks on the last word. "Wow...I'll be divorced at twenty-five. That sucks."

I let out a self-deprecating chuckle and finally pull back, wipe my eyes, and scoot past the guys to grab everything I need off my desk.

"We're coming with you to pack," Asher says. He's, by far, the most reserved of the group, but it hasn't stopped him from defending me over the years when players, agents, or managers tried to push me around because of my age and gender.

A quick glance at the other two and Jeremy tells me I don't have a choice, so I nod in resignation. "Alright, let's go then."

"Wren, babe, can you just sit down so we can talk about this?" Derrick shouts from the living room.

He's currently being held back by my pissed off entourage while I pack everything I own in this apartment, which sadly isn't much.

More muffled shouts come from down the hall, and I step out of the closet when I hear a yelp. "Why the fuck did you punch me, asshole?" Derrick growls. "You're really gonna pick some dramatic bitch over me?"

Another yelp—this one followed by a low groan and an audible gag that sends a shiver of disgust down my spine. I have a severe fear of vomiting so even hearing somebody gag makes me nauseous.

"If you ever talk about Wren like that again, I'll make sure you're never able to procreate, you lying piece of shit. You cheated on the sweetest person in the entire world and have the fucking *nerve* to call her a bitch? You're a pathetic excuse for a husband, and we're all glad she's getting away from your wandering dick," says Asher's deadly calm voice.

My jaw drops as my eyes burn.

I refuse to cry in front of Derrick, but that was probably the most Ash has ever said at once in front of other people.

Tossing the last of my clothes in my suitcases, I zip them and marvel at the fact that the last four years of my life fits into two large suitcases and a carry-on. Wes and Jamie saunter in, which lets me know Asher and Jeremy stayed back to keep an eye on my soon-to-be ex so I can get out without a fight.

Wesley's eyes widen like saucers when he takes in my bags. "That's it?" he chokes out. "Baby Reid, you've lived here for four years and that's really all you're taking? We have plenty of time if you need to grab the rest of your stuff."

My cheeks heat as I stare at the floor. "No," I murmur. "This is all I have. Derrick never wanted me to ruin the clean lines of his apartment with my 'stupid decorations and useless pictures of people we don't even see.'" My fingers make air quotes around the words I heard constantly the first two years of our marriage. After a particularly bad fight, I stopped trying to make this apartment feel like mine.

Fingers on my chin tilt my face up to meet Jamie's ocean eyes. "I'm so sorry we weren't able to help you before now." His voice is gruff. "If we had known…"

"J, no. He doesn't beat me or anything..." I pause, the words taste like ash on my tongue. Because he while he's never physically hurt me, he could get really loud and mean when he was especially drunk or angry. "I wasn't unsafe. I'm fine. The important thing is I'm out now, and I finally get to see my family again."

"You mean you get to see *Rhodes* again," Wes smirks, waggling his eyebrows at me.

I roll my eyes with a small smile. "Yes, Rhodes will be there too."

He gets serious then, gripping my biceps gently in his calloused hands. "You have to stay in contact with us, okay? Don't go back home and forget about your family in Seattle, Wren. I don't want to lose the closest thing to a sister I've ever had." He trails off in a whisper as his eyes flood with tears.

I've never seen Wesley cry before.

I throw my arms around him in a panic. "Wes, I would *never*. I promise. Y'all are my family too, and I have space in my life and heart for all of you. Rhodes is my best friend but *so are you*." Flicking my eyes over to Jamie, I grab his hand just as Asher walks in the room. "This goes for all of you. Y'all are irreplaceable in my life. The love and support you've shown me since the day I met each of you is priceless, and I will never take it for granted. Okay?"

They pull me into yet another group hug. "We love you, Wren. Even if you find your true love and decide to stay in hot-as-hell Charleston, you're still our Baby Reid, and you'll always have a place in Seattle as long as we're here."

I snort and shake my head at Asher. "You're just full

of words today, huh Ash? Better be careful or I'll start to expect full sentences from you all the time."

He smiles innocently as the other two chuckle and Jamie grabs my bags. "You ready to get out of here, Wren? The jet's prepared to take off as soon as you get there."

I take a deep breath and glance around the sterile-looking room one last time. "Yeah," I say with a sigh. "Let's go."

CHAPTER 2
WREN

THE RIDE to the airport is spent with the guys once again begging me not to forget them in the most dramatic ways possible while I try to get ahold of my dad. I'm on the verge of panic the third time I get his voicemail when he texts me that he's on his way to an astronomy conference and will call me when he lands.

The whole thing strikes me as odd, but I decide I'll interrogate him when he gets home...right after I tell him about Derrick.

With a groan, I drop my face into my hands and all the guys go quiet except Jeremy, who lowers his voice to a whisper as he talks into his earbud. "I feel so stupid." My voice is threaded with stress. "I knew something seemed off but honestly most of the last four years have been...not the greatest. I don't know where I went wrong."

"Hey!" Asher's firm voice surprises me as a hand rubs soothing circles on my back. He's sitting next to me in the middle row of Jeremy's large 3-row SUV. "You can't blame yourself for somebody else's bad decisions. Derrick has been a selfish asshole as long as we've known him, and you never deserved a second of it. He's lucky all he got today was a dick punch." He smirks as Jamie leans over the seat to hug me from behind and lets out a deep breath against my neck.

Jamie gets dizzy in cars, so I always encourage him to take the third row alone so he can stretch out. Turning my head, I take in his dilated pupils and slightly-green pallor. We're in bumper-to-bumper traffic in the middle of downtown Seattle, and even I'm a little queasy with all the quick stops and starts. The daily gridlock is one thing I absolutely won't miss about living here. It's bad on a regular day, but on game days? If I leave the stadium too early, it can take me two hours to go five miles.

"Jamie, do you need some meds?" He's weirdly embarrassed about his motion sickness and vision issues, which he developed after he was hit by a foul ball two years ago. He nods and I pull the anti-nausea tablets from my bag. "Under your tongue and sip some water slowly. Let me know if you need a bag," I whisper, kissing his clammy cheek.

His eyes and jaw are clenched shut, and he looks even more green, so I grab one of the barf bags I keep stocked in everybody's cars for this exact reason. Glancing in front of me to where Wes sits in the passenger seat, I point to the windows and mouth "roll them down" as I open the bag and hand it to Jamie. He snatches it from my hand and scoots closer to the open window.

"In the bag, J."

I barely get the words out before he's heaving into the bag. Grimacing slightly, I motion for Asher, who does *not* handle bodily fluids well, to roll down his own window and turn away. I climb over the back of the seat to sit next to Jamie so I can rub his back. I've gotten used to being the one to handle Jamie's episodes, so, even though I'm terrified of throwing up, I can breathe through my mouth and compartmentalize enough to take care of him.

We spend a good half hour still stuck in traffic and he finally gets the meds and some water down just as we pull into the airport. "See?" he rasps. "Only a big sister would take care of me as I puke in the back of a car. I can't wait to meet our dad."

I roll my eyes but take a few pills out of each bottle and put them in a baggie for him. "You're an idiot, but I can't wait for you to meet my dad either. Keep these on-hand, and when you fly be sure to bring the bottles I restocked in your bathroom last month, okay? If you need more, call me or the team doc."

His eyes are shiny and bloodshot when he wraps me up in a hug. Kissing the top of my head he says, "Blood or not, you're my sister in every way that counts, Wren. We love you, and we're here for anything you need."

Wes pops up in front of me like a demented jack in the box before I can respond. "Good lord, Wesley Black. You just took five years off my life," I say, with a hand over my racing heart. He smirks.

"I do love when you get all southern on us, Baby Reid. Your accent gets way more intense when you're angry or excited, and it's so fun." I roll my eyes at the thirtieth time hearing that name today. I'll never tell them, but I secretly love the nickname. I always wanted a sibling, and now it feels like I have three.

I'm tall and blonde with blue eyes the same color as my friend, and when I first moved here, everyone was stunned how much Jamie and I looked alike. Honestly, it is kind of weird that I was raised by a single dad and never met my mom, while he was raised by a single mom until she died, and he went into foster care.

Jeremy parks on the airstrip in front of the jet and puts his hand behind Asher's seat, turning around to look at us. "Alright, boys. Let's get our favorite girl off to warmer weather. We can visit in two weeks before the season starts back up, so no whining." I snort a laugh as we all climb out.

Wes grabs my suitcases while Ash snags my carry on, and they take off to load them onto the plane. Both ignore my protests as Wes races off, giggling like a little boy sneaking cookies before supper.

"Your dad's gonna pick you up at the airport when you land?" Jer asks in a gruff voice. I try to catch his eye, but he pointedly keeps his gaze away, and Jamie fights a smile next to me. We don't see the big guy get emotional very often, but when he does, it's always silent and as hidden as possible.

I don't really want to answer Jeremy's question because I know he won't like the answer. With Dad out of town and my plane not landing until late, I don't want to call anybody to come get me. I'd like to hold off the questions as long as I can, which means taking an Uber for the half-hour drive to Dad's house in Charleston.

"Daddy's out of town," I say quietly. "I'm just gonna catch an Uber from the airport."

Asher and Jeremy let out gruff sounds of displeasure.

"Not a chance in hell, Baby Reid." Wes's voice surprises me as he and Jamie speak at the same time before they point at each other and shout "*JINX!*"

Wesley rolls his eyes as he pulls me into a hug. "Be safe and call me when you land," he whispers in a choked voice. "I don't give a fuck how late it is. I can't go a month without talking to you so just...call me when you have time, okay? Or if you're sad or bored or need anything. You call me. And don't forget about us after you finally see your bestie again."

"You know I'll never forget you, Wesley Joseph Black," I say with a smirk. "We made the best friend pinky promise, remember? The only other people to have that honor are Jamie, Asher, and Rhodes. Y'all are stuck with me until we're old and gray."

"Miss Reid?" I'm startled by my favorite flight attendant, Amy, when she appears behind me. With a grimace, she mouths "I'm sorry."

I take one last glance at the guys before Jeremy gently pulls me to the side. "I ordered you a car service. They'll take you wherever you want to go after you land. He'll just need an address." He hugs me hard before pushing me gently toward the plane.

Asher smiles softly. "We'll see you in two weeks, Wren. Be safe and text when you can."

Nodding, I turn to follow Amy as tears burn the backs of my eyes. I can't even appreciate how stunning the interior of this plane is because there are so many thoughts running through my mind. It's like I have the weight of the world on my shoulders, and this is one of those times I wish I had a mom.

As soon as the cabin door shuts, I cry. The sad thing is, I'm more upset that I have to leave my friends than I am about Derrick cheating. I'm not sure when things got so messed up between us, but I now can admit that he wasn't good to me after we got married. When we first met, he was this larger-than-life, charming guy who showered me in affection.

He didn't even remember our anniversary last year.

There were a couple of good periods during our four-year relationship, like the first few months after we got together. And the days after he got drunk and made a fool out of himself at whatever bar or club I had to drag him out of between game days, he was sweeter than cherry pie. Those mornings, I woke up to coffee, flowers, and a new charm for my bracelet (the one I left back at the apartment).

One particular time sticks out in my mind, and I wonder how long he's been messing around on me.

One year earlier

"Night, babe," Derrick says as he slips into bed behind me. I groan, not happy to be woken up when I have a big meeting first thing in the morning. Cracking my eyes open, I see it's still pitch-black outside. When I check my clock, I find it's only two-thirty in the morning.

"Derrick, why the hell are you getting home so late when you have a game tomorrow?" As I roll over to face him, I see his bare back in the mirrored closet door and notice what look like scratch marks on his tan skin. "Are you okay? What happened to your back?"

I swear he had been nearly asleep, but at my words his eyes fly open and he scrambles into the bathroom, which floods our bedroom with bright light.

He strolls back out, rolling his eyes. "Those? I had a muscle scraping treatment done at the training facility yesterday. It always leaves those marks."

I raise an eyebrow at him. "Oh yeah? Because I was at the facility filming content all day and didn't see you. When did you have time to get muscle scraping done?" I put air quotes around the words because I know he's not being honest, but I can't figure out why.

"Will you mind your own goddamn business, Wren?"

he shouts angrily. "What I do for my career is none of your fucking concern, and I'm real tired of you tryin' to manage me all the time."

My mouth drops open in shock. "Derrick, I work eighty hours a week. When would I have time to manage you?" He's acting so weird, and my gut is screaming at me to dig deeper and get the truth out of him.

Before I can press further, he grabs his pillow and stomps out. "If you're done with the interrogation, I'll be in the guest room."

I cry myself back to sleep, wondering what he's hiding from me and how I can fix it.

The next morning, after de-puffing my tired eyes, the smell of coffee and something sweet hits me and my stomach growls on cue. I walk into the kitchen, suspicious when I see a small gift bag on the white marble counter. The bag has the logo from a local jeweler on the side and sits next to a large bouquet of roses. I lean in to politely smell them, grimacing after I'm rocked by a sudden sneeze.

"Hey, babe! You're finally up," Derrick kisses my cheek and hugs me from behind. "I'm sorry for how I acted last night. Practice ran late and some of the guys were harassing me about not making it off the bench again this year. I was upset and had a few drinks, but I know I shouldn't have taken it out on you. I got you a little something as a thank you for all you do for me and for us."

He hands me the bag with the same smile that drew me in more than three years ago. "Go on, open it."

I feel myself softening toward him already, and I wonder if I might have overreacted last night because I was tired and stressed about my meeting today. I open the gift slowly, pulling out a pretty silver bracelet. There are three smaller bags next to the bracelet, and I open them to find three small charms.

"One for each year we've been married. A rose, for your favorite flower. A ladybug, for your childhood nickname. And the letter D, for your favorite person in the world," he says with a smirk.

My smile is tight as he clasps the bracelet on my wrist, and I focus on my blurred reflection in the huge stainless-steel fridge in front of me so I don't snap or cry. "Thanks, Derrick. I love it."

"I also got your favorite pecan praline latte and some donuts from that shop on the corner. I have to run to the field for practice, but good luck at your meeting, babe. I'll see you later!" The second he walks out the door, I collapse onto the barstool.

There's a hollow pit in my stomach as I look at the bracelet and my drink. Maybe I would feel better about his apology if he hadn't gotten everything wrong. I'm allergic to pecans, and I hate roses because they make me sneeze. My childhood nickname was never Ladybug—Daddy always called me his Starshine. And the letter D is nice but unfortunately wrong. Derrick hasn't been my favorite person in a long time, if ever.

I left my favorite people in South Carolina.

Seven hours later, I walk up a paved driveway toward a white house taking a deep breath as I try to pull myself together. When I knock on the light-blue door, the familiar scent of lavender infiltrates my nose from the large pots on the porch, instantly settling my nerves. I've barely pulled my hand away when it swings open, and I'm enveloped into warm arms more familiar to me than my own mother's ever were.

"Mama Gray, can I stay here for a while?" I ask between sniffles.

Rhodes's mom looks at me with sympathy in her hazel eyes. "You never even have to ask, sweet girl. Welcome home."

CHAPTER 3
RHODES

I'M RUDELY awoken at the ass crack of dawn on my day off when my phone blares an annoyingly catchy Taylor Swift song. Groaning, I feel around my nightstand blindly for the offending device, swiping the screen to answer.

"You do know it's my day off, right?" I ask, my voice still thick with sleep.

"Oh, I know." My mom's chipper voice is even louder than usual on speaker. "I just thought you might like to know that a certain blonde beauty we've all been missing is sleeping in your old bedroom right now."

I shoot up straight and stare wide-eyed at the wall. "That's not funny, Mom."

I can *feel* her rolling her eyes at me. The woman has more personality than anybody I know. "I'm well aware, my dear son. But I'm telling the truth. Wren showed up here late last night in tears and asked if she could stay for a while. Naturally I put her in your room."

She hasn't even finished her sentence before I trip my way out of bed and rush to throw on the first set of clean clothes I can find. My mom cackles, but I can't find a single part of me that cares enough to stop. My girl is home, and something is wrong.

I stomp my way back to the bed to take my phone off the charger just as my mom says, "Grab her a coffee and see if you can find out what happened but do it *gently*. Dad and I need to head into the office, so we'll see you tonight." She hangs up.

I knew something was wrong when Wren never responded to my text yesterday morning. We may not talk as much anymore, but she *always* answers me. And now knowing she's here? Less than five minutes down the road? My stomach churns with anxiety.

Two minutes later, I'm in my SUV, heading to the coffee shop down the road. Wren is an absolute ray of sunshine ninety-nine percent of the time, but that other one percent is always in the morning before coffee.

After picking up her favorite iced chocolate dirty chai, I push every single speed limit on the way to my parents' house rather than enjoying the sights of downtown Charleston. I've lived here since being drafted more than four years ago and the incredible views of the water and colorful buildings never get old. Butterflies swarm in my gut, and my chest is so tight, I feel like I might lose my ability to breathe at any second. I haven't seen Wren in *two years,* and it's been killing me. I don't see my parents' cars, so I'm guessing they've already left.

I don't bother knocking when I arrive, instead going around back so I can slip in through the sliding door in the kitchen and up the back staircase. From there it's a short few feet to my old room. The door is slightly ajar, but when I knock lightly, there's no response. Checking my watch, I see it's only just after eight and grin. Wren is *not* a morning person, so this should be fun.

I open the door the rest of the way, and I swear my heart stops dead. There, on *my* queen-sized bed, under *my* blue sheets, is my dream girl. She's curled up tight on her side facing the door, and even in sleep, she's more gorgeous than I remembered.

Walking closer, I'm able to get my first good look at Wren in two years. Her mouth is parted slightly so her breaths come out as little snores, and I put my fist to my mouth to hold back a laugh. The early-morning sun shines brightly through the large double doors that lead to my second story terrace, highlighting dark circles under her eyes that definitely weren't there the last time we saw each other. She also looks a bit too thin to be healthy and worry spikes in my gut the longer I stare.

"I can feel your eyes on me. I promise I'm okay, Mama Gray," Wren says in a groggy voice, her eyes still firmly closed. Her voice scares the hell out of me, and I realize I have no idea how long I've been watching her sleep like a stalker.

I make my way to the side of the bed closest to the doors and set her drink down on the nightstand next to my favorite picture of us from college. It was right after one of the best games of my college career; she had hopped onto my back and kissed my cheek. Whoever took that deserves a raise because it's a perfect picture, and they caught me smiling at her like the lovesick bastard I was...*and still am.*

Chuckling, I push some of her messy hair out of her face. "I mean, I'm glad you're okay, but you've got the wrong Gray there, Starling."

She gasps, shooting up. "Roly-Coly-Oly!" In less than a second, she launches herself at me and then I have two arms full of a soft, sweet-smelling girl. Wren wraps her legs around my waist and my eyes widen as my heart thunders in my chest.

Do not get a fucking boner right now, dude.

"I missed you so much," she whispers into my neck. Her voice is raspy like it gets every time she cries, and then I feel tears wetting my shirt. I hug her tightly, one arm under her ass to hold her up and one hand running through her hair.

"I missed you too, pretty girl," I whisper back. She feels so damn good in my arms that I'm having a hard time concentrating, but her quiet sniffles bring my earlier worries to the forefront of my mind. "Don't get me wrong, I'm so fucking happy you're home, but why didn't you call me and let me know you were coming back? Is everything okay?"

She shakes her head against my chest and pulls back so her sleepy, bloodshot eyes meet mine. "You were right." Her voice is so quiet I almost don't hear her and confusion swirls in my brain. Panic and disappointment rapidly follow when she untangles her limbs from my body and drops down to stand in front of me.

I cup her cheeks and gently tilt her face up so I can see her stunning blue eyes. "Right about what, Wren?"

I've seen just about every look under the sun cross this girl's face over the years, but shame wasn't one of them until now. Her cheeks burn bright, and her eyes are downcast, making tears gather on her lashes again. "Derrick cheated on me, and somebody caught it on camera and emailed it to the PR account yesterday morning."

Fury burns fast and hot in my chest as a red haze clouds my vision. *"He fucking what?" I growl.* I never understood that word anytime I'd peek at one of Wren's romance books and see a line about the hero *growling*, but

I sure as hell understand it now. I feel fucking *feral* and the urge to go beat the shit out of that asshole for hurting this angel of a woman barrels down on me like a freight train.

She flinches, and my stomach drops all the way to the floors under our feet. "I'm sorry I raised my voice, Starling." Pulling her against me, I kiss her temple. "So, what exactly was emailed to the PR account?"

Her voice is shaky as she details the video she got and all the people who saw it. "Thankfully we were able to contain it so it hasn't hit the press yet, but Jeremy, my boss, encouraged me to take some time off and then work remotely while I file for divorce. I figured I would just stay with Daddy since I don't know how long I'll be in town."

My heart races with excitement when she mentions divorce, and I instantly feel like a selfish asshole for being happy, but *holy shit*. Wren is technically single now and living in Charleston for at least the next month while she takes some time off. "Stay with me," I blurt.

Wren's jaw drops. "Rhodes, I can't just move in with you. Won't that cramp your bachelor baseball player lifestyle?" Her tone is light, but there's a little crinkle between her eyebrows. She doesn't like whatever is running through her overactive mind right now.

I run a hand through my messy hair and fight to keep the blush from my cheeks. She doesn't need to know there's no *playing* that happens off the field, despite some of my teammates' best efforts since I joined the Raptors. It turns out I was right, and I am demisexual. I've been out so many times over the last few years, but any time I made it past a few dates and tried to have sex, I couldn't keep an erection. I was so mortified that I finally just stopped trying.

Scoffing, I level her with a serious look. "If you think for one second I'm going to pass up the opportunity to live with my best friend, even temporarily, you'd be wrong. Come on, Wren, we can hang out all the time and you can meet my teammates and see how we do things at the Raptors HQ. I'll even stock your favorite snacks, and you know I already have all of our favorite movies."

She waggles her eyebrows. "You gonna have a Marvel marathon with me, Rho? You know there's no breaks allowed."

It makes me happy that she's able to joke even though she's obviously upset over everything that happened yesterday. Her smile is still brighter than the sun in spite of living on the other side of the country with that oppressive fuckwad for four years. It seems obvious to the rest of her friends and family, but I don't think she realizes just how much Derrick managed to isolate her from her support system.

I twirl a long lock of her hair between my fingers. Wren's a wild sleeper, but her hair always feels like silk no matter how messy it is. "I can't think of anything I'd love more than hearing about your *god-awful* obsession with 'America's Ass' for two days straight," I tease.

She freezes mid-retort and grabs the hand that's still tangled in her hair. "Rhodes..." she whispers, her voice filled with awe. "Is that real?"

Teary, red-rimmed eyes are locked on my left hand, and I bite back a curse. I didn't even consider that she doesn't know about my tattoo. Hopefully, she isn't creeped out. Clearing my throat, I turn a sheepish grin her way. "Uhh...I plead the Fifth?"

Her eyes widen as the corner of her lip twitches, and I nearly let out a sigh of relief at that hint of joy in her expression.

At least she's not staring at me like I've only got one oar in the water.

"When did you do this? And why?" Her fingers run reverently over the intricate Starling tattoo, and shivers skate down my spine at her soft touch.

I clear my throat. "Um, yeah. Well, you know you've always been my good luck charm, and after you stopped coming to visit, my game went to shit." She eyes me guiltily and opens her mouth to, no doubt, apologize, so I run my fingers through her hair and smile at her. "I don't blame you, Wren. I never did. And I didn't tell you because I knew you would blow up your own life to help me with mine."

"Still, I'm sorry Rho." She sighs, nuzzling her face in my chest.

Kissing the top of her head, I take a subtle breath. As usual, she smells like apples and honey and *mine*. "Anyway, my game went to shit, and my friend Aidan figured out why my attitude changed and suggested I keep a piece of you with me to, and I quote, 'keep up the good bestie juju.'" She laughs, and it's such a relief to hear.

"Hey, circling back to your dad, where is he? I would have thought he'd be throwing a parade to have you back home."

My question makes her tense, and she shakes her head, pulling the strand of hair I was playing with loose from my fingers. "I don't know exactly...." She taps her phone to light up the screen and sighs. "He told me yesterday he was going to some kind of conference but didn't give me any details or tell me when he would be back. I'm a little worried about it, to be honest. We've never kept secrets from each other before, and I can't help but feel like he's hiding something."

I gently slide my hands down her arms and thread our fingers together, squeezing softly. "He's a grown man, Starling."

She opens her mouth to protest, but I press a finger over her lips, earning me the cutest grunt of frustration. "I know you worry. I know you've been doing your best to take care of him, but you and I both know that man can take care of himself and has been for a long time. Trust him to tell you when he's ready for you to know."

She sighs softly, and the way her breath fans over my finger causes a stir below my belt that I quickly turn to try and hide.

Clearing my throat, I walk towards the door only to peek back over my shoulder and catch her staring at my ass. "Why don't you get dressed, and I'll make breakfast?" I ask, intentionally ignoring the embarrassment on her face. "Then maybe we can hit up the training facility later, and you can meet some of the team."

Her eyes light up, and I once again marvel at just how much she loves baseball. When we were in college, if she wasn't studying or at my house, she was with me at the field. She started out in the stands and would study while I practiced, but eventually she got to know the team and became our unofficial good luck charm, attending every game she could to cheer us on. Archie definitely has it right when he calls his daughter 'Starshine'.

Even the coach liked having her around. Said her positivity rubbed off on the team and made us play better.

Heading into the kitchen, I peek in the fridge and see my parents have everything I need to make Wren's favorite huckleberry pancakes. I grab all the ingredients and throw them together as plans for the next four weeks swirl in my mind. The season doesn't start until early next month, so aside from some scheduled events and an endorsement shoot or two, all my time will be spent making sure my girl has the time of her life and never wants to leave again.

Game on.

CHAPTER 4
WREN

YOU WILL NOT *lust over your best friend, Wren Andromeda Reid.*

The words are a mantra in my mind as I watch Rhodes leave his old bedroom. His joggers showcase his muscular ass perfectly, and I discreetly wipe my mouth to make sure I'm not drooling. He's always handsome, but in the golden light of the early Carolina sun, he looks like some sort of saint. It's almost sickening how pretty he is.

My cheeks flame when he catches me ogling his toned backside, and I quickly avert my gaze, hurrying to get ready the second he's out of sight.

The day I met Rho I was so flustered by his looks, I didn't realize until too late he had friend-zoned me, and after that I had to work dang hard to tamp down my attraction to him. It got easier to ignore as the years went on, and then when I met and eventually married Derrick, I forgot about it altogether.

Rhodes went from somebody eighteen-year-old me lusted after every day to my friend and the most important person in my life after my dad, and it needs to stay that way. Not only do I not need another relationship anytime soon, but I also cannot lose him.

I take a quick body shower and fluff up my naturally straight hair before putting on some tinted sunscreen, mascara, and blush.

I'm digging through my suitcase when my phone dings a dozen times in rapid succession, so I hurriedly throw on my jean shorts and a Siren's hoodie, knowing it's likely the guys blowing up our group chat. I check my notifications and snort a laugh when I see some of the texts.

> JAMIE
> We would know if the plane crashed, right?
>
> WES
> Wren is fine. She's probably sleeping, moron.
>
> JAMIE
> Well that was rude, Wes. Are you spending too much time with Asher? Is that why you're so mean to me?
>
> ASHER
> Can y'all shut the fuck up? It's too early for me to play referee.
>
> WES
> Oh shit. Daddy Ash is mad.

I've just finished tying my high tops when my phone plays "We Are Family" by Sister Sledge. I roll my eyes, but I also can't help but giggle. The guys back in Seattle chose their own ringtones on my phone, so even before I answer, I know it's Jamie I'll see on the other end of the video call.

"Hey there, Baby Reid," he crows. "Why the fuck are you ignoring the group chat?"

"Yeah, Wren! One day gone and you've already kicked us to the curb? I'm hurt." Wesley's dramatic tone is clear through the phone, and I snort.

"As if, Wes. Your needy butt couldn't handle it, and you'd track me down," I laugh lightly before exhaustion hits me again, and a sigh escapes from my pursed lips. "Seriously, though, I had a ridiculously exhausting day yesterday, which is why I didn't reply last night. And then I talked with Rhodes for a few minutes before getting ready for the day which is why I've been AWOL this morning." I walk out of the room and briefly admire the wide staircase as I make my way down it, my hand grazing the white wood railing. "I literally *just* checked the group chat, but I did call Ash when I landed just like I promised, so it's not like y'all were totally out of the loop."

Jamie shoots a look of betrayal to someone off screen, and I can only assume it's Asher. My theory is confirmed when I hear him grumbling about how he doesn't have to report his every phone call to them. It quickly devolves into a yelling match between the two and Jamie huffs in frustration before making a swift exit.

"Sorry about that," he murmurs into the phone. "Things have been...tense this morning. And the fact that it's not even six a.m. isn't helping. Everybody is tired as fuck and edgy, which definitely won't help us do well in this last training game against Colorado."

I grimace and guilt overwhelms me as I plop down to sit on the last stair. "I'm sorry, Jamie. I didn't mean to cause any drama when I left," I whisper. Again, what does it say about my marriage that I'm more upset over making trouble for the team than I am about my husband cheating on me?

"Enough of that," he barks. My eyes widen slightly. Jamie rarely gets this upset about anything, and he's *never* raised his voice at me before. "This is on Derrick, not you. Wren, everybody in this entire program *adores* you. They're all pissed as hell at Derrick and figuring out what they can do to make sure you don't leave the team for good. There's even talk of releasing him from the team when his contract is up at the end of the season for the breach of our code of moral conduct. That video's been making the rounds around the office from what Jeremy has said."

My eyes water, gratitude for the men and women I've worked with every day for the last four years making me feel lighter than I've felt in days. Professional sports are notorious for cheaters and playboys, but I never thought I would have to deal with the fallout of being married to one.

"I don't want to leave the team, Jamie. You know that. I'm here for a month and then we'll see where things are at. It's gonna take at least sixty days to finalize the divorce unless we can get it expedited, according to Jeremy's lawyer, and I'll have to meet with a lawyer here, too. Derrick should actually be being served his papers today." I trail off, looking down at my watch. It's just before nine in the morning here, which means it's almost six there. "I would assume they'll be served sometime this morning."

Jamie's face lights up, and there's a mischievous gleam in his eyes. "Oh? Interesting. Wes, Asher, Jer! Let's go!"

"The fuck do you want now, Reed?" My boss's gruff voice comes over the speaker, and I wave excitedly when he looks over Jamie's shoulder. A smile lights up his grumpy face. "Hey Cupcake! Sorry, I didn't know he had you on the phone. How was the flight? Are you settling in okay? Do you need anything?"

I laugh. "Jer, I'm fine. The flight was good, and I have everything I need." Talking to the guys on video is great, but I miss them already. And I really miss Jeremy somethin' fierce, especially since I haven't seen my dad yet.

"Chill, Bossman. Baby Reid is fine. Can we focus on me now?" Jamie's voice is on the verge of a whine, and Wes teases him mercilessly for it. "We need to go find Douchey Derrick, *right now*."

Everyone goes silent, and even I'm confused. Jamie sighs in exasperation before he clarifies. "Monroe is being served divorce paperwork today, and if we do some light stalking, we can see it happen."

Whoops and hollers sound around the room, and I cover my mouth to hide my amusement. The phone is snatched from Jamie's hand and Wesley's face fills the screen. "We love you, Wren, but we gotta go. Text us back and call when you can!"

A chorus of "Love you, Wren!" fills the air before they hang up, and I take a minute to sit there and bask in the love from my friends when Rhodes's voice startles me.

"Were those players on the team?" He sounds angry, and I'm not sure why. He's leaning against one side of the kitchen doorway with his arms crossed over his chest and an irritated frown on his handsome face.

I smile shyly at him before I answer. "Yeah, that was my boss, Jeremy, and three of the guys from the team. They kind of adopted me when I first started, and after you, they're my closest friends."

His frown deepens as he cracks his knuckles, and

nerves flutter in my chest. Why is he so upset? "You'll get to meet them when they come to visit in two weeks. I promised I'd show them around Charleston before the season starts."

"And where will they be staying?"

"Probably in a hotel? Jamie will likely be begging to meet my dad, so it wouldn't surprise me if he or all of them try to finagle their way into staying with him."

I'm so confused. He's being really weird right now.

He breathes angrily out of his nose before visibly calming down. "Are you hungry?" he asks. The quick subject change gives me whiplash. "I made your favorite huckleberry pancakes and grabbed your chai from upstairs." That gets my attention. I gasp and make grabby hands, and I'm rewarded with a deep chuckle. He passes me the cold liquid-heaven with a smirk, and I take a long drink, nearly moaning at the perfect balance of spicy-sweet flavors.

My stomach growls loudly. "I'm starving. Lead the way Roly-Coly!"

"You know they won't let you into the training facility with that on, right?" Rhodes asks sarcastically, pointing to my Siren's hoodie. His mood has been better but every time my phone buzzes he looks a little irritated, so I silenced it to give him my full focus.

We're driving through downtown Charleston on our way to the facilities, and I can't stop staring out the windows at everything that's changed since I was last here. The sun is high in the sky and it glints off the water, nearly blinding me. Rhodes rolled all the windows down as soon as we got in his SUV because he knows how much I love the smell of saltwater and the breeze on my face.

I give him my best side eye. "What do you suggest I wear then, Rho?" I point at the massive gray stone building in front of us as he pulls into the sparsely filled parking lot. "Because we're here." The training facilities are attached to the back of the stadium and not nearly as colorful. Everything at Rebel Park is decked out in Carolina blue and white to match the team colors, whereas the training facility is constructed of plain gray stone and glass and sterile white and black on the inside.

Rhodes is still grumbling about my attire when he puts the SUV in park, and I snicker quietly. Could I have worn something different? Of course. But I love riling him up whenever possible and this seemed like the perfect opportunity.

What I'm not expecting is the wicked smirk that crosses his face as he leans over the console, gently dragging his finger over my chin and down my neck. My breath hitches when he hooks it into the neck of my hoodie, pulling until I'm inches away from his face.

"Oh, Starling," he purrs. "You clearly forget just how well I know you. If you think I didn't grab a backup shirt the second I saw the offending hoodie, you'd be wrong." As he reaches into the back seat, his warm breath fans across my face. I shiver, and warmth spreads between my legs. I jerk back and lean against the door with a hand on my chest, desperately trying to slow my racing heart.

Bad Wren. Get control of your libido before you make things awkward.

My inner voice is a bitch, but she's right. I'm fresh out

of a four-year marriage, but it's been nearly a year since the last time Derrick and I had sex. Not for lack of trying on my part. I took classes, bought sexy lingerie, and booked romantic weekend getaways. But every time I tried to initiate anything, he shut me down. He was too tired the first few months, and then when I started questioning that excuse, he'd get frustrated and tell me he "just wasn't into it anymore."

I suggested couples therapy several times, but he'd take offense and rant about not needing strangers to tell him how to be a husband, then he'd storm off to the nearest bar. Looking back, there were obvious signs he was cheating, but I chose to ignore them because I didn't want to lose another important person in my life. But as I sit here in Rhodes's SUV, I realize that Derrick was never really someone I couldn't live without.

The important people are here in Charleston and some are back in Seattle, and the latter are blowing up my phone asking for pictures and telling me all the things they want to do when they visit. I feel more settled and safer in this SUV than I ever did in that cold, clinical apartment.

I let out a startled squeak when something soft smacks me in the face, and my hands karate chop it down onto the seat, my eyes narrowing when Rhodes's deep laugh echoes through the small space.

"Sorry, Starling." He quirks his lips and boops me on the nose with a long finger. "You went all space cadet on me and I couldn't resist. Now hurry up and put on the hoodie or we're going to be late."

Finally, I look at the item in my hands. I unfold it and gasp. *"You didn't."*

His expression turns into a full-blown smile. "Are you

kidding? I've worn that thing every single game day since freshman year when you first gave it to me. It's never failed to keep me grounded whenever I got nervous or felt like I didn't deserve it." He trails off.

My eyes feel hot, but I don't let the tears fall. Right around the time Rhodes was being seriously scouted during our freshman year, we were in his room watching a Raptors game when he had an anxiety attack seemingly out of nowhere. When he was finally calm enough to talk, he broke down in tears and confessed he had been having them often because he was terrified that he would let everyone down.

He said that the pressure was getting to him, and he was so afraid to fail, he couldn't eat or sleep some nights. I spent the rest of that evening running my fingers through his hair while he dozed with his head in my lap, trying to figure out how to make him feel better.

The next morning, while he was putting on his sweatshirt, and idea hit me, and several hours, one bribe to a senior design student, and two specialty sports shops later, I gave Rho his very own 'Wren luck charm.'

I'm breathless as I sit in Rhodes's fancy SUV and take in the same sweatshirt I gave him so many years ago when we were just kids. I brush my fingers over the logo in awe.

"How does it still look this good all these years later?"

The tips of his ears redden, and I cock an eyebrow at him, slip my hoodie off and replace it with the giant one in my hands. I only have on a bralette underneath, but my bikinis cover less, and he's seen me in those plenty of times over the years. It shouldn't be a big deal.

And it isn't. Until I look up and see the banked heat in his hazel eyes as his gaze locks on my chest.

Forget breathless, the desire in his eyes has my heart stopping altogether.

I must make some sort of noise because the color drains from his face. He looks out the windshield, taps his fingers on the steering wheel, and clears his throat.

"Well...I... uh...replaced it?" His voice cracks on the last word and he snorts. "Fuck, that sounded bad. What I mean is, I wore the hoodie you gave me to every single game for eight years even when it started to get too small. It finally fell apart last year so I took it to like...three different shops until I found one that could replicate the exact hoodie and design. They had to cut it up, so I took the pieces to my mom and she's keeping them for me until I figure out what to do with them."

I'm stunned silent for a minute until the color returns to his face and embarrassment turns the tips of his ears bright red.

"Rho...you really did all that just for one hoodie I gave you our freshman year?" My voice is incredulous, but my heart feels like it's going to burst out of my chest with glee as my eighteen-year-old self does a happy dance.

It doesn't mean anything. You're just friends.

The problem is my feelings for Rhodes Gray have always been...*more*. I thought getting married and moving across the country would take away everything I shoved down sophomore year. But if anything, they're back and stronger than ever. Being surrounded by his warmth and unwavering support is bringing up so many things I thought I buried.

He scoffs and hops out of the SUV before rounding the hood to open my door. "Do you really not know how much that meant to me, Starling? I was drowning and you went out of your way to throw me a life preserver. You gave me a way to always feel connected to home—*to you*—no matter where in the world I ended up. That hoodie isn't *just* anything, Wren. It's everything to me. My most prized possession. My personal good luck charm."

I smile softly. Rhodes hooks his arm around my neck and leads us into the building, planting a kiss on the top of my head as he pulls the door open.

It takes me an embarrassingly long time to get myself together, but by the time we reach the upper-level offices, I'm back to poking fun at Rho even as I stare in awe at the state-of-the-art facilities.

"Well, who do we have here?" A booming voice startles me back into Rho's chest. Standing in front of us is a man I would know anywhere. At a bit less six feet tall, he's a only few inches taller than me with rich, dark skin, and a clean-shaven head.

"Benny!" I shriek, springing up onto my toes to hug him.

His chuckle is so deep, it practically rattles my bones as he picks me up in a spin that makes me dizzy. "Is that our unofficial mascot, Wren Reid? How you been, darlin'? Streaks here hasn't shut up about missin' you in the three years I've been wrangling these heathens." He leans in with a conspiratorial wink and says, "Between you and me, I was ready to trade him just to get a break from all the whining."

I stumble back dizzily when Benny puts me down. When the room stops spinning, I turn to see Rhodes with an embarrassed smile on his face as he rubs a hand across the back of his neck.

"Will you quit it, Coach? Damn. You would think after thirty years in the game, you'd have some couth. Or at the very least, protect your players." His tone is exasperated, but affection shines in his eyes as he greets the man.

Don Bennett, or "Benny" as we call him, was the baseball coach at our college and has been friends with my dad for a long time. I've known him since I was a little girl, and I'm sure it surprised him when I started hanging out at the stadium and training facilities with Rho and the guys all the time, but he also got a front row seat to my friendship with Rhodes and knows how close we are.

Benny laughs and gives me a genuine smile. "You stick with me, kiddo, and you'll know more than you ever wanted to about this team."

Rho grabs my hand and tugs me down the hall. "Alright, I'm gonna take Wren to the main office so she can meet everyone and see how things are done here. Who knows," he winks at me, "maybe we'll even convince her to stay."

CHAPTER 5
RHODES

"WHO DO we have to bribe to get her on our team?" Sarah, the team's junior PR associate, asks me. We've been wandering around for over an hour and Wren is a hit just like I knew she would be. Nearly every single person adores her.

Wren is so enthralled with the incredible offices and all the media team's filming equipment that I nearly had to drag her away from the cameras so she could meet the rest of the group outside of our tech guys. Then Sarah showed her the smart board in the conference room, which she said is great for making plans with the content creation team.

The only person who doesn't seem to like my girl is making her way over to me with a too-wide smile plastered on her face.

"Hey there, Rhodes," Whitney purrs as she wraps her hands around my forearm. "I was wondering when I would finally run into you again."

Whitney is an intern in the Public Relations department, and even though she's only been here a month, she's thrown herself at nearly every guy on the team. Sure, she's objectively pretty, but she knows it and doesn't take kindly to being told 'no.' She's been uncomfortably persistent even though I politely told her I was unavailable. *Several times.*

Wren looks over just as I try to extricate myself from her claws, and I turn pleading eyes to her, mouthing "help me."

She stifles a laugh, excuses herself, and saunters my way. I really hope I'm not imagining the jealousy in her eyes when she sees Whitney clinging to me like a leech in a shallow pond. My girl isn't the bitchy type, and I never saw her get territorial with her ex, so I'm interested to see how she plays this.

It takes a conscious effort to keep my jaw off the floor when she winds her arms around my waist and hops up on her toes to kiss my cheek with no hesitation.

"Hey Rho, you wanna go get lunch soon? I'm starving and I can practically hear the dumplings at Lotus callin' my name." She ends her words on a groan, and I hear the snort of derision that comes from Whitney. "Oh! I'm so sorry," Wren turns to Whitney and holds her hand out with a megawatt smile. "I don't know where my manners went; I'm Wren Reid, Rhodes's..."

"Girlfriend," I blurt, ignoring the wide-eyed stares being aimed my way. "Wren is my girlfriend." I smirk, wrap an arm around her waist, and tuck her tightly into my side. Whitney's mouth hangs open, but she finally lets go of my arm, so I pull Wren back several steps and look down at her with a genuine smile on my lips. "The relationship is new, but we've been friends for nearly a decade now, right Starling?"

If she's surprised by my declaration, she sure doesn't show it.

Batting her eyelashes at me, she turns to the shocked woman in front of us and leans in like she's telling her a secret. "That's right. Apparently, Rhodes here has been in love with me for *years* and never told me. Now that I'm single again he finally took his shot and clearly, it worked out." She beams, holding her hand out once again for Whitney to shake. "Sorry, I totally didn't catch your name! Do you work for the Raptors?"

Whitney's eyes are like saucers as she robotically shakes Wren's hand. "Umm... I'm uh..." Somebody nearby coughs, and it's enough to startle her out of her stupor. Clearing her throat, she sneers. "My name is Whitney Morgan. I work in the PR department, so the team and I spent *a lot* of time together, and yet I've never heard your name."

I have to give Wren credit; her smile doesn't falter in the face of the catty woman.

"That's funny," I chime in. "Because I've only seen you around the facility three times since you started working here, and I know I was talking about Wren with the guys at least two of those times." Her smug look drops, and she looks *pissed*.

Did she really expect me to back up her fake story?

I turn my attention back to the beautiful blonde at my side. "Either way, I'm sure you'll see a lot more of my girl around here for the next month. And I'm sure she would love to answer any questions you might have since she's head of PR for the Seattle Sirens." I don't even bother to fight my smug smile as I nuzzle my nose into Wren's hair. I'll obviously take any chance I can get to brag about this remarkable woman.

"Well, we should get out of here. Gotta keep her fed, you know?" I wink at Whitney and pull Wren away with a wave to the rest of the staff before leading us outside and down the stairs. We barely make it out to the parking lot before she absolutely loses it, laughing so hard tears start running down her face and little snorts escape her lips. The sound is so infectious I can't help but laugh with her.

Several minutes later, we're in my SUV when Wren throws a contemplative glance my way. I brace myself for questions I'm not ready to answer but instead she shakes it off and smiles. "Can we really go to Lotus? I haven't had dumplings or bao in for-ev-er, and I would commit serious crimes for some right now." Her hands are clasped together, and her bottom lip is stuck out in the same pout I haven't been able to resist for eight years. She's so goddamn *pretty*. Her blonde hair practically glows in the sunlight against the tan leather of my seats, making her look like some sort of angel. And seeing Wren in my hoodie that's easily two sizes too big for her, does funny things to my heart and my libido.

I shake my head and start the SUV, smiling over at the girl next to me. "Anything for you, Starling."

"Good lord, I forgot how good these are," Wren moans from across the booth. I clear my throat and move my hand under the table to adjust myself. She may have been okay with playing my fake girlfriend in front of Whitney, but I doubt she's ready to know that the little noises she's making have me ready to bend her over the table in front of the entire restaurant.

"It's been so long since I ate here, I kind of forgot how good everything is," I say around a bite of steamed pork bun. Lotus is one of our favorite places in Charleston, and for more than just the food. It's a tiny shop tucked away in a rundown strip mall just up the road from my house, but despite how the outside looks, the inside is warm and intimate, which makes it a perfect date spot.

She raises her eyebrow at me. "Rho, you live five minutes away and you love this place. Why's it been so long since you last ate here?"

I shrug and tilt my head back to stare at the ceiling. I can't face her when I know how pathetic I'm about to sound. "It felt too weird coming here without you, Starling. This was our place. We ate here every time you came home. Bringing anyone else here felt wrong, and coming by myself just made me miss you more than I already did. I haven't been since the last time you were home."

Prepared for the worst, I drop my head to gauge her reaction. I don't recognize the look in her eyes, but the best way I can describe it is soft. She doesn't look like she pities me or thinks I'm too intense, which gives me the courage to say what I do.

"I missed you so much, Wren. Nothing in my life has felt right since the day you moved to Seattle, and the only thing that kept me sane was knowing I'd see you every few months when you came to visit your dad. But two years ago, the visits just... stopped. You were quiet and distant. I missed my best friend." I'm not surprised I'm getting choked up.

She's quiet before she slides out of her side of the booth, and I drop my face into my hands, sure I just fucked everything up. I startle when her small arms wrap around my waist, and she buries her face in my shoulder.

"I'm so sorry, Rho. I never wanted to make you feel like you aren't one of the most important people in my life. Derrick got really controlling after my last trip home when he found out you had stayed at my dad's house with us, and it was easier to distance myself instead of dealing with the constant arguing. I can't even tell you how many nights I slept in my office or on a friend's couch after he picked a fight with me at work. When I look back now, it's obvious we didn't have a healthy relationship, and truthfully, I think deep down I knew it was over for a long time before the video came out."

I squeeze her to me tightly, holding back the fury that grips my throat knowing there were times Wren wasn't comfortable in her own home. I kiss the top of her head and take a deep inhale of her honey apple smell.

"I promise, Wren, you will never have to feel like that again if I can help it. Especially while you're living with me. You should never be afraid to go home, no matter what's going on in your relationship. You are sweeter than sugar cookies at Christmas, Starling. The fact that your dumbass ex treated you with anything less than respect pisses me off to no end. You should know if I ever see him again, I will be breaking his nose."

She chokes out a laugh. "Don't go being all violent on my account, Rhodes Colter. I let him bait me into fights and instead of going home to work things out, I always ran. It's what I know best. The few times I actually did go home after a fight, he wasn't there, so after that I stopped trying. My therapist and I have been working on my avoidance issues when it comes to conflict, but I know I don't want to fix things with Derrick."

Wren is so strong. It probably makes me sound selfish, but I'm so damn glad she left that idiot and came home. I know she told me not to get violent, but I don't think I'll be able to help myself. I've been so angry since she told me what happened and now that I know he treated her like that for years and still got to have her when I couldn't, makes me feel sick.

Before I can reply, her phone rings with a FaceTime call, "Crazier Best Friend" by Andi plays. I see the name Wesley on the screen, and I try not to jump to conclusions when her face lights up.

"Do you mind if I take this?" she asks excitedly.

I don't need her to think I'm some asshole who doesn't want her talking to anybody but me, so I give her a small nod and turn back to my food.

"Baby Reid! It's about damn time you answered your phone. How are you? Did you settle in okay? Can we come visit now? Sorry, let me rephrase. We're coming to visit tomorrow!" The masculine voice over the phone is familiar, but I can't place it.

Wren snorts and my breath catches as my jealousy flares watching her beam at her phone.

Who the fuck is this guy, and why is she smiling at him like that?

I'm brought out of my jealous fog when she thrusts her phone at me with a wide smile.

"Wesley Black, this is Rhodes Gray. Rhodes, this is Wes."

Looking at the small screen, I realize why his voice sounded so familiar, and my jealousy burns hotter. He's the Sirens' shortstop and my best friend's younger brother.

I slap a friendly smile on my face and glance at Wren. She looks nervous.

"You must be the Rhodes we've heard so much about! It's really nice to finally meet you, man. Wren's told us so much about you. I feel like you're my best friend, too," he says with a manic grin.

CHAPTER 6
WREN

"WES," I hiss. My cheeks are on fire, and I'm mortified. I really don't need Rhodes knowing how much I talked about him the last four years.

I hear more than one person in the raucous laughter that comes through the phone, and I groan, covering my eyes with my hands.

Jamie's familiar baritone makes me smile when he chuckles. "We're just teasing you, Baby Reid. It really is nice to finally meet the guy who's been such a big part of your life."

Rhodes looks at me with one eyebrow raised and a small smile. He puts his arm around me and pulls me closer to his side so we're both in the frame. "Actually, I already sort of know Wesley."

My eyes shoot to his in surprise, and he smirks as Wes shakes his head in confusion and refutes him on the screen. "Aidan is my best friend," he explains with a shrug.

Realization dawns on me, and I start to laugh. "What

a small world! I never realized your Aidan was Aidan Black. That's awesome!"

Wes's jaw is still hanging open when I turn back to look at him. "Holy shit. You're *Rhodes Gray*." He cackles. "God, am I that stupid, or did I just never put the pieces together when Wren told us about you? Aid talks about you all the time, man. It's nice to officially meet you."

Rhodes smiles as the guys razz him for being oblivious and my heart warms at the interaction.

All three of my Seattle boys are now on-screen giving us cheesy grins. "Wes decided we couldn't wait any longer to come see you," Asher says in his usual stoic tone. "Our flight lands at 11 a.m., and we can catch an Uber to the hotel."

I scoff. "Why did you get a hotel? I told you my dad won't mind y'all staying with him, and he's not even home right now, so it's actually perfect timing. And I will absolutely come pick you guys up from the airport."

Rhodes clears his throat and scowls at me. "*We* will come pick you up from the airport."

I'm a little taken aback by his tone, so I widen my eyes at him and mouth "What the heck?"

He grimaces. "Sorry, that came out harsher than I meant it to. I just meant I would be happy to come with to pick you guys up so we can all go grab lunch or go fuck around a bit." He turns to me and softens his voice. "Starling, I've missed over two years of your life because your ex didn't like our friendship. It would be nice to get to know the important people you spend all your time with."

My irritation fades. I should have asked him to come with us either way. With a nod, I turn back toward my phone to see the three stooges grinning like jackasses. I give them my meanest evil eye. Wes has his hand over his mouth as his shoulders shake with laughter.

I say goodbye to my favorite gossips and hang up before this devolves into them spilling secrets they have no business knowing in the first place. Two years ago, when I first stopped visiting South Carolina, Jamie cornered me after I ignored three phone calls in a row and demanded to know if I was being harassed.

I broke down in embarrassed tears and explained how Derrick hated Rhodes even though we were strictly friends. I gave him a watered-down version of all the problems we were having in our marriage and how when I cut Rhodes out of my life I felt like I was missing a part of myself.

Unfortunately, the very next night, the guys questioned me while I was drunk, and I blurted every single detail of my crush after being friend-zoned. They've been trying to convince me to leave Derrick ever since, especially since they know how he treated me.

"I'm excited to meet them, Starling. They seem like fun guys." Rhodes kisses the top of my head.

I smile up at him and lay my head on his shoulder. "They are, and honestly, they're like the brothers I never had. Jamie is totally convinced we're long-lost siblings, and I know he's going to bring up his theory to Dad." I sigh. "They weren't kidding when they teased me about how much I've talked about you over the years." My voice is barely more than a whisper as he threads our fingers.

"I talk about you too, Starling. I'm pretty sure every single one of my teammates knows everything about you without even meeting you. I really did miss you so much."

I squeeze his hand and clear my throat. In spite of the work my therapist and I have done, all this emotion still makes me feel itchy. "Alright, Roly-Coly. What are we doing the rest of the day?"

He checks his phone. "Well, I was gonna go meet the guys at the Fun Park…"

Disappointment surges through me, and I try to keep my face neutral. "Oh, that's okay. I can just head back to the house and hang out if you'd rather—"

"Wren! What the fuck, no. I want you there. I was just trying to figure out a way to say I wanted to introduce you to my friends without sounding pushy." I grin at him. "Of course, I want to meet them! Are you sure I won't be buggin' y'all or crashing guys' night?"

He chuckles. "Absolutely not. Let's go."

CHAPTER 7
RHODES

MY HANDS SWEAT the entire ten-minute drive to the park. I know the guys are gonna love her because I do, but they also know how wildly in love with her I am, and Aidan can't keep his mouth shut to save his life. And with him also finding out that Wren is friends with his little brother? I'm sweating bullets.

Wren is practically bouncing in her seat when we park and normally I'd laugh, but I'm too anxious. I face the door to hide a grimace, turn off the engine, and hop out to open her door.

"Hey, yo, Streaks!"

I whip around and grin. Every guy on the team earns a nickname eventually, but mine and Aidan's both happen to involve some unfortunate poorly-timed nudity. During his rookie year, Aid refused to date after one too many encounters with clingy cleat chasers. But like most guys in professional sports will tell you, winning a game tends to have an...energizing effect on you. Some guys work it off in the gym or party all night, and others chase a different kind of release. Aidan's roommate, on *three* separate occasions during away games, caught him *celebrating Palm Sunday*. It became the team's running joke to ask Aid if he'd be practicing his sermon so we knew not to walk in on him. And from that his nickname, Preacher, was born. That was seven years ago, and the nickname hasn't changed once.

Mine is only slightly less embarrassing. I got blackout drunk shortly after Wren moved to Seattle, and the idiots I was drafted with dared me to sneak into the stadium and streak around the bases. What I *didn't* know was that there was a scheduled team meeting in the conference room that overlooks the field. Needless to say, several of my teammates have some very incriminating stories about me, and I'm sure they'll be chomping at the bit to tell my girl every single one of them.

"Hey, Preach. Didn't know it was bring-the-cutest-kid-in-the-world day," I say to Aidan. I crouch down and hold open my arms for his son, Crew.

"Uncle Rho!" Crew gasps as he jumps into my arms. "I didn't know you were gonna be here today!"

I squeeze him tightly and turn around to see Wren staring curiously at us, a shy grin playing on her lips.

"I also brought a friend. Crew, this is my very best friend in the entire world, Wren. Wren, this is my honorary nephew, Crew."

Aidan raises his eyebrows at me. "*The* Wren?"

She smiles at him and holds out her hand. "The one and only."

He grins widely at her and swoops in to hug her. "There'll be none of that handshake nonsense here, darlin'. Any friend of Rhodes is a friend of mine."

"Did our lonely little Preacher finally get a date?"

Our other friend, Copeland, shouts from behind us as he slams his car door shut.

Aidan releases Wren and tosses an arm over her shoulder, waggling his eyebrows at Cope. "Sure did, Hawthorne. Jealous?"

I huff and cross my arms at his antics and turn to Copeland. "Hey Cope, this is Wren Reid. Wren, these yahoos are Aidan Black and Copeland Hawthorne. And of course, you already met Aidan's son, Crew."

Her pretty eyes twinkle with trouble, and the second she opens her mouth, trouble spills out in the form of sugar-coated shit-stirring.

"Oh, I already know Aidan," she purrs seductively, walking her fingers up his arm where it still rests over her shoulders. "In fact, I'm *very* familiar with him."

He gets a panicked look on his face, and I struggle to hold it together when his mouth gapes open like the fish he and Crew love to catch. "N-no," he stutters, horror overtaking his shock. "You must have me confused with someone else."

Her lusty expression cracks, and she starts giggling wildly. "I'm sorry!" she says between gasps. "I couldn't resist. Your brother is one of my best friends, so I've heard all about you and Crew from him! I didn't know you were the same Aidan that Rho was friends with though."

Aidan's stricken expression clears as Copeland barks out a laugh, ruffling her hair. "I like her."

I smile like a loon when he winks at me, but I'm honestly a little shocked. Copeland is extremely mistrustful of women ever since his fiancé cheated on him with one of his old teammates. It's been five years, and while I know he's over her, he's definitely not over the mountain of trust issues she left behind.

Aid snaps out of his stunned silence when Wren announces she's going to FaceTime Wes before we go in, and he moves to stand next to her. I hear the FaceTime connection sound and then Wren says, "I just met Rhodes's best friend! Wanna say hi?" and then she turns her phone towards Aidan.

"What the fuck little brother?" he laughs. "You're friends with Rhodes's bestie?"

Wesley lets out a sound that's part laugh, part groan. "Jesus, now my poor Baby Reid has to deal with you, too? Say the word and I'll rescue you from the heathens when we get there tomorrow, Wren."

She giggles and waves him off, promising him she'll call him later before she hangs up and turns back to Aidan. "I became friends with Wes like four years ago after I started working in PR for the Sirens. Your mom brings me cookies literally every time she's in town."

Aidan's jaw drops in mock-outrage, and Copeland practically cackles. "She makes those cookies for you?!" he asks incredulously. "I beg her for peach cobbler cookies all the time, but she only makes them on special occasions and before she goes to see Wes. I always assumed she made them for him, but it makes so much more sense now."

Wren groans. "I dream about those cookies, but she won't give me the recipe. She always says she wants a reason to keep seeing me and she won't have one if she gives up the goods."

Crew wriggles in my arms, so I set him down and he runs up to Wren. She crouches down to his level. "Do you think we can get Grandma to make cobbler cookies since you're here?" he whispers.

She giggles quietly. "I bet we can. How about we all

get together at your Uncle Rhodes's house for dinner tomorrow night? Uncle Wes will be there too!"

My heart races as I see her interact with Crew. She's always been so good with kids, and they absolutely love her.

I wonder if she wants kids.

"I'll arrange dinner stuff for tomorrow," I tell them. "But for right now, let's get inside so I can kick some butt on the go-kart track!"

"Remind me again why you haven't tried to lock that girl down?" Aidan asks a few hours later.

We're watching Wren help Crew steer his go-kart while we take a much-needed break. We've been playing nonstop for almost three hours, and apparently the only one who can keep up with the boundless energy of a 5-year-old is my 25-year-old best friend. They took to each other like ducks to water, and I think I may have been surpassed as the favorite if 'Auntie Wren's' new nickname is anything to go by.

"You know exactly why, Aid. She's literally *days* out of a terrible marriage and the last thing she needs is another big life change. What am I gonna do, huh? Casually bring up over breakfast that I've been in love with her since I was eighteen?"

He rolls his eyes. "I'm not saying declare your undying love, Rho. I'm tellin' you to buck up and make a move before somebody else does." He tilts his head to the side, and I follow his gaze to where some guy holds her attention. Crew stands next to Wren, animatedly talking to the little girl with him who looks to be about the same age.

A haze of irritation takes the reins as I stomp over to them to the tune of Aidan's laughter and toss my arm over Wren's shoulders, pulling her close.

"Hey baby," I say, kissing the side of her head. "You about ready to head out?"

She looks confused but smiles at me anyway and wraps her arm around my waist. "Yeah, sure. It was nice to meet you, Colton!" she says to the guy in front of us, who's now glowering at me.

Sorry, buddy. This one's all mine.

CHAPTER 8
WREN

WE'RE in Rhodes's SUV on our way back to his parents' house for dinner when I finally broach his weird behavior from the fun park. "So...what was that?" I ask.

He runs a hand through his wavy hair and keeps his eyes straight ahead, clearing his throat as he answers. "I don't know what you mean."

"You do know what I mean, Rho. Calling me 'baby' and that whole possessive act? Colton was just making conversation since Crew and his daughter hit it off and he thought I was Crew's mom." I sigh in exasperation. "Speaking of, did Crew's mom have to work or something today?"

Rhodes sighs sadly and offers me a brief glance before turning back to the road. "From what Aidan's shared with me, Crew's mom was a one-night-stand when he was drinking his feelings away shortly after he was drafted. She showed up on his doorstep like six months later super pregnant and high out of her mind. She gave birth a few months early and just...left. Crew was four hours old and unable to breathe on his own and his mom abandoned him. Aid's been parenting alone ever since."

"How awful," I whisper. "Is he okay now?"

His face brightens to a proud grin. "Crew is absolutely perfect. He's healthy and so strong you'd never know he was born weighing less than three pounds."

Relief fills me at the reassurance that the sweet little boy I met today is happy and healthy. I only got to spend a few hours with the kid, but he's precious. I laugh sadly as I think back. "I guess that's why Colton assumed I was Crew's mom and tried to set up a playdate for the kids. With the matching blonde hair and all, it makes sense."

Rhodes snorts incredulously and glances at me once before he makes the turn into his parents' driveway and shuts off the SUV.

"Are you really that oblivious? Or are you just ignoring the fact that he was blatantly hitting on you?"

I scoff and hop out of the passenger seat, shutting the door a little harder than necessary. His heavy footsteps follow me, but I keep walking up the driveway. Their house is absolutely stunning: a picture-perfect white farmhouse with a pretty blue porch and huge, comfortable-looking chairs placed under the large ceiling fans. It must be nice to sit out here in the evenings with a glass of sweet tea and a book.

Rhode's aggressive footfalls remind me that I'm irritated, and I sneer. "So what if he was Rhodes? What, am I just supposed to stay single and celibate forever because my stupid ex-husband cheated on me?"

"Damn it, Wren. That's not what I said!" He grabs my arm to stop me just as the front door flies open, and Kaci Gray envelops me in a warm hug.

"My sweet girl. We didn't get to see your pretty self

nearly well enough in the dark last night. Let me get a good look at you!" Kaci is a force to be reckoned with on the best of days, so I let her squish my cheeks while her assessing gaze runs over my face.

Her lips turn down into a frown. "You look tired, honey. I hope you take your time here to rest and recuperate. We're looking forward to having you around again."

She pats my cheek and lets me go, bustling all of us into the house, and I'm accosted by the most amazing smell in the world. "Mama Gray," I groan. "Did you make chicken pot pie?"

The only response I get is an incredulous look and Rhodes chuckles at my expense. When I turn a glare his way, he smirks. "Did you really think she wouldn't make her honorary daughter's favorite meal for her homecoming dinner?"

I flip him off, but my heart swells with appreciation for these incredible people as we follow her through the house. The Gray's, especially Kaci, have become family to me in every way that counts since the first time Rhodes brought me to meet them our freshman year. Not having my own mom around was always a burden I tried to keep away from my dad while I was growing up, but I don't think I realized what I was missing until I met Rhodes's mom.

My dad will always be my favorite person, and I know I can talk with him about anything, but there's nothing in the world like a strong woman to look up to, especially when you work in male-dominated fields like we do. Kaci Gray is an incredibly talented corporate lawyer.

Dad doesn't really talk about my mom or why she left, but I always assumed it was because she didn't want to be a mother. Otherwise, she would have taken me with her, right? Or at the very least visited her daughter at least once while I was growing up. Honestly, if it wasn't for the Gray's and my therapist, I think I would be a lot more bitter about it than I am.

When Kaci and Dominic moved here five years ago, they found this house and declared it their "dying house" because they want to die here. It sounds a little morbid, but sweet all the same. The stunning home sits on a large plot of land that they rent out to their neighboring farm, and the last time I asked, Dominic told me they charged the older man a dollar-fifty a month, "because renting that much space for a dollar would just be ridiculous."

When we walk into the brightly-lit kitchen, I smile when Rhodes's mom immediately goes to stand by her husband at the stove. Dominic moves behind Kaci, putting his arms around her and swaying to the soft sounds of Mitchell Tenpenny.

I take a seat at the large butcher-block island, leaning my head in my hand with a sigh. I've always been a little envious of the love they still share after so many years together, especially knowing their relationship was established *after* Kaci found out she was pregnant with Rhodes. Muscular tanned arms wrap around my shoulders as Rho rests his chin on the top of my head and clears his throat, catching his parents' attention.

Dominic beams when he sees me, comes around the island, and pulls me into a fierce hug. He knocks Rhodes off of me in the process, which elicits a grumble. "I know you got here last night, but I didn't get to squeeze you and tell you how happy I am that you're here." He kisses me on the top of my head. "We missed you something fierce, Wren."

Tears spring to my eyes before I can dam them back.

"I missed y'all, too. So much. I'm sorry it took me so long to come home and visit."

Dominic and Kaci share a look over my head, and I brace myself for the question I know they've been dying to ask. Raising his eyebrow at me, he strokes a big hand down my hair and gives me his no-nonsense "dad look" that I've seen him give his son a thousand times. "You ready to tell us what prompted this sudden trip home, Wren? Aside from missing your family?"

I groan, bury my face in my hands, and use the heels of my palms to rub my eyes. I'm sure I look like a raccoon running on two hours of sleep now, but I can't bring myself to care.

Clearing my throat, I keep my eyes trained down, not brave enough to face the pity in their expressions. "Derrick cheated on me, and I found out when somebody sent a video of it to the team email," I whisper.

Kaci gasps as Dominic's hand tenses up where it rests on my shoulder. "He *what?*"

"Wren...honey, I am so sorry you had to go through that on your own." She rushes over and envelops me in a warm hug.

I hug her back and take a deep breath, allowing myself to soak in the comfort she's always offered so freely. "It's okay, Mama Gray. There were signs for a long time. I just chose to ignore them for the sake of what I thought was love. And I wasn't alone! Four of my great friends and my boss immediately cheered me up and helped me get my stuff so I could come home. As a matter of fact, a few of them are flying in tomorrow for a visit."

Thinking of the guys and Ella always brings a smile to my face, and a little of the hurt fades away. I have so many people who love me unconditionally; focusing on them takes away some of the sting from Derrick's betrayal. I send off a quick text to Ella to see if she'll be visiting with the guys.

"How exciting! I can't wait to meet them. Do you have any idea how long you'll be in town? You know our house is yours, and we'd love to have you stay with us as long as you'd like." Kaci smiles at me, kissing my cheek, then moves to take dinner out of the oven.

"Well, I know I'll be here for at least a month. I don't have a place to live in Seattle, so I guess I'll start looking for a rental. I could stay with one of the guys, but I don't want to put anyone out if I don't have to." I hear a grunt and peek back at Rhodes. He looks angry. "And while I appreciate your offer to let me stay with you, I think I might stay with Roly-Coly-Oly for at least some of my time here."

He beams at me and reaches out to hold my hand. Out of the corner of my eye I see Dominic shoot him an unreadable look, but when I turn back to the island, he's all smiles.

"Good!" Kaci says cheerily. "I think it will be just great for you to spend some time together. Has she met any of the guys yet?" She directs the question to Rhodes.

He nods. "Wren actually already knew Aidan in a roundabout sort of way. One of the friends she mentioned is his younger brother, Wesley."

Rhodes takes the seat next to me as Kaci titters on excitedly about our friends, simultaneously setting plates of food down in front of us. I nearly moan at the smell as Rho tells them about our day with Aidan, Copeland, and Crew. I don't think I'll ever stop marveling that Kaci has a successful career as a lawyer and somehow still managed to raise an incredible man and run their house. And damn if the woman can't cook a mean pot-pie, too.

As I eat my favorite meal surrounded by the people I love, I realize I wasted so much time on Derrick and his needs when I could have been doing this every week–smiling, laughing, and feeling more myself than I have in a long, *long* time.

It's good to be home.

CHAPTER 9
RHODES

I'VE HAD a goofy smile on my face all day. After dinner last night, Wren packed up her stuff and came home with me, where she immediately made herself comfortable in my guest room. Waking up to my girl making coffee in my kitchen felt like a dream.

And if it was, I never want to wake up.

We're in my SUV on our way to pick up the guys from the airport, and I can't lie, I'm really fucking edgy. These guys are so important to Wren, and I need them in my corner if I ever have any hope of escaping the friend zone.

I chuckle as she fiddles with the radio for the millionth time and reach over to wrap my hand around her smaller one.

"You nervous, Starling? I thought these guys were your best friends...after me, of course?" I smirk at her.

She huffs a laugh. "I'm excited! And I know they're gonna love you..." Her voice softens. "I just really want them to like it here...to like *you*. My worlds are colliding, and I guess I might be a little bit anxious because of it."

Wren is so goddamn sweet. She's still always worrying about other people's feelings before her own. Grabbing her soft hand in mine, I thread our fingers together and rest them in her lap.

"Wren, listen to me. These are guys you consider family, and I fully trust your judgment," I wink at her, and a little thrill goes through me when I see her blush and glance away. "We'll get along great, and I know they're going to love it here because *you* love it here. This place made you the girl we all know and adore, and I'd bet my favorite glove they're out-of-their-minds excited to finally see it."

A loud sigh gusts out of her mouth, ending in a small groan. "You're right. It's not like I haven't spent every day of the last three years with them. I don't know why I'm so nervous. It's gonna be great."

But I struggle to keep my own nerves from showing as we pull up to the airport.

Wren throws me a sidelong glance with her delicate hand on the door handle. "Seems like I'm not the only one feeling things."

I smirk at her cockily. "Who, me? Nah baby, I'm right as rain."

She looks like she's getting ready to argue with me when three boisterous voices fill the air. Wren practically dives out of the SUV, squealing as she runs to hug the guys I really hope only have brotherly feelings like she claims.

I exit the SUV and walk straight up to the tallest one —Jamie, I think. He surprises the hell out of me when he pulls me into a hard hug.

"Hey, man! It's so nice to finally meet the infamous Rhodes. I'm Jamie Reed, this is Asher Linwood, and obviously you know Wes." He lets go and points behind me when another hand claps down on my shoulder, and I turn to see a familiar smiling face.

"God, you really do look just like Aidan," I laugh, shaking Wesley's hand.

He laughs, too, and tosses his arm around the third guy, who's just released Wren from a lingering hug. I raise my eyebrows at the contact and look between him and Wren suspiciously. It's obvious he notices because he rolls his eyes and clasps my hand in his and pulls me in for a quick 'bro hug.'

"Don't worry, Wren is family, nothing more. We love her, but none of us will ever be *in love* with her," he says low in my ear.

I grin at him in relief and clap my hands together. "Alright, well, first things first we have lunch with the parents—"

"SHOTGUN!" Wesley shouts, cackling like a little kid as he sprints to the front seat of my SUV.

Wren shoots me an elated grin and scoots to the middle of the backseat. Jamie and Asher climb in behind her as I hop in and buckle up. With a quick check around me to make sure everybody has their seatbelts on, I give the guys a knowing grin.

"Ready to meet the parents?"

"Look at your handsome faces!" My mom says, squishing Wesley's cheeks in her hands. "You sure do know how to surround yourself with pretty men, honey," she says to

Wren in her version of a stage whisper. My hand is over my mouth to cover my laughter, but Wren is giggling like mad where she stands with Asher.

We've been at my parents for half an hour now, and my jealousy about her and the guys fades the longer they interact. They really do treat her like a little sister. Even Asher, who seems to have the closest physical relationship with my girl, doesn't come off as the touchy-feely type *at all*. Wren pulled me aside when we first arrived and explained that he's got extreme social anxiety, so she would likely stick near him.

"Mama Gray, you might want to let go of Wes's cheeks now so we can take a tour and maybe pop over to Dad's house," Wren says.

Wes waggles his brows at my mom, making kissy noises. "You can squish my cheeks any time you want, Mrs. Gray."

I'm mildly mortified when my mom blushes, but she just flicks him on the nose and moves to stand by my dad, who's smirking at Wes. "Trust me, Black, you couldn't handle Kaci on her calmest days."

I exaggerate a gag and turn a pleading look to Wren. She's laughing at my expense with Asher and Jamie. Wren gives me a playful look and opens her mouth to speak when there's a loud banging on the front door. I look at everybody and notice my parents are doing their best to keep neutral expressions. And failing miserably, might I add.

My mom's voice shakes as she speaks, and I can't tell if she's trying to hold back a laugh or tears, but she points to Wren. "Sweetie, would you mind grabbing that? I ordered a few things when I thought you would be staying here, so it's probably for you."

Wren, who seconds ago was suspicious because she can read my mom as well as I can, turns to her with a look of gratitude and a touch of awe. "Mama Gray, you shouldn't have. I don't need anything. I'm just happy to be home." Her voice wobbles, but she clears her throat and opens the door with the rest of us following behind her like her loyal fans.

Her squeals reach my ears a second before I turn the corner, and I smile as the reason for my parents' odd behavior walks in with Wren in his arms.

CHAPTER 10
WREN

"STARSHINE," my dad says as he picks me up in one of his famous bear hugs. "I missed my baby girl so much."

I'm so freaking surprised and excited to see my dad that the only thing that comes out of my mouth is an embarrassing squeak as I hug him. Being in his arms brings up all the emotions I've pushed to the side the last week. Tears burn the backs of my eyes until his scent hits me, and with it, a memory.

Wren, Eight Years Old

I rub at the side of my head underneath one of my pigtails, stomping up the driveway.

Stupid, mean, hair-pulling boys.

I slam the front door and jump when I hear daddy's voice behind me.

"Wren Andromeda Reid." I cringe at his stern tone. I'm not supposed to slam doors because I'm supposed to use my words when I have big feelings. "Wanna explain the attitude, Starshine?"

Silly tears burn my eyes and spin away, shrugging while I put my backpack away. "It's nothin'" I mumble.

He doesn't say anything for a minute until I turn back around. Daddy almost never gets mad at me, but he does tell me I give him lots of gray hairs. "Wanna try that again, kiddo? You pounded in here like a bull raring to get out of the chute."

I giggle as I picture the last rodeo we went to and wonder what I would look like as a bull. "It's nothin', daddy. Just some rude boys acting like big ol' babies."

He frowns and drops down to his knees next to the shoe bench so that I'm taller than him. "Starshine, do you remember what I told you about boys when you started school this year?"

I nod my head and play with the ends of my hair. "You said some boys are dumb and don't know how to act around girls, but if one ever hurts me, you'll be there to patch me up..." my voice trails off, unsure if I can say the next part, but he nods at me. "And then you'd help me kick his ass."

Daddy smiles, big and proud and happy, and hugs me super tight. He always smells good. Like books and the ocean and home.

"That's right, Wren. The reason I call you Starshine is because you've always shined brighter than anybody else, and that means sometimes people will be mean and try to steal your shine. But you won't let them. And if anybody ever breaks your heart and steals your shine, I'll patch you up and help you get it back."

"So, whose ass do we need to kick, Starshine?"

I laugh and finally let go of my dad. My brows furrow when I notice how tired he looks. Being a single parent, my dad always looked a little tired, but this is next level. His normally dark blond hair is streaked with gray, and his blue eyes look duller than the last time I saw him. Add that to the dark circles underneath his eyes and it has me wondering where he's been.

Just as I open my mouth to ask, two of the three stooges behind me butt in and fight each other to get in front of me. Wesley beats Jamison and thrusts out his hand.

"It's nice to meet you, Mr. Reid. I'm your daughter's best friend Wesley Black." An irritated huff sounds behind us, and Wes rolls his eyes. "Sorry, her best friend *after* Rhodes," he snarks.

My dad stifles a chuckle as he takes Wes's outstretched hand. "My name is Archie or Arch. None of that Mr. Reid shit; it makes me feel old."

Everyone laughs, and when Dad's gaze catches on the two men standing next to me, his eyes widen. He blinks several times before rubbing the heels of his palms on his eyes. "Whoa..." he whispers to me out of the corner of his mouth. "Is it just me, or did you find a male clone?"

My eyes widen and Jamie snickers next to me. I choke on a laugh. "No, Dad. I didn't find a clone."

He ignores me, staring at Jamie for a few seconds longer. He snaps out of it with a shake of his head and a bright smile and holds out his hand. "Sorry! I swear I do have all my mental faculties. You just look exactly like my father did at y'all's age. It's nice to meet you boys."

Jamie throws me a confused look but shakes Dad's hand with enthusiasm. "My name is Jamison Reed. It's so good to finally meet the man who raised such an incredible woman." His words start out heavy with inflection, no doubt because of his sibling theory, but turn soft when he compliments me.

"Aww, J. You're such a softy." I wrap an arm around his waist. As much as I tease him, he really is one of the best men I know, and I'm so thankful to have him as a friend.

His eyes light with mischief as he smirks down at me. "Anything for my *sister*."

Everybody is chattering on around us, but I see the way my dad's eyes rake over Jamie curiously. But when I arch an eyebrow his way, he waves me off. I'm distracted when Kaci claps her hands together and smiles fondly at Dad and me. "Why don't we give you two a few minutes to catch up. Rhodes, be polite and give the boys a tour of the house."

The four of them clear out, and Rhodes kisses the top of my head before doing the same. He stops to raise an eyebrow, asking if I'm okay, and I grin at him and nod. He smiles back before joining the others.

As soon as the room clears out, the tears I managed to hold off earlier come back full-force. "Daddy," I sniff, throwing myself into his chest.

"When Dom called and told me you showed up in the middle of the night, I caught the earliest flight back I could." He strokes my hair like he did when I was a little girl. "Whose ass do I need to help you kick?"

I let out a choked sound, burying my face in his gray polo. "Asher kind of already punched him in the dick."

His chest rumbles under my cheek with his soft chuckle. "He's the quiet one, right? I didn't really get to meet him, but it sounds like we'll get along just fine."

"Yeah, he has pretty bad anxiety, so meeting new people is hard for him. I'm sure you'll get him to open up at some point since I told them they could stay with you," I mutter sheepishly.

He barks out a laugh, startling me. "Of course, you did. I haven't had this many boys around since you told

FINALLY HOME

Benny we could host the baseball team's bonding dinner at our house your sophomore year." He ruffles my hair and shakes his head. "You know our house is always open for friends and family."

Appreciation for my dad overrides my stress, and I feel like I can relax for the first time since I opened the email that changed my whole life. "Derrick cheated on me," I whisper into his chest.

My dad stiffens and pushes me back to arm's length. I'm worried he's going to blow up and insist on saying his piece, but instead he inspects my expression, heaving a sigh and leading me toward the large sitting room just off the foyer.

We sit on the plush, cream-colored loveseat that faces the street. He tosses an arm over my shoulder and hauls me into his side. "I'm sorry, Starshine." He's quiet for a long minute before he grunts and turns sideways on the seat to look me in the eyes. "You know you can tell your old man to mind his own peas, but you don't seem all that upset about your marriage ending."

I cringe and grimace. "I'm not *not* upset," I sigh. "Things weren't good between us for a long time—longer than I wanted to admit even to myself. It hurts, but mostly I just feel stupid for ignoring the signs. I left my family for him, Dad!" Angry tears burn the backs of my eyes, but I refuse to let them fall. I don't want to spend another minute crying over a man who made his indifference to my feelings so painfully clear.

He nods and brings me even closer so my head rests on his shoulder. "The day your mom found out she was pregnant, she was getting ready to leave me," he says quietly, pain lacing his tone.

My body jolts against the couch and I pull back to

stare at my father with wide eyes, too afraid to say anything and stop his story. My mom was always kind of a taboo subject, but I caught my dad staring at some of their old pictures a few times when he thought I wasn't home. I know next to nothing about the woman who gave birth to me—only that her name was Madelyn.

"Your mother was a nurse at the local hospital, and we started dating while I was completing my doctorate degree. I was on a fast track for a professorship at Ridgeview and Lyn was someone I never knew I wanted until she made space for herself in my hectic life. She said she didn't mind how busy I was, and for a while, it really seemed like she didn't. We moved in together after only three months of dating just so we could see each other a little bit more often between my classes and her twelve-hour shifts."

His eyes gloss over as the tops of his cheeks flush. "I wasn't a perfect boyfriend by any means, Starshine. I won't lie and say I didn't understand why she wanted to break up. I was so obsessed with my career and school that I wasn't able to give her the consideration she needed. And then one day she came to me in a panic with a positive pregnancy test."

I can't even imagine how stressful that must have been for them, especially in such a new relationship.

A radiant smile takes over Dad's face and that brings a smile to my own. "And then a few months later, just days after I got my doctorate, I was holding you in my arms. In the space of a single moment, my entire world turned upside down in the best way possible, and suddenly, nothing else mattered. Not my job, or how much your mom and I were fighting, or how little you slept those first few months. All it took was one of your tiny pink fists wrapping around my finger to know I'd always have a little bit of starshine in my life no matter how hard things got."

The tears finally fall unbidden from my eyes, and I throw my arms around the only person who's loved me unconditionally for my whole life.

He hugs me tight, smoothing my hair back. "I know growing up without your mama wasn't ideal, but I hope you know I wouldn't change a thing, Wren. Raising you was the highlight of my life, and I'm so damn proud of the woman you are now."

Sniffling, I give him a squeeze before pulling back and waving off his words. "Having Kaci around through college took care of any absence I felt from not having a mom, but I wouldn't change a thing about my childhood, Dad. You made me feel so heard and loved every day, just like you do now. I didn't *need* another parent when I had you."

"I love you, Starshine. I thank our maker every day that I was blessed with you."

"I love you more, Dad."

CHAPTER 11
RHODES

"DID you see Wren's face, Dom?" My mom whisper-screams as we file into the kitchen after our brief tour of the house. "I don't think I'll ever get over the way that girl loves her dad. Maybe I should whip up something sweet to match the mood..."

Wes raises his hand like a kid in class, and I smack it down. He gives me a dirty look, then switches up his expression and gives my mom wide, innocent eyes. "Actually, Mama Gray, I was gonna ask my mom to swing by Rhodes's house later and bring some of her famous peach cobbler cookies since they're Wren's favorites."

Mom points an accusing finger at him, and he flinches slightly. "Wesley Black!" she scolds. "Your mother lives close enough to stop by my son's house, and you didn't invite her over for dinner?"

Asher notices the subtle reaction and puts an arm around Wesley's shoulders.

Hmm, I wonder what that's about. I'll have to remember to ask Wren about that later.

Wes's shoulders slump in relief. He flashes my mom a

sheepish grin and holds up his phone. "I'll go call her right now if you'll give me your address."

Mom shakes her head at him and writes it down, handing him the sticky note. "It's a good thing you boys are so cute because it seems like common sense is lacking in some of you." She gives me a look of disapproval as Asher follows Wes out to the back patio, and I must look surprised because she scoffs. "Don't act like you haven't been following that girl around like a lost puppy since she got here, Rhodes Colter. When are you going to wise up and make a move?"

My face is on fire, and I try not to glare at my mom while my dad guffaws at my expense. "She just got out of a terrible marriage, Mom. How do you honestly think that would go? 'Hey, Wren, I know Derrick just broke your heart and your trust, but I've been in love with you since we were eighteen, and I think we belong together.'"

They glance at each other and roll their eyes. "We're not saying bombard her with nearly a decade of feelings all at once, son. Wren didn't really love that dumbass Monroe, and you know it. She was looking for love in the wrong places and assumed she found it. We all know she was too loyal to call off the wedding after she made the commitment."

Mom sighs and wraps me in a hug that makes me feel like I'm nineteen again, watching my best friend marry the wrong man. "Rho, she was never meant to be with Derrick, and everybody knew it except for her. She might be hurting right now, but I don't think she ever looked at him the way she looks at you. All you can do is try to show her that the right man was beside her all along. Take it slow, and trust that she'll see it when she's ready."

I hug her back and nod against the top of her head. "You're right. I have to try."

"I'm so tired, I swear I could sleep for a month straight."

Wren and I just made it back to my house after saying our goodbyes to Jamie, Wes, and Asher. The last few days have been a whirlwind as the guys and I got to know each other. Not to mention all the time we spent with Copeland and Aidan. My girl has been an absolute trooper dealing with six ball players over the last week, and I'm excited to spend some time alone together.

"I know, Starling. Tell you what. It's still early, so why don't I order dumplings for delivery and load up a tray with all of our favorite snacks, and we can have a movie night. It'll be just like college, only this time the alcohol will be legal." I smirk at her, and she giggles, a blush creeps up her neck as she no doubt remembers some of our drunken mishaps—most of which happened before she met her controlling ex.

"That sounds perfect, Roly-Coly. Let me shower really quick, and then we can play movie roulette." She turns and skips up the stairs.

I make the mistake of watching her go and have to bite my knuckle to stifle a groan. Her ass is always amazing but her ass in leggings? *Phenomenal*.

Shaking my head, I give myself a stern pep talk about not fucking this up by acting like a horny teenager while I order our favorites from Lotus and load up the snack tray. I've just gotten everything on the table when Wren comes into the room in a cloud of apples and honey. My gaze is drawn to her like she's gravity and I'm the moon, helplessly stuck in her orbit. And damned happy about it.

Holy shit.

She's in an old pair of my sweats, rolled and tied tightly at the waist, and a cropped tee with *no bra*. Any hope I had of getting through tonight without having to conceal a painful erection just vanished in a cloud of Wren-scented smoke.

"Okay." She claps her hands and rubs them together mischievously. "Are you ready to play movie roulette?"

I pull her over to my couch and relish in the contented groan she lets out. I spent a fortune on the damned thing based on a recommendation from one of my teammates, but it's comfortable and plush as hell, so I knew Wren would love it.

"The only person I'd ever play movie roulette with is you, Starling. I hope you realize that."

Movie roulette is a game we came up with our freshman year because Wren is indecisive and can never pick a movie. We each write down five movies and toss them into a baseball glove, and then, we mix them up and take turns picking out the scraps of paper. It takes the decision out of our hands and is the only way we actually get to *watch* the movie.

She gets up to grab a sparkly blue pen out of the purse she tossed on the entry table and sits back down next to me with a smirk. "You know the drill, Roly-Coly, five movies in the Rawlings. Sparkly pen completely mandatory."

We really could have used anything to put the choices in, but I had baseball gloves all over my dorm in college, so now it's a tradition. I snag my favorite one off the table, and we both write our picks down on tiny torn slips of paper before dropping them in the glove.

I pick it up, close my eyes, and mix the folded papers. Then, I hold out the glove and peek one eye open only to see Wren with a radiant grin on her face. It takes my breath away that I was able to make her that happy by doing something so simple. "You wanna do the honors, Starling?"

She nods, her grin morphing into a mock-serious expression. She's not wearing any makeup and her skin is glowing after being outside so much this week. Her freckles stand out like crazy, and I can't wait for the day I can kiss every single one on her face just to make her laugh. Or find constellations in them when she's sleeping like I used to.

I'm so caught up in watching her, I don't notice her pull out a paper until she holds it up triumphantly. *"Forgetting Sarah Marshall!"*

I groan. I've seen this movie no less than eight thousand times since we became friends because it's one of her favorites. The doorbell rings as I stand, so I give her finger guns as I divert to the foyer. "That's probably the delivery guy, so you get the movie started and I'll grab the food and the alcohol."

Two hours and *many* drinks later, we're both well past tipsy and much closer on the couch than we were earlier.

"I'm just saying, Starling, that position is one-hundred percent not possible. I mean really think about it."

I have no idea how we landed on the topic of the infamous backbend but here we are, arguing about it while I pretend I'm not in desperate need of a cold shower and a date with my left hand.

"Roly-Coly-Oly, how do you *know* it's not possible? Have you tried it?" Her face screws up at her question, and she shivers. "Actually, never mind. I really don't want to know."

The liquor is loosening my tongue. "I haven't tried *any* position, Wren." I pick up the vodka bottle from the table and take a swig, staring at the ceiling. "Not with any girls anyway."

I turn toward her loud gasp and squint one eye to make the second Wren go away so I can focus on the first.

"Rhodes. Are you seriously trying to tell me you're gay?" Her voice is a shriek, and I put my hand over her mouth to make the sound stop. Unfortunately, that worked a little *too* well, and she licks my palm, which sends a pulse through my already painfully hard cock.

The hurt look on her face distracts me from my wet hand. "Why wouldn't you tell me? We've been best friends for *eight years!*" Honest-to-God tears form in her eyes, and I scramble to come up with a response through the alcohol brain fog.

It's hard to focus on anything, but I manage to answer her question with a shake of my head, gripping her shoulders tightly. "God, Wren. No! I mean…I was never really attracted to any girls in college, and yeah at one point I thought I might be gay. I did some stuff with a guy when I moved out here, but that didn't do *anything* for me. So yeah, definitely not gay." I'm going to regret the vodka in the morning, but I'm not sure if it will be because of the hangover or because I can't seem to shut my fucking mouth.

"Hold on," she grips my arm hard where it's still clutching her shoulder. "Okay, so you're not gay, but you tried *stuff* with a guy? What kind of stuff?"

Her question has me covering my face, mortified. But it's the open curiosity and lack of judgment in her eyes that makes me comfortable enough to answer honestly. "I didn't technically have sex with anyone, if that's what you're thinking," I murmur. "But I kind of...gave a blowjob. But then when he tried to reciprocate I couldn't keep it up."

I feel sick with nerves admitting all of this to the girl I've been in love with for years, but it's also sort of freeing. I've never been able to tell anyone about this. Even Cope and Aidan don't know the extent of the encounter. "It felt fine, good even. But I just couldn't get into it. I didn't love blowing him either, so I'm pretty confident I'm not into guys."

The next part of what I want to tell her is arguably the most embarrassing, so I say it as fast as possible, hoping to just rip off the damn band-aid before I puke from the anxiety rolling through me. "The truth is, Starling, that I've never had sex with *anyone*. Male or female."

Wren gapes at me, but she doesn't say anything, so I ramble on nervously. "It's not that I didn't want to! For most of college I actually thought there was something wrong with me because I wasn't getting the sexual urges or feelings all the other guys on the team seemed to have. After a lot of research, I finally figured out I'm demisexual."

"What does that mean?" she asks quietly.

I'm grateful she's not freaking out or making a huge

deal out of me being a twenty-five-year-old virgin, so I take a deep breath and try to release some of the tension from my jaw before I get a migraine. "It basically means I don't feel sexual attraction for a person until I develop a close emotional connection with them. So, theoretically, I could develop an attraction towards a person regardless of their gender, as long as I was emotionally attached to them as well."

I hold my breath, waiting for some profound words of wisdom and acceptance from my brilliant best friend, but in true Wren fashion, she doesn't do what I expect. Instead, she curls back up against my side and hums. "That's really cool, Rho. Is it weird that I'm proud of you for being able to explore your sexuality like that? Because I am. You're braver than me."

Something in her tone strikes me funny, and I turn slightly to study her profile. "What do you mean, I'm braver than you?"

She's quiet for long enough that I nearly start to doze off, but her next words make me snap my head up because I'm not sure I heard her correctly. Then, I groan, dropping it back down into my hands to stop the spinning and choke back the bile that threatens to rise from the sudden movement.

I clear my throat and slowly open my eyes to stare at Wren. "I'm sorry, did you just say you *never* had an orgasm with Derrick?"

There's no way...

Wren clumsily rolls off the couch, landing on her back on the floor. She peeks up at me with her hands over her red cheeks, and a tiny whimper escapes. "God, this is mortifying. It's not like I never had one at all, but... I just couldn't *get there*... from sex. He always made out like I was the faulty one, and there must be something wrong with my body that I needed... *more*."

"You're joking, right?" The anger from her words sobers me up a bit, and I'm livid. "What a fucking prick. Wren, Starling, I've never been with a woman like that and even I know that they rarely come from penetration alone. I swear, next you'll tell me he only ever wanted to do doggy."

I glance down in time to see her cringe, and my jaw nearly hits the damned floor when I gasp. "*No.*"

She groans. "Rho, it's not like I didn't ask! I'm not a prude, and I've watched porn. I thought it was normal to just not experiment with sex once you were married!"

I don't bring up that her ex-husband might be the one who needs to experiment sexually, and instead, focus on her words. My dream girl talking about porn and experimenting with sex has me rock hard again, and I shift uncomfortably on the couch. Risking an awkward glance at her, I adjust myself and sigh at the release of pressure.

"But enough about my pathetic sex life!" She sits up quickly and grabs her head for a second squinting like she's in pain before she points at me. "Let's talk about you and your lack of attraction."

I cut her off with a grunt, not wanting to spill any more liquor-fueled secrets. "Can we just pretend I never said anything? This whole conversation has been mortifying, and I need to stop drinking unless I want to deal with a wicked hangover during our lazy day tomorrow."

I stand up slowly, throw our trash away, click the TV off, and head to the kitchen to pour two glasses of water. Grabbing those and the bottle of Tylenol, I wrangle the tipsy girl up the stairs and into the guest room, where she collapses onto the bed and is asleep in seconds. All talk of my attraction blessedly ceases with her cute little snores.

Crisis averted.

I leave the water and pills on the nightstand and grab the soft blanket from the end of the bed, tucking her in. Using one finger, I gently brush some of her long hair off of her face and lean down to kiss her forehead. I let my lips linger on her skin for a few seconds too long, inhaling her sweet shampoo and taking the chance to tell her the truth while she can't hear me. "It's only ever been you, Starling."

CHAPTER 12
WREN

A BEAM of sun wakes me up, and it takes less than three seconds for the pounding in my head to let me know I drank way too much last night. I always get the worst hangovers, no matter how much I drink. My mouth is dry and tastes disgusting, so I'm assuming I didn't brush my teeth before bed.

Gross.

I roll over slowly and squint at the small clock on the nightstand. It's just after eight, and Rhodes, the perfect man that he is, left me Tylenol and water after I passed out. As I sit up to take them, I try to remember how I got to bed last night, but everything after our third shot is a little fuzzy. My last clear memory is watching Russell Brand gyrate on a stage in Hawaii.

I snort a laugh and make my way to the shower slowly so I don't get sick. The hot water does wonders for my headache, so I allow myself to stand under the spray for an extra-long time before I finally start my routine. I'm midway through washing the conditioner out of my hair when last night's memories flood back, the first one to hit me is the position debate, which is quickly followed with *Rhodes is a freaking VIRGIN*.

"Holy shit," I whisper. I don't know what it says about me that him being more inexperienced than me is so...*hot*. A crazy idea takes root in my head the longer I think about it, and I use the rest of my shower to mull it over. I consider every possible outcome and wonder if it's something he would even consider since he's always been so adamant that we're *just friends*.

Plus, what if he's not attracted to me? Or what if he's actually asexual and just doesn't realize it? The fact that we have a close emotional connection doesn't automatically mean he'll be attracted to me. Could our friendship survive a rejection like that?

I guess we'll find out.

Rhodes is still asleep when I head downstairs so before I grab my keys I leave a note on the fridge, that way he knows I'll be back with breakfast.

This conversation is going to require mimosas and something covered in gravy. Lots and lots of gravy.

A short while later, I arrive back at the house with a precariously-balanced pile of boxes and a drink carrier full of champagne and juice. Two hands I'd know anywhere grab the containers from me, and Rhodes's smirking face comes into view. But the smirk drops when he opens the box to see biscuits and gravy from our favorite breakfast spot. "Starling, you absolute *angel*. You went to Huck's?"

I scoff. "Obviously, I went to Huck's. Where else are you gonna get the best hangover breakfast in Charleston?"

His smile is way too bright for this early in the morning as he takes the food from my hands, but just like always, it sends butterflies cascading through my belly.

Only knowing what I do now sends them further south than usual, which makes my cheeks flush.

As soon as he sets the food on the island, I take a seat and dish us both up. His bare chest is directly in my line of sight and I quickly shovel food into my mouth to distract myself. I really don't need damp panties while sitting at the kitchen island before 9 a.m.

I clear my throat, suddenly more nervous than I've ever been around him. "Hey Rho?"

He doesn't lift his eyes, mumbling around a bite of food. "Yeah?"

"Do you, uh, remember anything about last night before we went to bed?"

He freezes and pushes his food around the plate. A blush that matches mine creeps up his neck and over his cheeks. "I was kind of hoping you didn't. I never have a problem keeping my mouth shut when I'm drunk unless I'm around you, Starling. It seems like you're always the exception."

Hope blossoms in my chest. Maybe he won't think my plan is so crazy after all. I realize I might not get a better opening, so I choose my words carefully and lay out my proposition.

"Listen, Rhodes, I think I have a solution to both of our...situations." I start. "You've never done anything, and there's so much I want to try that I wouldn't feel comfortable doing with someone I barely know. I'm here for a month, so what if we used that time, and each other, to just...experiment?"

He opens his mouth to speak, and I hold my breath. My heart beats so hard, I think I might throw up. "Wren..." He grimaces.

Oh, no.

"You know what? Never mind. Honestly, it was just a silly idea, and I didn't even consider the fact that you literally said you've never been attracted to any girls." I have to get out of here. "Gosh, it is just such a gorgeous day outside. I think I'll go for a nice long walk! See you in like, half an hour, yeah? Call me if you need anything!"

I barely stop long enough to grab my keys and AirPods out of my purse before I sprint out the door, desperate to run his impending rejection out of my mind.

What did I just do?

RHODES

Did she just...?

I'm speechless as Wren backtracks and bolts out of the house for a run. I can't form a coherent sentence right now even if I tried because I think Wren Reid, *my best friend,* just offered to take my virginity. And every single drop of blood in my brain rushed south leaving me with yet another inconvenient erection.

A million thoughts run through my pounding head but the one I keep coming back to is *did she mean it?* This might be just an experiment to her, but it could also be a chance for her to see me as more than a friend without pushing things further than she's ready to go. But at the same time, it could just as easily be a surefire way to get my heart broken if she doesn't feel the same.

After a quick cleanup of the kitchen, I head upstairs for a shower, praying I have enough time to take the edge off before she gets back. The water warms quickly, and I step in as images from my dreams play out in my mind. My cock is rock fucking hard as I wrap my hand around it and hiss at the sensation as I drag it up and down.

I close my eyes and picture Wren on her knees in front of me, looking up at me with those stupidly-gorgeous blue eyes. "Goddamn, Starling." She wraps her hand around my aching length with a smirk as she drags her tiny hand up and over the head. My knees nearly buckle at the pleasure, and I curse quietly when I mimic the action with my own hand. It's not long before I'm fucking my fist faster and moaning her name, but just as I feel pressure at the base of my spine signaling my orgasm is close, the bathroom door opens.

My eyes fly open to see the object of my fantasies frozen just inside the doorway with her jaw dropped, staring at the hand still wrapped around my dick.

Wren squeaks and stumbles back into the doorframe but makes no move to leave. Her eyes quickly shoot to mine and widen.

"Rhodes," she gasps. "I'm so sorry. I heard you calling my name and I didn't...I wasn't expecting..."

She still isn't leaving.

I make a split-second decision to pull the glass shower door open, not giving a single fuck that I'm leaving a puddle in my path as I stalk towards her. She still hasn't moved, and her chest heaves with each breath. Stopping inches from her, I wrap my hand around the back of her neck and tilt her face up to mine. I search her eyes, and see exactly what I need to do next.

"*Fuck it.*"

I slam my mouth to hers.

CHAPTER 13
WREN

FIVE MINUTES *Earlier*

I got less than half a mile from the house when I realized I couldn't just leave the conversation like that, so I turned around and came back. Rhodes isn't in the kitchen where I left him, and the house is quiet.

Did he leave?

Walking up the stairs, I hear water running, so I assume he's getting ready for the day. I jog the rest of the way up. "Rho?" I call. "You up here?"

I'm just turning the corner into his bedroom when I hear him say my name from the bathroom, so I knock lightly before walking in and I stop dead in my tracks.

He wasn't saying my name, he was *moaning it.* Through the glass walls of his giant walk-in shower, I see Rhodes with a hand wrapped around his long, thick cock. And *wow.* I can confidently say that being with him would be nothing like being with Derrick.

He makes a small sound, and my eyes snap to his. They're locked on my face as I take him in. It takes me way too long to realize he knows I'm frozen in place, staring at him.

"Rhodes, I'm so sorry!" I gasp out. My heart races, and suddenly, I feel like I can't take a full breath. "I heard you calling my name and I didn't... I wasn't expecting..." I can't seem to get more than a few words out. Each explanation stutters and dies on my dry tongue the longer my eyes are glued to his incredible body. Toned from a lifetime of baseball workouts and tan from months spent under the hot South Carolina sun, Rhodes Gray would make a nun drool on her habit.

His expression intensifies, and he yanks open the shower door, ignoring the water that runs off his glistening skin as he stomps across the tile floor. He doesn't stop until I can feel the heat that radiates off of his muscular body. Shivers run down my spine when his hand slides behind my neck, tilting my face up toward his. For once I have no idea what's going on in Rhodes's head.

"Fuck it."

Suddenly, his soft lips cover mine and my senses are overwhelmed as he kisses me. His muscles are taut, and he tastes like mint toothpaste. I'm so lost in the kiss that I don't notice we're moving until my back presses against the shower wall, and I'm drenched from all sides by warm water.

Panting, I slide my hands from his shoulders to his pecs and push him back, only far enough so we're still sharing air as we gasp for breath. "Rho...are you sure?" I know we need to talk about rules and what this means, but I won't turn him down if this is what he really wants. At least, not before taking the edge off for him. The fact that he's attracted to me at all is blowing my mind, given what he told about his sexuality.

He smiles and runs his nose along the side of my face. "Starling, there's nobody else I would rather do this with."

The second the words leave his mouth; we struggle to remove my now-wet clothes in a flurry of movement. Limbs are everywhere, and I can't stop the laugh that bursts free when my arms get stuck above my head, tangled in my soaked sports bra.

"I can't believe you're laughing right now." Rhodes's words are muffled as he kisses down my chest and stops to lightly tug on my nipples with his teeth.

I gasp, and my laughter stops. I try to bring my hands down to tangle in his hair only to be stopped by my still-stuck bra. My giggles return in full force, and he finally lifts his head from my breasts.

"Wren, I'm naked and nearly on my knees in front of you. I gotta be honest, my ego isn't loving the laughter." His eyes dance with mirth despite his serious tone.

I wiggle my trapped arms above my head, catching his attention. His lips tilt up in the corner, and he snorts, barely holding back a chuckle. "Aww, Starling, you should have said you were trapped."

"Rhodes Colter," I say with a glare. "If you don't get this stupid thing off me in the next five seconds, I'm going to leave and instead of losing your virginity, you can go celebrate *Palm Sunday* all by yourself."

He barks out a laugh as he yanks my bra off. "You call it that too?"

I just shrug with a smile and gently trace my newly-freed fingers over the rigid lines of his abdomen. "You know what? I think I'd like to see that."

The amusement on his face is replaced with confusion and apprehension. "You'd like to see *what*?" His voice is skeptical.

"I want to see you touch yourself, Rhodes. Show me what makes you feel good." My words are more of a plea. I've never been in a situation like this before, and I don't want to show my own apprehension and make him any more nervous than he is. Derrick was *very* experienced when we got together, so as much as I learned from him, I've never had to do the whole virgin thing with somebody else.

He looks shocked for so long that I worry I've pushed him too far, too fast when he blushes, and his mouth forms a small, shaky smile. He keeps eye contact as he moves to the other side of the shower and sits down on the stone bench, spreading his legs.

I lean back under the spray of the shower and grab the body wash, my gaze trained on Rhodes as he takes his hard length and strokes it slowly. My focus splits between the task at hand and the way his eyes flutter in pleasure as his fist squeezes over the head of his cock with each stroke.

My fingers glide across my sensitive nipples as I wash my chest, and I moan softly. Rhodes's eyes flare at the action, and I circle one nipple, pinching it lightly.

Before long, his breathing speeds up and his muttered curses get louder. "Stop." My voice is a quiet command as I step forward. Rhodes is stunning: angular cheekbones flushed bright red, either from being turned on or from nerves or maybe both; wide eyes showcase his blown-out pupils that mask most of the hazel iris; and his plush bottom lip is trapped between his perfect white teeth.

The man is literally a walking wet dream.

"What's wrong?" Rhodes gets out between heavy breaths. "Is everything okay? Did you change your mind?"

Instead of answering him, I add extra sway to my hips and approach until there's hardly any space left between us. The look of reverence in his eyes as they rake down my body makes me feel like a goddess and gives me confidence.

He inhales sharply when I drop to my knees and slide my hands up his thighs. His voice is raspy when he speaks. "If this is a dream, I hope I never wake up."

I peek at him through my lashes with a small smirk and lick a line up his shaft, which pulls a sexy moan from him. I take him into my mouth as far as I can without gagging and pull back, using my saliva to slick the path for my hands as I grip and stroke him firmly.

"Jesus Christ, Starling. I'm not gonna last," he groans. "Fuck, Wren, pull off." His hands fist in my hair, gently tugging as he holds off his orgasm.

Too bad I'm desperate for a taste.

I double down on my efforts and use both my hands and my mouth to bring him right to the edge, taking him in as far as possible when the first ropes of his release hit the back of my throat.

"*Holy shit,*" he chokes through another moan. That single masculine sound of pleasure has me dripping with need.

When I pull back, Rhodes stares like I might not be real. Hesitantly, he runs his thumb over my bottom lip and pulls me in for a deep kiss.

It's ridiculous to feel shy after what I just did, especially with him, but I do. I grip his outstretched hands and let him help me to my feet. The anxiety of what just happened builds in my chest, and I blurt out, "Want me to help you wash up?"

He looks confused but smiles anyway and guides me

under the water with him. I douse a soft cloth with his body wash and glide my hands over his toned chest. As I work my way to his back he places a soft kiss on my forehead that nearly has me melting into a puddle on the shower floor.

"Where's your head at, Starling?" His deep voice sends shivers down my spine despite the warm water that cascades over us. He pulls my chest flush to his soapy back, trapping my hands beneath his on his mouthwatering abs.

"Firmly planted on my shoulders, Roly-Coly-Oly."

Rhodes's laugh thrums through me, and the same thrum echoes between my legs, reminding me just how much I want my best friend.

"You going to tell me why you freaked out or do I have to massage it out of you?" He punctuates his words by turning around and moves his hands to my shoulders, massaging the tension from them.

I groan and cover my face in embarrassment. "I just..." I consider my words carefully, so he doesn't think I'm rejecting him. With a sigh, I cup his face in my hands, stand on my toes, and give him a soft kiss. "I don't want this to change our friendship, Rhodes. I feel like this could be really fun, and I trust you more than anyone, but what if we do this and it's terrible? Or what if things get awkward when I go back to work in a few weeks?"

He's silent for a minute until suddenly, he rolls his eyes and pulls me in for a hard kiss.

CHAPTER 14
RHODES

SHE CLEARLY DOESN'T REALIZE *she's already ruined me for anybody else.*

"Wren, listen to me," I tilt her chin up, forcing her to meet my steady gaze. "Our friendship is solid. A little sexual experimentation isn't going to rock our foundation to the point where it cracks. Make sense?"

She scrunches her nose with a dubious look, and it takes me a considerable amount of self-control not to boop it, but I don't want her to think I'm not taking her concerns seriously. I am. I just don't see a scenario where we don't end up together anyway, so all this worry is pointless in the long run.

She huffs a laugh and wraps her arms around my waist in a tight hug. "Yeah, that makes sense. But I still think we should talk and maybe set some rules or boundaries, so the lines don't get blurry."

I'm thankful she can't see the expression on my face. We've never been good at following rules. I don't know why she thinks we will be now. "Sure, Starling. We can do that."

Turning off the shower, I grab the towel from the warmer (silently thanking Copeland for the house-warming present) and wrap it around her. I take another from the small closet for myself and breathe a sigh of relief when she's fully covered because if I had to stare at her wet, naked body for another second, I would say fuck her rules and drag her to the bed like some kind of deranged caveman. Instead, I rifle through my drawer for one of my softest shirts and slip it over her head and then put on my favorite pair of light gray joggers.

"So," Wren says "rules."

I nod and wait patiently for her to gather her thoughts.

She sighs deeply. "I think it should be obvious that if either of us starts to develop non-friendly feelings, we should call it off early."

Too late, Starling.

My thoughts spiral for a moment. What do these rules mean about her feelings for me, *or lack thereof*? But I manage to keep a straight face and nod with a noncommittal, "mhmm." If I have to, I can nurse a broken heart when she leaves town, but I don't think I'd ever forgive myself if I missed out on a chance to be with Wren.

Exhaling in relief, she smiles at me. "That was the big one, but I also think maybe we shouldn't tell anybody about our little...arrangement. It'll just make things more complicated."

I actually agree with that one. We should probably keep things quiet in case I end up alone and devastated when she calls things off. I wouldn't want to get my parents' hopes up.

"And then finally, no judgment, and nobody else. If we're going to play sex scientists, there's no room for condemnation. And I think we should keep it to just us. So no other people while we're...together."

I stare at her incredulously. "Did you even have to add that one? Wren, even if I was attracted to someone else, I wouldn't disrespect you like that, especially given the whole reason you're here." I hate to bring up her ex, but I hate even more that she feels like she has to *ask* me to stay faithful to her while we're sleeping together.

Her face falls, and I feel like a jackass. "Starling, I'm sorry. Even if this isn't an official relationship, I would *never* run around on you. As long as we're doing this, it's you and me. I promise." I hold out my pinky, so she knows I'm serious, and she smiles.

"We haven't pinky promised since we were in college." She giggles.

I smirk at her. "And the difference now is I get to seal it with an actual kiss." I cup her face in my palms like the precious woman she is and kiss her softly once, then I part her lips with my tongue and deepen it. Kissing Wren is like having somebody flip on a light switch I didn't know I had. Or like the first time you light up your Christmas tree for the season. She sets my damn soul on fire, and one day soon I'll tell her exactly that.

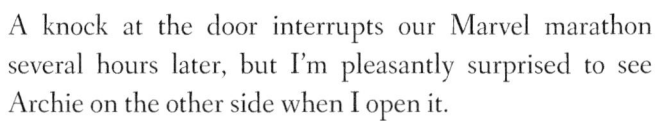

A knock at the door interrupts our Marvel marathon several hours later, but I'm pleasantly surprised to see Archie on the other side when I open it.

"Well, if it isn't my favorite major leaguer! How are you, son?" His voice is as jubilant as ever, and he looks worlds better than the last time I saw him. The dark circles under his eyes are almost gone, and the exhausted look he was sporting is gone too.

I smirk at him and lean in for a hug. "I'm good. Even better now that I know I haven't been usurped as the favorite now that you've met the other men in Wren's life."

He guffaws loudly. "You can't ask me to pick favorites among you boys, Gray. That's just cruel." He winks at me, and my heart warms that he still sees me like a son after all these years. "Speaking of favorites, is my baby girl here?"

"Hey Rho, who's here?" The woman in question walks into the room with an adorably irritated expression. She takes her movie marathons *very* seriously, but any annoyance disappears when she sees her father. "Daddy! What are you doing here?" The way she beams whenever she sees him never fails to make me smile. Her laugh rings out through the foyer when Archie picks her up and spins her around.

"I thought I'd swing by and take my favorite daughter to lunch. What do you say, Starshine? Wanna hit the town with your old man?"

Wren and I share a knowing look. "You're not old, Arch. If anything, we keep you young." I eye the gray hairs on his head with a smirk. "Then again...maybe we don't."

He pulls me into a headlock as I laugh, and Wren clears her throat. "Not to interrupt your bromance or anything, but I'm going to go change so we can head out," she says pointedly to her dad.

When he finally lets me out of the headlock, I eye him

warily. "You're looking much better today, Archie. You okay?"

He sighs wearily and shakes his head. "I'm completely fine, and I promise I'll tell you and your parents everything, but I need to tell Wren first. I don't really know how she's going to react, so I'll need you around here to make sure she doesn't take off."

I nod in agreement. "For what it's worth, it really seems like therapy is helping her. She doesn't seem to run from confrontation anymore. But if it's something big, I can see why you would be worried."

"Just keep an eye on her for me, would ya Rhodes? I worry about my girl."

Promising to look out for Wren is the easiest promise I've ever made.

CHAPTER 15
WREN

I DON'T REALLY THINK anything of my dad taking me out to eat since we used to do it all the time when I lived here, but he seems more nervous than a long-tailed cat in a room full of rocking chairs. When he offers to take me to our favorite Italian spot, I get suspicious of his motives. It's our special-occasion spot, so I feel like he might be trying to butter me up for something big.

Gino's is the cutest little restaurant in Mount Pleasant, a booming suburb of Charleston that consists of families and people who want to live in a quiet but active community outside of the hustle and bustle of the city. I always loved coming here and wandering the different shops and restaurants with Dad when I was a kid, but it's been ages since I've been. I think the last time was when we went to Gino's for my goodbye party before I moved to Seattle.

We walk in and it's like coming home in a weird way, and the red leather booths and checkered tablecloths lend to the cozy atmosphere. They're not busy, so the hostess lets us choose whatever seat we'd like, and my dad leads us to a booth below a large window so we can people-watch.

Nothing has changed since I last visited. There are empty bread baskets on every table, the green cloths waiting to be filled with fresh in-house baked bread. And there are half-melted candles that litter nearly every flat surface. We've always come here during the day, but I've heard after their dinner service they light the candles, and it's super romantic.

The owner's wife greets us and gushes about how long it's been since we were in, making me smile. Gino and his wife Francesca have been running this place for more than thirty years and still treat every single customer like family, which is part of why I love it so much. It was just Dad and I growing up, so coming here made it feel like we had even more family to celebrate the big moments with us.

After Francesca finishes fussing over us, she takes our orders and brings our drinks, telling us our food will be out soon. The minute she leaves, I fold my hands together and set them in front of me on the table. "Okay, spill. First the mysterious business trip you didn't tell me about and now lunch at Gino's? What's going on with you, Dad?"

Color dots his cheeks as he fiddles with his straw wrapper, tearing it into tiny pieces. "I was visiting my girlfriend for a long weekend."

I choke on my soda and launch into a coughing fit, grabbing my napkin to catch the liquid that dribbles down my chin before it stains my white tee. "I'm sorry, I must have misheard you. It sounded like you just said you were visiting your *girlfriend*."

He straightens in his seat, a stubborn expression sliding into place. "That's exactly what I said. I didn't want to tell you until I knew it was serious because I've never introduced you to a woman before."

I don't know whether to be happy for him, angry that he kept it from me, or hurt that he feels like I'm so fragile he couldn't tell me until now. "Wait...a serious girlfriend? How long have you been dating, exactly?"

A hint of shame flits through his eyes before he clears his throat. "That trip was to celebrate our one-year anniversary." He cringes.

"I'm sorry, are you seriously telling me you've been with this woman for a *year,* and you didn't tell me?!" I slap my hands down on the table, rattling the dishes. I know I should lower my voice given the setting, but I'm pissed.

He gives me his stern "dad" look; he means business, and I barely manage to conceal my incredulity. That look used to scare me when I was a kid but I'm a 25-year-old woman now. "Wren Andromeda." His stern voice matches mine in volume, and I jump a little bit. My dad hardly ever raises his voice.

Well shit, I guess that does still work.

I straighten in my seat, give him a sheepish smile, and glance around the restaurant. "Sorry, Daddy."

He gives me an exasperated look, but it's easy to see the love shining in his eyes. For so long it's been just him and me against the world, and I'm a little worried our relationship will change because of this new development. My dad will always be my person, but I've literally never seen him with a woman before. What if this hurts our close relationship?

"Like I was saying, I didn't say anything because I didn't want to hit you with a curveball until I knew for sure whether it was serious or not. You're my Starshine, Wren. And something like this might have made you feel like you wouldn't be my priority anymore. I guess I was just scared you'd be angry with me. You're a grown woman, but I'll always see you as my little girl. I'm sorry I didn't tell you, but I'm not sorry for protecting my baby girl's feelings."

And just like that, all my anger dissipates, which leaves me feeling hurt. "I just wish you felt comfortable enough to confide in me the way you've always encouraged me to confide in you. I may be your daughter, but like you said, I'm not a child anymore. I can handle the hard stuff without losing my cool." I raise an eyebrow at him. "And I definitely could have handled knowing you were dating before now."

He has the decency to look a little chagrined and nods. "I know, but I can't change the past. And honestly, Wren, I wouldn't want to. I needed time to get to know her and figure out my own feelings before I brought yours into the mix. I really think you'll like her, Starshine."

The idea of my dad potentially marrying someone isn't as jarring as I thought it would be, and I wonder if that's because I never saw him with my mom or anyone else. He's always just been my dad, not somebody's significant other.

Offering him a small smile, I place my chin in my hands. "Tell me about her."

His eyes take on a dreamy quality that nearly has me snickering, but I want him to know I take this seriously, so I hold it back. "Her name is Caroline, and she teaches biology at a college in Tennessee. She's... God, she's wonderful, Wren. She's brilliant and kind and funny, not to mention so full of life. I really do think you'll love her."

The way my dad talks about Caroline is the way I want someone to talk about me someday. He goes on to tell me how they met and some of the things they've done over the last year, and by the end of lunch I'm nearly in a sugar coma over just how sweet he is on her.

"Caroline sounds amazing, Dad. I'm really happy for you."

He beams and takes my hand in his with a nervous smile. "Part of the reason I wanted to tell you about her now is because she was offered a job at Ridgeview, and I considered asking her to move in with me. But I needed to know how you felt about it before I offered."

Mixed feelings bubble up in my chest. To know he's with someone is one thing, but them living together is a whole different type of scary. But I refuse to let him spend any more of his life putting my happiness before his, so I push all of that aside to dissect later and smile widely. "As long as you're happy, I am too."

Relief softens his tense posture, and I know I made the right decision.

"I'm not naïve enough to think this whole situation won't take some adjustment on all of our parts, but you really surprised me today, Starshine. You've had so many big changes the last month and are handling it with more grace than anybody would ever expect. You have a wonderful head on your shoulders, and I hope you know how proud I am of the incredible young woman you've become."

Tears fill my eyes before I can blink, and I do my best to hold them back. "I love you, Dad."

He looks at me warmly and grabs my hand across the booth. "I love you more than you'll ever know, Wren."

Later that night, Rhodes and I sit in the living room channel surfing while I tell him about lunch with Dad.

"And he really didn't say *anything* for an entire year? Not even to my parents!" His tone betrays his surprise, and I don't blame him a bit. I'm still processing the news.

I nod and collapse back against the couch with a huff. "I don't know if I'm really ready to talk about it, honestly. He's happy and that's all that matters."

Rhodes practically melts into the soft cushions. "Yeah, alright. But I wonder what she looks like. God, I can't picture Archie dating anyone."

We sit in comfortable silence for several minutes until he clears his throat. His cheeks are flushed when I look at him and he's fidgeting anxiously. "Hey, Starling?"

I keep my voice soft and expression gentle when I answer. "Yeah, Rho?"

"Will you...um..." he sighs loudly before turning to look me in the eyes. "Will you kiss me?"

My eyebrows raise, but I can't help my huge grin. Instead of answering him with words, I get to my knees and crawl across the couch slowly until I'm straddling his lap. His eyes are as wide as saucers as he takes in my position. His hands land on my hips in what seems like an unconscious move. "Is this okay?"

He nods frantically. "Yes. Hell yes. You on my lap is always okay, Starling."

I grin. "Well, okay then." I lean in and initiate the kiss. I'm hoping if I lead him a little bit, he'll feel more comfortable taking what he wants. And sure enough, after a few seconds he flips us so he's hovering over me, using his forearms to support his upper body.

His tongue demands entrance to my mouth, and I give it without hesitation, running my fingers through his soft hair and letting my nails scratch his scalp lightly when he nips my bottom lip.

He groans hoarsely and thrusts his rapidly growing erection into my thighs. I wiggle underneath him, desperately trying to get some friction on my neglected clit. The kiss turns frantic and needy the longer it goes on, and I push Rhodes back as both of us breathe heavily.

"Are you good?"

I nod and lift my shirt, giving him an eyeful since I'm not wearing a bra. "I have an IUD, and I'm clean." My cheeks burn hot. "I mean, if you're ready…" The last part is embarrassing to admit, but he deserves to know. "I got tested while the guys were in town. After everything, I needed the reassurance."

Understanding dawns on his face and he smiles softly, bringing his hand up to cup my cheek. "We get tested before the start of every season, so I'm good."

"Are you absolutely sure this is what you want, Rho?" I ask one more time.

He pulls off his shirt in response, and I'm momentarily struck dumb at the sight of his exquisite chest. It doesn't matter how many times I see it up close, I will never get over how he looks like a Greek statue. His pecks are clean shaven and rock hard, which flow into a ridiculously well-defined eight-pack. And he's got an incredible V-line and a dark happy trail that starts below his belly button, leading to what I know is an extremely impressive cock.

"Like I said yesterday, I've never been more sure of anything. If I could choose anyone to do this with, it's you Wren." He's barely finished his sentence before he pulls down my leggings and panties, glancing up at me with a blush on his cheeks. "Will you tell me what to do? All I've been able to think about since the shower is tasting you."

My cheeks flush hot, and I nod. My anxiety about screwing up our friendship has improved since we talked, but it flares again as Rhodes leans down and takes a deep inhale.

He lets out a ragged groan and glances up at me through his long eyelashes. "Fuck, baby. You smell so damn good."

Licking a tentative stripe up my core, my surprised whimper encourages him to continue. He flattens his tongue and licks a path from my opening to my clit and back. "Holy hell."

I *feel* his laughter against my clit, and it makes me shiver as I thread my fingers through his soft hair. His hands roam over my lower back, stopping to cup my ass in a tight grip. I tug his hair in response, and he growls, diving in with renewed vigor.

Rhodes practically *devours* me, and even though he's a little clumsy and wild, it's still the best oral ever. My back bows off the couch when he sucks my clit into his hot mouth, and the second he sticks a hesitant finger inside me, I'm clenching down on him in the best orgasm I've ever had.

"Oh my god, Rho."

He looks shy but also a little smug, and it's such a sexy combination on him, I can't help my dreamy post-orgasm sigh. "Was that okay?"

"Are you sure that was your first time going down on

someone?" The question is innocent but comes out slightly jealous.

Probably because the thought of him doing that to someone else makes you a little ragey.

His proud smile transforms into a dirty smirk, and holy shit, did it just get really hot in here?

"I've had more than a decade to research and imagine this moment, Wren. I'm practically a fucking boy scout with how prepared I am. Plus, you know I've given a blow job before, and I've done other things, but I've never gone down on a woman before you. It just felt too intimate to do with someone I barely knew."

The giggle that escapes me is unavoidable in the face of his confession. "God, you're too cute Rho." I yank him down to kiss me. I thought tasting myself would be a turn off, but if anything, I'm even more eager to have him inside me. I'm silently thanking my younger self for taking up yoga because I'm able to get my feet up and use them to push down his shorts and boxer briefs.

His cock bobs free, and Rhodes reaches down to stroke it a few times, which causes his knuckles to graze my clit. We both groan and he breaks our kiss to glance down as he lines himself up with my entrance. His hands shake and with the way his face is tilted down, I can't tell what he's thinking.

"We don't have to do this if you're not ready, Rhodes." I do my best to keep my voice even and soft, so I don't influence his decision.

His warm hazel eyes flash to mine. "I'm good, Starling. I'm ready. Just kind of nervous. Are you having second thoughts?"

I lift my hips in silent answer and moan loudly as he chuckles and works his way inside slowly. Each thrust is tentative and small, and even though I'm not the virgin here, I can't deny that the stretch is borderline painful. Derrick wasn't exactly well-endowed, and it's been a while.

"Jesus Christ, Wren," he chokes. "You're so fucking tight."

The pain is finally starting to recede as I squeeze my eyes closed and do my best to breathe through it. Rhodes seems to sense my discomfort because as soon as he's seated fully inside me, he presses his forehead to mine and stills.

"You okay, Starling?"

Taking several deep breaths, I open my eyes to see Rhodes staring. His eyes are dilated and full of heat. I gasp when he adjusts his position and his gaze darkens, becoming greener. He kisses me slow and deep as he gently pulls out halfway, thrusting back in and tilting his head to make sure I'm still okay. I smile shyly and nod.

No words are necessary as he begins to thrust faster and harder, finding an unsteady rhythm. Then, he pulls out so he's kneeling over me on the couch. I nearly whine at the loss of him inside me until he yanks me by the hips so my ass is between his legs with my thighs resting over his as he slowly slides back into me, hitting a spot that causes me to see stars with every thrust. In this position only my shoulders are touching the cushion, so I toss my head back, letting my hands play with my nipples.

"Oh my god, right there! Don't stop, Rho, please."

He grins wickedly and holds eye contact while he licks his thumb and brings it down to rub circles over my sensitive clit.

"Fucking hell, Wren. If you clench around me any

tighter, this will be over way too fast," he pants out breathlessly, thrusting in a steadier rhythm now.

"I'm gonna come, Rhodes. Don't stop!"

"Fuck, me too." He picks up the pace with his thumb and just as his thrusts falter, he pinches my clit and I come with a scream that does nothing to mask his roar of pleasure.

He collapses on the couch on his side and rolls me with him so he's still inside me.

It's several minutes before I'm able to speak, and my voice is a hoarse whisper when I do. "Was it everything you hoped it would be?"

He heaves a deep sigh and wraps me up tightly in his arms, kissing the top of my head several times as he murmurs, "It was more, Starling. So much more."

CHAPTER 16
RHODES

I WAS worried Wren would freak out after we had sex, but if anything, she's more affectionate than ever. After losing my virginity yesterday, we cleaned ourselves up in time for dinner with my parents, where she stuck to my side like glue. I could tell my mom wanted to ask questions, but a stern look was enough to deter her until now.

I came over to my parents for breakfast this morning while Wren went to a yoga class with Aidan's mom, Shelly, and I wasn't even all the way through the door before the inquisition started.

"Did you tell her you love her yet?"

I groan and rub the heels of my palms against my eyes. "Mom, no. Not yet. Don't you think I would be shouting it from the damned roof if I told her I love her, and she acted like *that*?"

My mom looks confused, and I don't blame her since I'm not much clearer than she is. I'm not about to point out to Wren that she's acting like a girlfriend rather than somebody who wants a temporary friends-with-benefits arrangement. Her behavior is so far from what I expected that it's throwing me for a loop.

It started small, with little touches and holding my hand. But by the end of the night she had sat herself on my lap and was half asleep, nuzzling my neck. *In front of my parents.*

Mom clears her throat and looks at me with an emotion I can't name in her eyes. "Honey, I really think you should tell her while she's in town. The way she looked at you last night is the way I've looked at your dad for more than twenty years, and I don't want you to miss out on a love like that because you were waiting for the perfect moment."

I stare at her incredulously and open my mouth to speak, but she holds up a hand.

"Yes, Wren is fresh out of a terrible marriage, and she's likely skittish right now. I get that. But you love her more than Derrick probably ever did, and you've been pining after her since college. You need to remember I know that girl almost as well as you do. Her actions last night didn't seem like she would be against being with you romantically." She raises an eyebrow at me.

My cheeks flush. One night in college, shortly before Wren and Derrick got together, I went home to Oregon for spring break and came home absolutely hammered after a night out with some old high school buddies. I didn't even make it all the way in the house before I drunkenly confessed my pathetic lack of a dating life to my parents. I told them how I didn't want anybody but Wren and how I knew I wasn't gay either. It felt like my body's way of saying Wren was the only girl for me, and I would likely be alone forever and die a virgin. My dad still laughs about it to this day. In his words, "I almost taped you and sent it off to Hollywood, son. The level of dramatics was fit for a movie screen."

Obviously I know now that it's just my sexuality, but I still want Wren more than anything.

Needless to say, I wouldn't go out as often when I'd visit home and stopped drinking so much when I did go out to avoid any more inebriated confessions.

"Mom, I'm well aware of her current relationship status and the details of what brought her home. Trust me when I say I'm trying to woo her while also doing whatever I can to make sure she doesn't feel pressured or uncomfortable. Wren is...." Sighing, I run my fingers over the Starling tattooed on my left hand and glance up at my parents across the kitchen table. "She's everything to me. My dream girl in every sense of the word. I think I'm holding back because I just don't know what I'll do if she doesn't feel the same."

I drop my head into my palms and groan. I don't want to see the pity on their faces. A heavy hand on my back startles me out of my crisis and my shoulders drop slightly when I raise my head to meet my dad's understanding gaze.

He looks almost exactly the same as he did when I was a kid other than the light smattering of gray at his temples. I hope the Gray genetics bless me so I look as good as he does when I'm his age. The man is 49 years old and still gets confused for my older brother on a pretty regular basis. It drives my mom up a wall and boosts his ego every single time.

"Rhodes, that girl is crazy about you. We could see it back then, and we see it now. But it's likely buried under years of feelings for someone else and preconceived notions about how she should be handling her divorce. I don't really see why jumping into a relationship would hurt either of you in the long run, but we will always support the both of you no matter what."

Having their support lifts a weight off my shoulders I didn't realize I'd been carrying, and I know I'm lucky to have such incredible parents.

"Plus," I glance over to see my mom sporting a too-wide grin. "The sooner you legally make Wren my daughter, the sooner we get beautiful grandbabies."

I choke on my spit and cough violently while my dad beats my back. Even the sound of me gasping doesn't cover their laughter. When I finally get enough oxygen to my brain to function, I turn a dirty glare their way just as my dad slides back onto the stool next to Mom.

"What if we don't want kids?"

Mom raises her eyebrow and quickly looks at my dad before she turns to me with a shrug, that grin still wide and wild on her face. "Then we'll get adorable grand-dogs. Seems like a win-win either way."

They continue to plan out our entire future, but the incessant buzz in my ears drowns out their words. My mom doesn't know it, but she just gave me one more idea of how to convince Wren to stay.

"Now, you know this breed takes work, right? I won't give him to you if you aren't prepared to put in the effort to train him proper-like and keep up on his grooming."

I nod vigorously. I want the man holding my new "child" hostage to know I'll take his care *very* seriously.

After a lengthy phone call and a check-in text to make sure Wren was still in meetings until later this afternoon, I left my parents' place and drove an hour to Archie's friend's farm.

"I know exactly how much work Newfoundland's take, sir. I've loved this breed since I was a kid and have done a ton of research over the years in the hope that I'd be able to own one someday." I might be laying it on a little thick, but the dog is cute and fluffy and staring at me with small eyes that are a much lighter shade of blue than my girl's deep-ocean color.

Mr. Hendrick's deep-set gaze appraises me critically, causing me to subconsciously straighten my spine. At 70 years old and nearly a foot shorter than me, Walter Hendrick is still a scary son of a bitch. I'd never say it to his face, but the man has made me nervous ever since I met him five years ago when he came to one of my college games with Dad and Archie. Back then, he had thick brown hair and a larger-than-life personality, but now his hair is mostly gray, and though his presence is still intimidating, it's more subdued.

Back in the day, Walter was a guest lecturer on animal husbandry and Archie took his class as a filler-elective in college. Mr. Hendrick said Archie was a major pain in his ass from day one but eventually grew on him. They stayed in touch over the years, and he's been kind of a pseudo-grandfather to Wren since she was born. I'm honored he was willing to give me the time of day, let alone one of his precious pups.

He nods but still looks suspicious as he holds my baby and strokes his fur gently. "You play ball professionally, don't ya?"

I nod, keeping my mouth shut.

"Well then, what makes you think you have time for a dog at all? Let alone one that needs so much time and attention?"

His question doesn't faze me since I've been thinking about this for years. Now that Wren is here, I'm finally ready to take the plunge. *And if it helps convince her to stay, that's just an added bonus.* "I'm a very active person even during the off-season, and I already have full permission from my coach and the training facility to bring him with me to practice. And on the days that I can't, my parents are thrilled to have a grandchild around—even if he's not human." I quirk my lips.

Walter never had any children, instead choosing to become a licensed breeder alongside his late wife, Elizabeth. He's slowed down significantly since cancer took her three years ago, so I was lucky he had any pups at all.

My comment gets a small smile out of him and fucking *finally*, he hands me my baby. "Mhmm, I see. And this sudden need for a pup has nothing to do with the pretty little thing I heard is back in town?"

I freeze mid-snuggle and send a wide-eyed, panicked look at the old man with my face still buried in the puppy's fur.

He smirks at me and scratches his sun-wrinkled fingers under the pup's jaw, his eyes mist over as a faraway look crosses his face. "My Lizzie didn't want a thing to do with farm life until the day she came out here from the city to visit and saw the brand-new litter of pups my first dog had whelped the week before. To this day I don't think she would have agreed to marry me without the dogs."

I met Mrs. Hendrick a few times before she passed after I moved out here to play for Charleston, and she was a kind soul. The woman never met a person or animal she didn't like and raising dogs was her passion. I prayed that someday Wren and I would have the love she and Walter shared, and now with that dream closer than ever, I desperately hope I don't fuck it up.

With a slight shake of his head, his eyes clear and he holds out a hand for me to shake. "You're a good man, Rhodes. I couldn't pick a better home for my last pup."

My mouth parts in shock. "Of the season, you mean?"

He smiles sadly. "Ever. I'm too old to handle them by myself anymore, and it just isn't the same without Lizzie by my side. I've been doing this for damn near forty years, and as much as I love it, I'm ready. Your dad callin' me today felt like a sign and the look in your eyes just now reminded me of how I looked at Lizzie all those years ago." He sighs. "Do whatever you have to do to make it work, son. There's no greater feeling than spendin' your life with your best friend, and that sweet girl of yours deserves nothing but the best."

His words reaffirm everything I've been thinking, and I gently squeeze the puppy in my arms. "Don't worry, Mr. Hendrick. I plan to. I also plan to bring this little guy back to see you every once in a while, just so you know your last pup is doing alright."

His grin grows, and he gives the sleeping pup one last gentle pet. "Call me Walt."

CHAPTER 17
WREN

I'VE JUST WRAPPED up my meeting with the divorce attorney when I hear Rhodes's front door open.

"Hey! How was your day with Mama and Daddy Gray?" I call out, still typing up the last of my notes on my tablet for my call with Jeremy and his lawyer later this week. I haven't done much more than update him through texts since I got here, and I miss the big guy like crazy.

There's no response, so I close out my tabs and set my tablet on the coffee table. "Rho?"

I go to stand when out of nowhere, I'm tackled back to the couch by a blur of shiny fur and puppy breath. "Oh my God!" I squeal and pick up the huge fluffball, holding it under its soft arms to get a better look at what is an absolutely precious boy. "You are the cutest thing I've ever seen in my *life*. Whose baby are you, huh? You're absolutely dashing. Yes you are!" He squirms in my arms and attacks my neck with aggressive licks and little nips, and I can't contain my laughter.

"I can already feel myself being replaced." Rhodes's deep voice is filled with warmth. He's in the entry to the living room, a blinding grin on his handsome face as he watches the surprisingly big dog attack me with affection.

As soon as I see him, a wide smile makes its way onto my face until what he said registers, and then my jaw drops. "He's yours?" My voice is practically a squeal and the pup yips in response. I immediately squish his little face between my hands and plant a kiss on his nose in apology.

My best friend laughs, walks over, and drops down onto the couch next to me. He ruffles the little guy's fur. "Sure is. You know how Mr. Hendrick has a farm out past Ridgeville?"

I nod with a smile. I need to go see Walt soon; it's been way too long, and I miss the old grump somethin' fierce.

"Well, you know I've wanted this breed for pretty much my whole life. So, when my dad told me Walt only had one pup left, and he was a *gray* Newfie? I knew it was meant to be. I drove out there this morning, and he glued himself to my side right away."

I smirk at him. "So, he's like the dog version of you? Because I seem to remember you doing the exact same thing to me eight years ago."

He winks and leans in to drop a too-short kiss on my lips. "Totally worth it." My surprise must show on my face at his show of innocent affection but he just chuckles. "Anyway, this wild little one still needs a name. Got any ideas for me?"

I'm beyond touched that he's asking for my opinion, and a little part of me is secretly thrilled at the prospect of naming a pet with him, even if it's technically not *my* dog. I run my fingers through his soft, silvery gray fur and look at his light blue eyes while I contemplate my answer. It only takes a few seconds for it to hit me, and I grin at Rhodes.

"I think his name is Finnegan. Finn for short."

He glances back and forth between me and the puppy with a mix of emotions on his face before finally settling on joy. "Finnegan Gray. I love it. What do you say we take Finny here outside to go potty and then we can head to the pet store to get all the things he needs to feel comfortable in his new home."

My heart swells with affection for this man. Rhodes has wanted a dog as long as I've known him and the childlike awe in his eyes now that he finally has one is making my feelings dip into dangerous territory–the kind of territory that usually precedes three little words that would change everything between us.

Panicked at the direction of my thoughts, I set Finn aside and jump up off the couch. "That sounds great!" My voice is high and reedy, so I clear my throat and plaster on what, I hope, looks like a genuine smile. "You take him outside and I'll just go... get ready." I turn and rush up the stairs before he can respond.

You have got to chill out, dude. The number one rule you suggested was no catching feelings.

Confused thoughts swirl around my mind while I strip out of my slouchy clothes. Just as I lean over to pull on a pair of jeans, my door opens and I squeak in surprise and turn around, holding the material to my chest.

"Jesus, Rho. You're fixin' to send me to an early grave. What are you doing just barging in here like that?" I'm not actually mad about it, just startled.

He doesn't say anything as his eyes rake down my mostly naked body. My panic from earlier begins to fade when I see the desire in his eyes and heat pools low in my belly. His expression gives nothing away as he takes slow, measured steps towards me.

My heart beats faster the closer he gets, and I barely feel the jeans fall from my fingertips, too distracted by the way he backs me up until my knees hit the edge of the bed. His long, calloused fingers push my hair behind my ear. I expect him to drop his hand but instead he pushes it to the base of my skull and grips a fistful of the strands, pulling it hard until I have no choice but to drop my head back.

I gasp and my fingers grip his soft shirt as his mouth crashes onto mine. His tongue licks along the seam of my lips, demanding entrance as I moan. I feel my panties growing damp, and I know he feels it too when he moves his leg between mine and drops one hand to my lower back to encourage me to grind on him.

Rhodes breaks the kiss with a ragged groan when I do exactly that, leaning his forehead against mine. His minty breath washes across my face as he lets out a small laugh. "Goddamn, baby. You're ruining me in all the best ways."

My pulse soars, and I don't want to think about the implication of his words, so I slam my lips back to his. The friction against my clit is almost too much, and I whimper into his mouth.

"Panties off and get on the bed, Starling," he pants. I scramble to do as he asks and nearly trip when my panties get caught on my foot. I would feel embarrassed, but I'm too turned on. Finally, I win the fight against my bra clasp and collapse onto the bed, rolling onto my back and sliding up until my head rests on the pillows.

The heat in Rho's eyes is unmistakable, and I feel myself getting wetter by the second the longer he stares. My clit starts to throb, and I squirm around on the bed. I try to find some friction by rubbing my legs together but he lets out a snarl as he dives on top of me and immediately takes one of my stiff nipples into his mouth to suck on it. My back arches, and I let out a cry at the unexpected jolt of pleasure.

"Seeing you naked and writhing for me is something I only ever thought I'd see in my wildest fantasies. It's so much fucking better than I imagined." His words are a growl against my breast as he sucks and laps at my skin before he moves to do the same on the other side.

My mind catches on the way he worded that.

What does he mean, better than he imagined? Why did he make it seem like he's been waiting forever for this? Is it possible... that he's wanted me for longer than this arrangement?

A small part of me screams to be cautious as a dangerous seed of hope starts to form with his words. Luckily, all coherent thought leaves me when he kisses his way down my torso, stopping to dip his tongue in my belly button. I giggle wildly and push his head. "Rho! Stop it."

He chuckles. "Sorry, Starling. If I only get you for a little while, I figure I should taste every part of you while I can."

Something in my gut sours at his mention of how temporary this arrangement is, but I force it away and lock my feelings back into their pretty little box where they've comfortably sat for the last eight years. It still takes considerable effort to unstick my tongue from the roof of my mouth and swallow past the sudden dryness so

I can answer him. "Don't let me stop you, then. As long as I get to return the favor later."

A wicked grin tilts the edges of his mouth, and he licks his full lips. "Promise?"

CHAPTER 18
RHODES

WREN LOOKS SO GODDAMN beautiful spread out for me. I wonder if I could implement a no-clothes rule for the rest of her time here, at least around the house. The way her eyes light with desire has me leaking precum into my boxers as I make good on my promise to taste every inch of her.

The apprehension doesn't kick in until I finally reach her center. Outside of our rushed first time and the research I've done, I still have almost no experience or confidence in what I'm doing. What if she hates it and is too nice to tell me? What if I'm worse than a fumbling teenager?

Small hands frame my cheeks and pull me from my mini-crisis. "Where'd you go?" Wren's sweet voice soothes some of my panic and staring into her startling blue eyes calms me further.

Laughing nervously, I kiss her and speak against her lips. "Will you, uh, tell me if I ever do something you don't like?" My cheeks are on *fire,* but I know she would never judge me for my lack of experience.

"Oh, Roly-Coly, of course I will. But I promise I'll love anything you do because it's you."

My heart nearly beats out of my chest, and I swear to God, I forget how to breathe. She probably only said it to reassure me, but it felt like more. Without responding, I pull back and trail open-mouthed kisses along the inside of her thigh, using my hands to spread her legs even farther so I can fit my wide shoulders between them.

She whimpers when I briefly flick my tongue against her clit, and then I move to her other thigh so I can drop kisses up that one too. When I finally make it to her core, I toss her legs over my shoulders and dive in. I slowly lick up her drenched slit and dip my tongue into her tight hole before I shower extra attention on her clit. I'm gently circling it with just the tip of my tongue when she tugs on my hair lightly.

I look up. Her cheeks are flushed pink, and her eyes are bright with arousal, her hair a disastrous halo of blonde on the pillow. I'm not sure she's ever looked more beautiful.

"Flatten your tongue and use more pressure over my clit," she begs.

I do as she asks, and I'm rewarded with another whimper as I add my fingers to the mix and gently thrust them into her. It's not much longer before she clamps down and starts mindlessly begging and says she's about to come.

"That's my girl. Come on my tongue. I want to taste you for the rest of the day."

Her pussy flutters around my fingers, and I know she's right at the edge. Leaning down, I nip at her clit, and she goes off like a rocket, praising me as she cries out her release. I work her through it softly with my mouth and fingers until she pulls my head up and kisses me deeply.

I sweep my tongue into her mouth and grunt into the kiss. I'm hard as a fucking flagpole right now, but I wanted to get her out of her own head. I'll take a cold shower and call it good.

"Wow." Her breathless voice meets my ears and I grin. "You're really good at following directions."

With a snort, I drop kisses all over her face, ending with a long one on her luscious lips. "You're talking to a professional baseball player, Starling. Of course, I'm good at following directions."

She tries to push down my sweats, but I grip her hands in one of mine and hold them above her head. "Nuh-uh. This was about you, Wren. You needed to get out of your head, and I was more than happy to help you do that."

She grins slyly and tugs her hands free. In an impressive show of strength, the darling woman pushes me on to my back and straddles my knees. "And what if this helps me get out of my head too?"

A wicked sense of déjà vu hits me. I've seen this exact moment play out in my dreams no less than a hundred times. Only the real thing is so much better. "I'm down for anything that helps you relax, Starling."

Her smile is triumphant and sinfully sexy as she slides her hands beneath the waistband of my sweats and boxer briefs. The smooth skin of her fingers glides across my lower abdomen, sending a shiver down my spine and a pulse to my throbbing cock that makes me squirm.

Her eyes track the small movement as she jerks my sweats down, my dick slapping against my abs with force.

Her beautiful eyes open a fraction wider, and she licks her lips, making me feel ten feet tall.

Wren places gentle kisses across my chest, flicking her tongue across my nipple as she passes, which forces an embarrassing sound from me. She traces the lines between my abs with her tongue, and my hips thrust up involuntarily. "Fuck, baby. That already feels so good."

All coherent thought leaves me the second her tongue touches the head of my cock. She licks the precum that's gathered on the tip and hums before taking me into her mouth.

"*Fuck!*" My shout is loud in the quiet room.

My breaths speed up as Wren licks me like a fucking lollipop, and I have to avert my gaze to the ceiling so I don't immediately come in her hot mouth. Taking a chance, I glance back down, tangle my fingers in her hair, and guide her just a bit deeper, watching her closely for any sign of discomfort.

I'm shocked when she moans, her eyes fluttering closed as she sucks with renewed vigor, taking me as far into her mouth as she can. She gags when my crown taps the back of her mouth. "Fuck, baby, you're incredible. Keep doing that and I'll be coming down your pretty little throat in seconds."

She pulls off with a gasp and shoots me a sexy-as-hell wink before diving back in. The next time she deepthroats me proves to be too much, and I pull on her hair, which elicits a deep moan that vibrates through my cock. "I'm gonna come, baby," I choke out quietly. "Oh, fuck. Wren!" I come with a hoarse shout, flooding her mouth and watching in awe as she swallows every drop. "You're a fucking dream, Starling."

She looks up with glassy eyes and flushed cheeks

before she crashes down next to me and cuddles her still-naked body to my side. I turn and pull her in for a deep kiss, uncaring that I can taste myself on her tongue.

A tiny yip fills the space as Finn barrels onto the bed, making us both laugh into the kiss. I pull away and laugh even harder when Wren squeals and attempts to cover herself with the small throw blanket on the end of the bed. He must take her pulling the blanket as an invitation to play because Finn takes the edge between his tiny teeth and yanks, catching us both by surprise when he's able to dislodge it from his mama's grip and pull it out of the room.

Wren looks at me with wide eyes, one arm covering her perfect tits. I bite my bottom lip as I pull her arm down, taking in every inch of smooth, tan skin. She shakes her head and climbs to her feet. I force myself out of my boob-trance and smile. "You're so beautiful, Starling."

Her expression softens as she puts her panties on, then she sits in my lap and kisses me softly before leaning against my chest with a sleepy sigh when I hold her tight. Ideas flit through my mind of what I can do to make her happy, to make her want to stay. We sit together quietly for a few minutes and soak up the comfort.

I'm trying to decide the best thing to do on a free Friday when the perfect idea comes to mind. "Starling, what do you say tomorrow we pick up a bat for you and head to the cages for the day?"

She looks confused but excited, nodding her head. "Of course! You know I've always loved going to batting practice with you."

She doesn't need to know that we aren't going to practice. I'll let the real reason be a surprise. "Great," I say with a wide grin. "Let's just relax tonight then. We're headed out first thing in the morning." I push her off my lap and smack her on the ass, ignoring the way my cock perks up again when she sticks out her tongue at me.

There's plenty of time for more later. Operation 'Woo Wren' starts first thing in the morning.

"Well, I'll be! If it ain't my future wife." My teeth grind in irritation. I swear to God if Aidan wasn't like a brother to me, I might kick his ass for the way he flirts with my girl. He winks at me when Wren hugs him, and I flip him off discreetly, trying to be mindful of our present company.

I spot my favorite kid across the room and I almost wish we had brought Finn so they could play, but leaving him with my parents was a better idea. They work from home most of the time, and until he's had all his shots, I don't want to drag him around so many new people and places.

A tiny gasp rings out behind Aid. "Auntie Wren!" Crew screams. She giggles and crouches so she can catch him when he bounds into her arms, but the kid is moving so fast he takes them both down.

After they manage to stand, Wren looks around the batting cages in awe. There are around forty kids of all ages here today as part of our annual kid's camp with the local foster care program. We do this particular camp twice a year: once right before the season starts and again a month after it ends.

The program serves a dual purpose. The first is to give the kids a chance to let loose and have fun twice a year without worrying about work or school or any other responsibilities. And the second is to scout potential talent from a group who otherwise might never have the opportunity to get on the MLB's radar. I knew Wren would love this, which is why I brought her. Plus, the more time she spends with the guys on the team and the back-of-house crew, the higher the chance of her potentially accepting a job and staying in town.

I toss my arm over her shoulder and lead her and Crew to where Copeland stands with four boys and one girl. The boys must be about twelve, and their excitement is obvious. It makes me smile. The girl can't be much older than maybe eight and seems much shyer than her male counterparts, clinging to the boy next to her.

I slap my hand down on Cope's shoulder and hear several gasps. "Hey y'all," I aim a wide smile at the kids. "How's it going?"

One of the smaller boys looks at me reverently, and my heart expands in my chest. I'm recognized often since I play professionally, but it's a whole different level of pride when a kid looks at me that way. "Wow," he whispers. "You're Rhodes Gray. My dad and I used to watch all your college games, and I even got to go to one of your last ones." His gaze glosses over, and my heart breaks for him as he hurriedly wipes his eyes and glances around to make sure no one saw.

I hold my hand out with a smile. "It means the world to me that y'all supported me even way back then, bud. It's really nice to meet you." He shakes my hand timidly and doesn't say anything. I hold back my chuckle because I don't want him to feel self-conscious, but hopefully, he gets a little more comfortable around me over the next few days.

"What's your name?"

He startles like he didn't expect me to continue our conversation. "Oh! Sorry, I'm Noah. And this is Matteo, Josh, Chase, and Ava. We all live in the same group home, so we came together." He points out each kid in turn, and I make note that Chase is the one Ava clings to in case she gets nervous later. They look thrilled to be here—even Ava looks happy to be included, which is awesome. We don't see a lot of girls at this camp, so we're always excited when they show up.

"It's really cool to meet y'all! You might already know some of our names, but I'm Rhodes, and this is Copeland, Aidan, Crew, and Wren. The guys and I will be here all week, and Wren is here to help out today."

Ava, the most subdued of the bunch, sends a small smile towards Wren and scoots closer. "Do you work for the team too?" Her voice is quiet, and she looks excited to see another girl.

"I don't work for the Raptors, but I do work for the Seattle Sirens." She leans in conspiratorially. "I run their Public Relations department, so basically I handle all of the crazy stuff the players do and make sure it doesn't get the team in trouble."

Ava's eyes are wide with awe, and I feel like mine are the same as I watch Wren patiently explain her job and how she got hired there and what she studied in school. They're so engrossed in their conversation, neither notices when the guys and I take the rest of the kids over to their first activity.

CHAPTER 19
WREN

"THAT WAS the most amazing day I've had in *years*, Rho. Those kids are so sweet in spite of some of the awful things they've been through and seen in such a short amount of time."

Rhodes and I are lying in the outfield on a blanket he grabbed out of his SUV, along with dinner from Lotus. Camp is over for the day and everybody but us has gone home, so we're relaxing under the stars as we talk about everything and nothing.

He sighs happily, rolling on his side so he can prop himself up on one elbow. "You were a natural with those kids, Wren. They adored you."

My stomach clenches with anxiety. I know where he's going with this, and I'm not ready to have this conversation. I don't know that I'll ever be. Glancing around desperately for a distraction, my eyes catch on the dugout, and a plan forms. Before Rhodes can say anything else, I hop up, back away slowly and unzip the jacket I borrowed from him. "You know what I've always kinda wanted to do?"

He looks like he wants to continue the conversation but then is distracted when I make it another ten feet away and pull off my top. I watch his eyes widen and smug satisfaction glides through my veins when he chokes on his own spit. "Wren I—"

"I've always wanted to have sex in a dugout," I interrupt with a smirk. "I was wondering if you might want to help me make that fantasy come to life."

A mischievous glint enters his eyes and before I can turn to run, Rhodes is right there, tossing me over his shoulder as he sprints to the home team dugout. I screech when he slaps his hand against my ass. "Shush, Starling. You need to be quiet in case anybody is still here." There's laughter in his voice, so I don't really think we'll get caught, but knowing there's a possibility turns me on in a way I didn't expect.

When we make it to the dugout, he drops me on the bench and then we're a frantic tangle of limbs, lips, and clothing as we rush to get naked. The thrill of getting caught makes my heart race and I'm already wet.

Rhodes glides his hand through my slick core and growls. "Look at you, my dirty girl. Does the thought of getting caught turn you on? You're fucking dripping."

He pulls out his fingers and brings them to his mouth, sucking them clean with a deep groan that reverberates through my body. We're on the same page without words, so when he sits down on the bench and pulls me into his lap, I straddle him without complaint.

Lifting up on my knees, I line his cock with my entrance and sink down slowly as our moans echo around us. "Jesus, Starling. You're practically strangling my cock in this position." Rhodes's words sound like gravel, and I squeeze around him to increase the pleasure.

I love that sex with him feels just as good when it's slow and sweet as it does when it's quick and dirty—like right now. The sound of slapping skin, grunts, and praises echo around the empty field, and I must get too loud because Rhodes slaps his hand over my mouth and growls in my ear. "Hush, Wren. You wouldn't want anybody to come out here and catch us defiling the dugout, would you?"

Even if I tried to deny it, the way I clench around his thick length would show just how much I'm affected by his words. Voyeurism has never been something I thought I'd be into, but I think it's the idea of someone catching me with *Rhodes*.

Being caught might force us to confront whatever this thing is between us, and a small part of me wants that. I'm sure it's just my hormones talking, because someone actually seeing us would be a nightmare. Just as my thoughts start to spiral into anxiety, Rho licks his thumb and brings it to my hypersensitive clit, rubbing in circles.

"Fuck you feel so good when you tighten around my cock, Starling. Are you gonna come for me?"

I nod frantically and grind down on his shaft. He takes his thumb off my clit and wraps both hands around my hips, using the leverage to buck up into me. His pelvis hits me at just the right angle to add new pressure to my g-spot. A warm sensation that I've never felt before floods through my core, and I writhe on top of him. "Oh my god, Rho. Don't stop!"

He grits his teeth, "I'm there, baby. Come for me, *now!*" He yanks me down hard one last time and the combination of friction on my clit with the pulse of his cock as he comes inside me sets off the most intense orgasm I've ever felt. I scream and white dots float across my vision, leaving me a sticky, panting mess.

"Holy shit, Wren." Rhodes's voice is full of awe that I barely hear through my post-orgasm haze.

I'm sure my words are slurred when I ask him what's wrong, but he seems to understand because he glances from his lap to my face repeatedly. He's quiet for long enough that the fog starts to clear from my mind, and I get nervous.

"Are you okay?" He still doesn't say anything, but his lips tilt up in a feral grin.

He pulls me into a filthy kiss and chuckles when he releases me, both of us struggling for air. "Have you ever squirted before, Starling?"

My mouth drops open and when I glance down, I notice the bench and his lap are both way more wet than they should be. "Oh my god, I did *that*?"

Rhodes tries really hard to mask it, but he still looks smug as hell. "Not bad for a recently reformed virgin, huh?"

I can't help the laugh that bursts free at his words, and I smack his chest playfully. "Shut up. I swear if you weren't so cute, I'd take your car and leave you to find your own way home." I move to get off of his lap and moan at the feeling of his semi-hard cock dragging along my sensitive core.

He snickers as he helps me clean up with a towel he pulls from...somewhere.

Where the hell did he get that?

With a yawn, I get redressed and hum in satisfaction when Rhodes cuddles me into his arms.

"Tired, pretty girl?"

"Yeah," I say through another yawn. "It kind of just hit me all at once. It's been a long day."

He smiles and bends down in front of me. "Hop on then, Starling, so we can get you home to bed."

I know he means *his home*, but in my sleepy, satiated state I can't help but think about how nice it would be if he meant *our home*. Butterflies fill my chest at the thought, and that scares me more than anything. I survived growing up without a mom and having a cheater for a husband without losing my optimism. But if I lost Rhodes because I fell in love with him when he doesn't love me back?

I'm not sure I'd ever find my shine again.

"Okay, kiddos! Today is our last day, and if you're new to camp this year, this is your free day! We have stations set up around the field for y'all to play at and we'll break for lunch in two hours, but otherwise be safe and have fun!"

I can't conceal a wide smile when Aidan stands at the home plate to ring in the end of camp. I guess normally Rhodes would be the one doing the honors, but he had a brand photoshoot he couldn't get out of and had to miss today. He asked me to accompany him to the shoot, but I wanted to be here with the kids. This program has been so fun and informative.

My dad offered to tag along and so far; the kids love him. Dad turns to me with a wide smile as everyone disperses across the field to the different stations, a large group walking to the makeshift batting cage in the outfield. "This is so much more involved than I was expecting after how you described it to me, Starshine." He links his arm with mine as we head to Aidan's station near one of the dugouts.

"Right? I was surprised when Rhodes brought me here the other day, but it's been so much fun. Twice a year they host between twenty and fifty local foster kids, and God, Dad, some of the things these kids have dealt with are heartbreaking."

Just then someone crashes into my back and if it weren't for my dad, we both would have gone sprawling. "Wren, you're here!" Ava screeches excitedly. I regain my balance, turn, and hug her back; suddenly, I'm even more happy I chose to come here today instead of sitting in a stuffy studio with Rho.

I introduce a clingy Ava to my dad. "Dad, this is Ava. She's been my shadow in a bid to learn everything there is to know about Public Relations in professional baseball. Ava, this is my dad, Archie."

Dad holds out his hand to shake hers, and even though she scoots behind me, she tentatively reaches out and accepts the shake. "It's nice to meet you Ava! Has my girl been showing you the ropes?"

Ava nods enthusiastically. "I want to be just like Wren when I grow up!"

My dad laughs, but I nearly burst with pride. I've always loved my job, but I never really thought of it as something a kid would aspire to be. Ava is such a sweetheart, and I'm pretty sad that I may not see her again after today. I ruffle her hair and smile down at her. "I bet you'll be even better than me, Ave."

She smiles and skips off, presumably to find her foster brothers. Dad turns to me with a twinkle in his eye and a knowing grin quirked on his lips. I groan, fully aware what's coming.

He laughs at my feigned irritation and tosses an arm over my shoulders. "Oh, come on, Starshine. You can't blame an old man for wanting a grandkid or two."

We've had this conversation more times than I can count since Derrick and I got married, and my answer still hasn't changed. "Daddy, I love you, but I'm not built for the whole mom thing, and you know that. Does Caroline have any kids you can pressure into procreation?"

His expression grows somber, and he glances around and guides me to the empty dugout, encouraging me to sit with him. "She doesn't, but that's not the point." he sighs. "Wren, I know growing up without your mom was hard, but that doesn't mean you wouldn't be wonderful at it. You're so good with the kids here and if you could see the way your face lights up around them, I think you'd realize that. If you truly don't ever want human children, I support you. But I don't want you to miss out on something so big because you're scared."

I know we're talking about kids, but I think about Rhodes when he says it. This friends-with-benefits thing we have going on has been incredible so far, but I only have a couple of weeks left before I return to reality, and I've started to realize that I don't want to leave. But *I'm* the one who made the rule about not catching feelings. *I'm* the one who insisted we stay just friends.

Like he can read my damn mind, Dad turns to me and waggles his brows. "That goes for *all* aspects of your life, Starshine. I couldn't help but notice the way a certain ballplayer looked at you the day I came home."

I try to disguise my panic with an eye roll. "I don't know what you're talking about. Just because you're blissfully in love with Caroline doesn't mean everybody else wants hearts and butterflies too."

He snorts. "You're just as bad of a liar as when you were fifteen and would sneak my truck out at night to practice driving in the empty fields next door."

My glare is ice cold, and he gives a boisterous laugh. "I'll keep pretending you haven't been in love with that boy since college, and you can keep bein' a river in Egypt. Your old man is here when you're ready to talk."

"Dad, I got *married*. Pretty sure that's a good indication I wasn't in love with my *friend*."

I turn away so he can't see my face, and I hear him sigh loudly before he pats my knee. "Alright, I'll drop it." He pauses while we watch Noah, Chase, and Ava run by, playing what looks like a game of tag. "That Ava sure is a sweet little thing, isn't she?"

Thinking about my eager shadow brings my smile back and I nod. "She is. She's a fantastic kid from what I've seen. I just hate that she's had such a hard life. I mean to not even be ten years old and lose both of your parents in a car accident, only to be shipped off to a foster home where you don't know anyone? It breaks my heart."

He looks contemplative and pulls out his phone, sending a text. I'm about to ask him about it, but he turns to me with a small smile. "Have you considered becoming a foster parent?"

My eyes widen in surprise at the question. I haven't; I was too focused on not wanting biological children. "I haven't..." I start slowly. "But I'm not sure I could do that. I travel so much for work, and I'm a single woman—that doesn't exactly scream stability. Somebody like Ava, like any of these kids really, deserves more than that. I do think I'll find a way to work with this program in the future though, even if I have to fly here from Seattle to do it."

"Hey there, Reid fam! Y'all wanna help set up lunch for the kiddos?" Aidan's voice startles me, and when his words register, I check my watch. I'm shocked to see more than an hour has passed.

Smiling up at him, I quirk a brow at my dad. He slaps his palms on his knees and groans obnoxiously as he stands. I laugh at his theatrics but take his proffered hand. "You're barely fifty, Dad. Cool it with the grunts and groans."

Aidan stands there quietly shaking his head in amusement. "I brought somebody along who's more than willing to help y'all set up too."

Rhodes steps out from the side of the dugout, and I grin before I can stop it. "Hey! I thought your shoot was an all-day thing."

He smirks, and I quirk an eyebrow when I realize his gaze is locked on the bench behind me. "Nah, they got the shot they wanted pretty quick and let me leave, so I figured I'd come see my favorite people. I was a little surprised when Aid said y'all were hanging out in here though. I figured it would still be wet after we hosed it down a few days ago."

Oh. My. Fucking. God. He did not just say that.

My voice is high and squeaky when I answer, and Aidan and my dad cast me concerned looks. "NO! Nope. Totally dry." I look at Aidan, clearing my throat. "What do you need us to do, boss man?"

As the four of us make our way to the makeshift picnic area, I shoot visual daggers at my *ex* best friend, nearly growling when he winks at me. *Payback's a bitch, Rhodes Colter.*

CHAPTER 20
RHODES

WREN LOOKS so fucking pretty first thing in the morning. I mean she's pretty all the time, but when she first wakes up with pillow lines on her face and her hair a total disaster, I don't think I've ever been more attracted to her. I nuzzle my face into her hair and take a deep inhale of her mouthwatering smell. I don't think I'll ever be able to smell apples again and not get hard.

It's the Monday after baseball camp, and I'm in bed with Starling's back against my chest, switching my attention between my eBook app and watching her sleep like a fucking stalker. Wes recommended this book, *The Signature Move,* to me after finding out their boss was reading it, and even though I didn't think I'd like it because hockey isn't my thing, I'm hooked.

Waking up with my girl next to me the entire last week has been nothing short of heaven on earth. A month ago she was married and across the country, so I'm beyond thankful that she ended up here with me against all odds.

"Mmm, good morning." Her raspy voice hits my ears

as she stretches and grinds her ass back against my morning wood.

I groan, dropping my phone so I can grab her hips and hold her still. "Good morning, Starling. How would you like to go on a little adventure today?"

That gets her attention, and she flips over to stare at me with sleepy, curious eyes. Through a long yawn, she asks, "What kind of adventure?"

I smirk at her and pull her in for a kiss, ignoring her protests about morning breath. "How about we take a shower and then I'll think about telling you." The pout she gives me is too fucking cute, and I bite my lip to hide my smile. "Come on, dress light, but bring a bathing suit and a jacket."

Her eyebrows shoot up, but she does as I ask. She rolls out of bed with a groan, stretching her arms above her head. Apparently, she took off her pants at some point during the night and is wearing only one of my t-shirts, and I nearly choke on my own spit. "Jesus Christ, Starling. Are you trying to kill me?"

She peeks at me over her shoulder with wide, innocent eyes. "What do you mean? I'm just stretching."

And then she bends over.

"On second thought, let's take separate showers." I glance at Wren's perfect ass and the sliver of her bare sex that peeks through her legs and bite my fist to hold myself back. We really do have plans today and don't have time to play right now.

That adorable pout quickly makes a reappearance as she huffs. "Fine, but this whole adventure thing better be worth it because I had plans to spend your entire day off in bed.

I groan as she exits the room and fall back to my bed,

FINALLY HOME

scrubbing my hands down my face. This woman might actually kill me.

"This is the most perfect day I think I've ever had," Wren sighs dreamily. "I've lived in South Carolina my whole life, but I've never been out on the water like this. It's crazy how peaceful it is." She's stretched out on our family yacht in the tiniest blue bikini I've ever seen and let me tell you: trying to solo navigate a thirty-eight-foot boat down the Charleston harbor while her tight body was on display in front of me was *not easy*.

Wren appreciating the view settles some of the nerves I had while planning this yesterday. I come to Folly Beach once or twice a month to sit out on the water and relax. The press and fan attention during my first two years with the Raptors was a hard adjustment for me, especially with my comfort person across the country. So, whenever my anxiety would overwhelm me, a few hours on the water really helped bring me back to my center, and I'm hoping it helps Wren feel the same way after everything that's happened the last few weeks. First, Derrick cheating, then coming back to Charleston, getting divorced, navigating our little arrangement, and now discovering her father has a long-term girlfriend for the first time in her life is a lot to handle.

I smile at my beautiful girl affectionately and keep my eyes locked on hers. "I'm glad, Starling. You've been through so much lately I felt like you deserved a day off, and what better place than on a boat with nobody else around?"

She gets a mischievous look in her sparkling blue eyes that puts me on alert, and when she hums, I know I'm either going to love or hate whatever comes out of her mouth next. With an exaggerated glance around, she sits up and stretches her arms above her head. "Man, it's just such a nice day, I think I'll work on my tan."

And then she takes off her fucking top. My jaw drops at the same time those triangles of fabric do, and I have to wipe the back of my hand over my mouth to make sure I'm not drooling. "Wren," I hiss. My gaze darts around us. "Somebody could see you!"

We're far enough from the beach that nobody there could see us, and it's the middle of the day on a Monday, so the water is fairly empty. But the thought of somebody seeing *my girl* exposed has me wanting to wrap her in the biggest towel I can find.

Her only reply is to smirk before she lowers her sunglasses into place and lays back on the lounger, her perky breasts exposed to the warm air. Wren's skin is perfectly tan already, so I'm pretty sure she's doing this to get back at me for this morning. Or for teasing her in front of Archie the last day of camp.

I shiver with desire when I think about what happened in that dugout, and I realize all of my favorite places are being taken over by memories of this woman naked and coming on my cock. It wouldn't be right to defile the white leather lounge bed the same way.

But wouldn't it be wrong not to?

With that thought, I strip off my white Raptors tee I'm only in my blue board shorts and drop a knee to the bench at the end of the lounger before I crawl my way up, bracketing a knee on either side of Wren's hips. She raises a brow but stays silent, so I offer a sly grin and lower my head to suck one of her rosy nipples between my teeth, biting it lightly.

She lets out a breathy gasp but still doesn't say a word. If she wants to pretend I don't affect her, I guess I'll just have to try a little harder to prove I do. I spend a few minutes on her breasts, licking and sucking at the stiff buds. Each sound that escapes her tightly closed lips feels like a victory in its own right, and it urges me on.

I place a kiss on her belly button, and she rubs her thighs together. "Something you want to say, Starling?"

"Rhodes, Please!"

"Please what, baby?"

Letting out an exasperated sigh, she finally takes off her sunglasses and glares at me. "*Please,* touch me."

It takes serious effort not to smirk at her impatience, but I can't pass up the chance to tease her a little. "I *am* touching you." I murmur, punctuating my words with a tiny kiss over her bikini bottoms.

She whines and thrusts her hips up so her mound hits the bottom of my chin. "I need more."

I can't deny this woman anything. Slipping my fingers up her hips, I tug on the strings that hold her bottoms together and watch them unravel, leaving her bare. I glance up at her glassy eyes and hold her gaze as I drop to my knees on the floor so I can run my tongue leisurely through her soaked core, savoring her drawn-out whimper.

Her taste coats my tongue, and her needy whines make my cock jump eagerly. I undo my shorts and pull out my dick, giving myself a solid stroke while I keep my mouth over her pussy. "I want you to come on my face, Starling. Can you do that for me?"

I could stay between her legs for the rest of my life, but I'm already close from her teasing this morning, and I need her to come first. I push two fingers into her tight channel and curl them upwards, using enough pressure that she cries out.

"Oh, God, right there! Just a little more."

Adding a third finger, I suck her swollen clit hard, and it sets her off. Feeling her pulse around my fingers brings me even closer to orgasm so I sit up and straddle her hips again, protesting when she knocks my hand from my rock-hard cock to take over.

"Wren, baby, I'm gonna come." I rasp. Sweat beads on my forehead. I can't focus on anything but the subject of my fantasies lying naked beneath me, her tan skin shimmers from the sun and her orgasm. It only takes another minute of her stroking me before I groan out my release, ropes of come landing on her perfect tits. "Jesus, Starling."

She glances down at herself and then back to me with lust darkening her sparkling eyes. She drags a finger through the mess on her skin and without breaking eye contact, she slips it into her mouth and sucks it clean. "Holy fuck," I choke. The sight alone is enough to have me hardening again.

I collapse next to her on the warm leather and pull her sticky body to mine as we breathe in the salty ocean air. Wren giggles and when I tilt her chin up so I can see her face, her eyes are filled with mirth. "What?"

"Sex on a boat wasn't on my list when we started this, but I'm glad I got to check it off anyway. I never imagined this is how I would spend my time in Charleston."

Her words are like a bucket of cold water over my

post-orgasm glow. The blatant reminder that this situation is temporary feels like a hot poker in my gut. When she leaves at the end of the month, she'll be taking my heart with her. But despite the impending misery, I can't bring myself to regret a minute of my time with Wren.

I shake off the serious thought and smirk at her, picking up a strand of blonde hair that came loose from her bun. "How about we take it a step further and check off 'sex in the ocean', too?"

The smile she gifts me in return is brighter than the sun doing its best to burn my shoulders, and I know that even if all I can have of her are her firsts, I'll still be happy. Either way, she'll always be my everything.

CHAPTER 21
RHODES

I CAME DANGEROUSLY close to confessing my love to Wren after that first day at camp late last week week, but then she shut me down brutally when I mentioned how good she was with the kids, so I worried she might not be ready for another commitment right now.

"Brutally" might be a strong word there, Gray. She distracted you with sex and then gave you the most incredible orgasm you've ever had.

Wrinkling my nose at myself in the mirror, I smooth out my shirt nervously. Wren meets with Jeremy today to discuss her leave and the possibility of working remotely from Charleston, and I'm headed to meet Archie so I can pick his brain about his daughter. She said she had a great chat with him last week, so while I don't expect him to break her confidence, I'm at least hopeful he'll give me some advice. I just want to know where she stands emotionally.

She's in our kitchen sipping her chai when I walk in, and she wolf whistles. "You look handsome, Roly-Coly. Where ya headed?"

I'm pretty sure I hear a little bit of jealousy in her voice, but maybe that's wishful thinking on my part. "I'm actually headed over to meet Dad and Archie for brunch and maybe a round of golf, so I probably won't be back until late afternoon. Will you be okay here?" Obviously, I want her to feel comfortable being alone in our home—and it is *our home*—but there's always a little niggle of worry in the back of my mind that she feels like I'm not giving her enough attention.

She laughs, and I'm struck dumb again by how incredibly beautiful she is in the mornings. Her cheeks are pink from yesterday's sun and her freckles are out in full force. Her hair is a disaster, half of it in a braid and half of it hangs in tangles off of the side of her head.

Even though she's talking, I need to kiss her *right now*, so I do, wrapping my arms around her and lowering her in an exaggerated dip. She's breathless when I pull back, eyes bright with happiness.

"What was that for?"

I shrug with a sweet smile and kiss her forehead. "I just love you."

Her eyes widen slightly, and I realize too late that what I just said sounded way more than a friendly I love you.

Holy fucking shit. Backtrack, you moron.

Coughing, I clear my throat. "And I love having you as a friend. I couldn't imagine my life without you, Starling." I boop her on the nose for good measure and slowly back out of the kitchen before I do something even more stupid like give her finger guns. "If you need anything while I'm out today, just call or text me, okay? I might not be able to answer right away if we're on the course, but I promise I'll check my phone as often as I can."

She's laughing and practically shoves me out the door. "Rho, I have meetings all day, and I'll have Jeremy for virtual company. I promise I'll be fine, okay? Go and have fun! Tell Dad and Daddy Gray I say hi."

"So let me get this straight," Archie says between loud guffaws. "You're not only in love with my daughter, but you actually *told her today*. And instead of going with it like a normal human being would, you threw her a changeup and said you love 'having her as a friend?'"

Archie and my dad have taken every opportunity the last hour to razz me about my colossal fuck-up this morning, and I'm about ready to ditch the gossipy old assholes and head back home to my girl and our puppy.

I scowl at him and cross my arms like a petulant child. "Well, what would you suggest I do then, Arch? She's been through so much in the last month, and I don't want to push her before she's ready. I don't even know if she has feelings for me beyond friendship and physical attraction."

Okay, yeah. So I sort of accidentally let our little arrangement slip when I spilled my guts earlier, and I'm damned lucky Archie loves me. Otherwise I think I'd already be buried six feet under the green right now. I overshare when I'm nervous, a trait I have in common with Wren—or maybe one I picked up from her since I was never like this before college.

Archie and my dad exchange a long look before they break out into raucous laughter. I put my club away and wave at them. "Alright, it was nice to see y'all. I'm gonna go waste my life away, never knowing what true love feels like."

That just makes them laugh harder.

We're getting dirty looks from a few of the old timers on the course so I wave at them with a polite smile, not even the slightest bit embarrassed about their behavior. After so many years, you get used to it.

"Rhodes, I love you like my own son, but you're an idiot." Archie finally gets out when his laughter fades.

My mouth drops open. "Well, that's a little harsh. I would think you would be grateful that I want to protect your daughter's feelings and not just dive into something she might not be ready for because I'm selfish and impatient."

He and my dad just shake their heads at me, and Dad gives me a look that says "really?"

I give them a pointed look at and hold my hands out, palms up. "What am I missing? Because I'm just trying to do right by the love of my life so our relationship doesn't start with her having regrets."

That finally pulls a smile out of Arch. He throws an arm over my shoulders, which is a little awkward since I'm a good four inches taller than him, but it's comforting nonetheless.

"Do you really not know how much she loves you? Or are you just letting your fear get in the way?"

I roll my eyes slightly. "Of course she loves me, Arch. We've been friends for nearly a decade."

He gently smacks the back of my head and chuckles softly. "Rhodes, that girl has been in love with you since she was eighteen years old."

It takes a solid minute for my brain to process what he

said, and then I'm the one who's laughing. "Right, good one. The girl of my dreams has been in love with me for years, and I had no idea. In fact, she loves me so much, she decided to go off and marry another guy! One of my fucking teammates. My *roommate,* no less!"

He shakes his head and places his warm hands on my shoulders, looking me directly in the eyes. "The first day she met you, she came to my office and told me every single detail of your meeting. The look in her eyes was like nothing I had ever seen before. And when her face fell when she said you wanted to be friends, I suspected it might be just puppy love that would pass. But then y'all got closer, and she brought you to meet me, always insisting you were *just friends.* So I never pushed. But then she came home in tears from a party one night. She drank herself sick because she saw you kiss another girl, and she said it hurt to know she would never be able to have the one person she wanted. Y'all were nineteen, and I assumed that was the push she needed to move on."

He grimaces. "And she did, with your awful ex-roommate. I thought for sure that was the end of her being hung up on you, but I saw you two on her wedding day. I saw the way you comforted her, the way you offered to drive the getaway car. And most importantly, I saw you break down after all was said and done."

My eyes widen and my breaths come faster. Before the anxiety attack can fully take hold, Archie wraps me in a tight hug. I haven't had one in over a year, but knowing he saw me that night, at my absolute worst, has me ready to crawl out of my skin.

"I saw the way you cried when you thought everyone was gone for the reception, son. I saw the panic, and I watched your heart break, unable to do or say anything to make it better. I knew then that she married the wrong man, but as long as she was happy, I couldn't say anything. I've always said I love you like you're my own, Rhodes. I meant it then, and I mean it now. So if you want my advice? Go get your girl and put you both out of your misery."

He's not even finished with his speech before I run for my SUV to the tune of their catcalls and shouts of good luck. I'm pretty sure I break at least four laws on the way back to the house, and when I get there I push past the crushing fear that threatens to swallow me whole.

"Rho is that you?" Wren's melodic voice greets me as I walk in the door, shutting it harder than necessary in my agitated state. Finn must be outside or asleep upstairs because he doesn't greet me at the door.

She looks almost exactly the same as when I left her this morning, but she's brushed her hair and slicked it into a high ponytail. Just like every time I see her, she takes my breath away with no effort.

"Hey!" She sounds so happy to see me. "How was your time with the dads? I didn't expect you home so soon, but I can't say I'm upset about it." She giggles and wraps her arms around me.

My entire body relaxes as I finally consider that Archie might be right. Has she really been in love with me for all these years? And did I really friend zone myself that first day?

There's only one way to find out.

"You okay?" she asks.

I clear my throat several times before I can speak, and even then, it sounds like my words are being raked over hot coals. "I love you, Wren."

Tilting her gaze up to meet mine, she smiles. "I love

you too, Rhodes."

I shake my head and gently remove myself from the hug. "No, Starling. I'm *in love with you.* I've been in love with you since we were eighteen years old, and I saw you for the first time in that cute yellow shirt and those shorts that showed off your stunningly perfect legs."

Her jaw hangs open and she tries to speak, but I interrupt. I'm in too deep to stop now—not until she knows the full truth.

"I fell in love with you because of every drunken ride in Archie's truck. Every time I held your hair back while you puked. Every time one of us was sick and we took turns taking care of each other—even when we'd pass it back and forth for months because we couldn't stay apart long enough to get better. I fell in love with you while I watched you fall in love with Derrick. I fell in love with you when you held my hand through the draft. For Christ's sake, I fell in love with you while I watched you *marry another man*, and I've loved you from afar every single day since then."

My chest heaves as I struggle to breathe, but I need her to know.

"I felt like the world's worst friend and biggest asshole because when you showed up on my parent's doorstep three weeks ago, I was *ecstatic*. I knew you being here would give me every chance to convince you to stay in Charleston forever. I'd finally have a chance to make you fall in love with *me*. Because that's the truth of it, Starling—you never belonged with him. You were always meant to be mine."

She's silent for several long minutes and when she starts to cry, my heart plummets into the pits of hell.

Am I about to lose my best friend?

CHAPTER 22
WREN

AM I DREAMING RIGHT NOW?

Tears streams down my face and all coherent thoughts have left the building while I process Rhodes's confession. So many conflicting words fight for dominance in my brain, so I go with the loudest ones.

"I love you too," I whisper.

He's still rambling but at my words his jaw gapes open. "I'm sorry," he chokes out. "You what?"

"You heard me," I say with a smile. "For every reason you listed, I have all the same ones and a thousand more. I wanted you that very first day, but after seeing how excited you were to be friends, I didn't want to risk your presence in my life by asking for more." I sigh and take his hand in mine. "I don't know where we go from here, Rho. My job is in Seattle, and yours is here. I'm plum *petrified* of things changing between us and losing you. But I do know that I love you. If what you and I could have is half of what your parents have, I think it might be worth the risk."

I wait for him to say something, but he sighs and his

whole body seems to sag. "Thank fuck. If Finny didn't make you fall in love with me, I wasn't sure what else to try."

I can't help my obnoxiously loud cackle, and I hold up my finger before letting Finn in from the backyard. On my way back, something occurs to me, and I start to giggle again. "You're really tellin' me you got Finn just in the hopes that he would convince me to love you? Is *this* the real reason you said I was your girlfriend that first day at the stadium?"

His cheeks turn pink, and he shrugs bashfully. "I did really want a dog, but Walter seemed to think it might help. As for the girlfriend thing, I panicked! It was the first thing that came to mind. Also, Whitney creeps me out."

That sets off another round of giggles because I can absolutely see Walt saying something like that to Rhodes and him taking it literally, not to mention the absolute absurdity of us dancing around our feelings for so long. "So," I ask quietly once my laughter fades. "What do we do now?"

His answering grin is the biggest I've ever seen on his handsome face. He's practically *glowing* with happiness. "Now, Starling? We start the rest of our lives together."

A knock on the door startles me awake. Lifting my head up off of a very sexy chest, my mouth lifts in an amused smile when I see Rhodes still knocked out, cute little snores puff from his parted lips. The knock sounds again, louder this time, and I straighten my clothes and make my way to the front door.

A tiny blond head is visible just above the glass panes that start halfway up the double doors. I barely have the door unlocked when a tiny body tackles me to the ground.

"Auntie Wren, you're here!" Crew's sweet voice is threaded with giggles and almost covers Aidan's exasperated sigh. He lifts Crew off me and sends me an apologetic grimace.

"Sorry, Wren." He rubs his son's head affectionately. "I think it's safe to say he probably won't follow in our baseball footsteps with a tackle like that."

Laughing, I nod at his words and stand up so I can move to tickle Crew. "What do you think, buddy?" I ask him between rounds of giggles. "Are you gonna be a big, tough, football player?"

"Crew would never play lame old football, right? Baseball is in his blood." Rhodes's warm breath ghosts over my ear, and it sends a shiver down my spine.

"Right Uncle Rho! I'm gonna be a pitcher just like Uncle Cope... *after* I play football." Aidan and Rhodes gasp, clutching their hearts like they rehearsed it, and Crew and I break out into loud laughter again.

The guys exchange smirks and Rhodes wraps his arms around me, dropping a kiss on my cheek. "Not that I'm not happy to see you guys, but what are you doing here?"

Aidan raises an eyebrow and coughs lightly. "Uh, dude? It's our monthly guys' night? Copeland is on his way."

My eyebrows rise. "I had no idea, or I would've been gone already. I can go hang with Mama Gray or my dad. I've barely seen them since I've been here. I'll grab my stuff and get out of y'all's hair and come back later!" I take off up the stairs and stop in my room to change my clothes, double checking that I have everything I need.

When I turn around, Rhodes is leaning in the doorway with his hand up on the frame. I swear he has an honest-to-God *pout* on his face, but I'm too distracted by the bulging muscles in his arm to figure out why. His tan skin is taut and covered in a light layer of hair that does nothing to distract from the prominent veins that stand out when he flexes.

So I have a thing for forearms; sue me.

"Wren?" He snaps his fingers in front of my face, and my jaw drops.

"Excuse me, did you just snap at me?" I place a hand on my hip and raise an eyebrow.

His smirk widens as he copies my stance, and I roll my eyes. He prowls toward me slowly and grabs my hips in his big hands. "How else was I supposed to get my beautiful girlfriend's attention when she was busy drooling over my muscles?"

My heart stutters at the word "girlfriend" on his lips. I don't know where the sudden shyness comes from, but my cheeks flame with the heat in his eyes. A flash of insecurity crosses his face when I stay quiet, and he starts to pull away, but I fist his shirt gently.

"Is that what I am?" I ask. My own insecurities are making themselves known despite my best efforts to keep them hidden. Not that I can truly hide them from someone who knows me so well.

He pulls his hands free from mine and my heart falls, but he moves to cup my face. "I guess I never really asked, did I? You're everything I've ever wanted, Starling, and I would love nothing more than to have you as my girlfriend."

I don't even let him finish his sentence before I nod. Tears well in my eyes, but I don't have a chance to bask in my happiness before he crushes his mouth to mine in a deep, soul-searing kiss, which is cut short when a quiet "Oh, shit," comes from the hallway. We jump apart like we've been burned, breathing hard. Aidan stands next to a clapping Copeland; both of their mouths open in shock.

Grabbing my bag, I smirk at the boys and pop onto my toes to give my *boyfriend* one more quick kiss goodbye. When I make it to the door, Aiden and Copeland are still frozen in place, so I pat them on their cheeks and turn to smirk at Rhodes. "Looks like the porch lights are on, but nobody's home. You might wanna check on them."

I manage to keep my laughter in check until I'm halfway down the stairs and yell, "See y'all later! No hospitals or morgues or I'll tattle to Mamas Gray and Black!" I stop on the landing and laugh silently when I hear their last names together out loud. "Copeland, have you ever considered changing your last name to White? Y'all could form your own boyband and call yourselves *Three Shades of Gray*."

I hug Crew goodbye and don't stop laughing the whole way to the Gray's house.

CHAPTER 23
RHODES

"DUDE, WHAT THE FUCK WAS *THAT*?!" Aidan's voice is borderline screechy as we walk down the stairs. "And did she just make fun of our last names?"

I can't help the laugh that bursts free because the little shit totally did.

I wonder if I could spank her for it later?

Clearing my throat, I quickly hop off that train of thought before my pants get uncomfortably tight in front of my friends and my nephew. "*That* was a kiss, and yes she did. She's a sassy little thing when she wants to be." Pride swells in my chest as I answer Aidan's questions, and I thank my lucky stars that she feels the same way I do and is willing to give us a shot.

"No shit it was a kiss," comes Cope's smartass response. "What Aid meant to say is how did that happen? *When* did that happen? And more importantly, were you gonna tell us?" Copeland isn't an emotional guy by nature, but he knows how I feel about Wren and has been rooting for us just as much as anybody else but in a quieter way.

I turn a shit-eating grin their way when we make it to the kitchen. "I confessed my feelings when I got home from golf this morning after Archie told me I was being stupid."

Their eyes widen in sync, and I scratch the back of my neck as my ears heat under their scrutiny. "Our dads raked me over the coals, so I rushed home, told her I love her and that I've loved her since college, and now she's my girlfriend."

Aidan smiles widely and rounds the island to hug me. "Congratulations, man. I know how long you've waited for this. And the more I see of her, the more I realize how perfect y'all are together." He laughs. "She's you in girl form. But, you know, much prettier."

I scoff and flip him off, but Cope's expression has me glancing worriedly his way. "Do you not like her?" I ask him quietly. He seemed to like her at the fun park a few weeks ago, but maybe something has changed since the camp. I wouldn't break up with her if he didn't approve, but it would suck. I'd just need to work that much harder to make them friends.

His startled eyes dart my way, "*No!* Dude, that's not it at all. Wren is amazing, and she really is the perfect girl for you. Plus, you love her, so that's all that matters to me." He trails off and fidgets nervously. "But...her divorce isn't final yet, right?"

I nod, because I know where he's headed with this. "She won't go back to him."

He only looks mildly relieved at my words. "How do you know?"

I didn't share the details of why Wren came home; the guys just know she's getting divorced and needed a place to land. Hopefully, she won't mind me telling them now that she knows they won't betray our confidence.

Shaking my head, I sigh, grab my laptop, and set it on the counter. "Wren went to work one day about a month ago and opened her email to this." I hit play on the video Jamie sent me last week. He claimed he gave it to me so I had a backup copy should she need it, but really I think he wanted to make sure I knew not to hurt Wren any further.

Sounds of shock and outrage come from them when Derrick comes into focus, and something in my chest relaxes now that I see she has two more people on her side.

"Are you fucking kidding me?" Copeland is *seething*, no doubt reminded of his ex, Carly. Ever since she screwed him over the guy hasn't had more than a one-night stand and gets tattoos whenever he starts to get the urge to settle down. According to him, getting something as permanent as a tattoo settles his need for commitment.

I can't wait for him to meet a girl that knocks him on his ass.

I wince and clamp a hand down on his shoulder. "Apparently it wasn't the first time either. At least, that's what we all suspect, so, she's definitely never going back to that bastard. It even sounds like the Sirens might drop him for breaching their morality clause. I personally don't think that's enough."

Aidan snorts. "Of course, you don't. He married your girl and then fucked around on her. You probably wouldn't be satisfied unless a time machine or a coroner were involved."

I tilt my head in contemplation. "You know, you're probably right. But I also don't really want to leave Wren alone while I rot in prison for killing the asshole, so unless you personally know somebody with a time machine, he gets to live another day alone and hopefully jobless."

Cope's answering grin is downright evil. "You just leave the plotting to me, yeah? I never got revenge with the she-devil, so let daddy Copeland play a bit."

Aidan and I crack up, but I nod at him. "Do what you need to do, *daddy Cope*. Just don't cause permanent bodily harm. I'm not in the mood to bail your ass out of jail."

He smirks. "No worries. My personal brand of revenge is more psychological."

His words make me nervous, but I know he won't take it too far. And maybe we just won't tell Wren right away that we set Copeland loose on her ex. I'll mention it after my crazy teammate has a chance to fuck up Derrick's life a bit.

CHAPTER 24
WREN

RHODES'S PARENTS grin like loons when I show up at their house and beg to hang out until the guys' cute date night is over.

"Honey, you know those boys wouldn't have minded you crashing guys' night," Kaci says sweetly. "They all adore you."

I sigh happily and hug her hard. "I know, but then I wouldn't be able to see you and Dominic, and I miss y'all. I feel like I haven't seen you guys or my dad hardly at all since I've been home, and I'm having parental withdrawals."

Dominic makes his way over and pulls me from his wife so he can bear-hug me. "We miss you too, Wren. You know you're welcome here anytime. Especially now that —*oof*." He cuts off abruptly when Kaci elbows him in the side.

His words register, and I pull back to gape at them, my cheeks flaming with embarrassment. "It's been like... six hours! He already told you?"

Of course, he did.

The pieces click together and my mouth drops even further as my heart speeds up. "Wait a second...he went golfing with you and Dad this morning..."

Kaci sighs exasperatedly and smacks Dominic on the shoulder. "I swear, Dom. You don't have the sense God gave a goose sometimes."

He winces, rubbing a large hand over the back of his neck. "So, your dad and I may have had a come to Jesus with Rho this morning." He holds up his hands and backs away slowly. "But it seems to have worked out, so that's great! Now, I'm just gonna..." he stops, hooking a thumb over his shoulder before he turns and sprints down the hall to his office.

Kaci and I look at each other and erupt into laughter for several minutes, and then she sighs. "Never a dull moment with those three. Come on, sweetie. You want a sweet tea? I think we need some girl time."

A weight lifts off my chest, and I nod gratefully, following the only woman I've ever considered a mother into the kitchen to spill my guts.

"So," she sings. The way she adds an extra syllable to the word tells me she's ready to grill me. Normally, the playful look in her eyes would make me nervous, but I'm brimming with the need to talk to somebody about this—somebody who's *not* a father figure to me.

I force a deep breath and hold it for three seconds before I let it out, utilizing a calming technique my therapist taught me. I've begun to uproot all the stuff I've buried over the years in therapy, but that doesn't alleviate the anxiety sneaking in. "Mama..." unexpected tears spring to my eyes and quickly spill over when I try to blink them away.

"Oh, my sweet girl. It's okay." I cry harder when she

wraps her arms around me, and everything all comes flooding out. I tell her about the first time I met Rhodes. How I liked him from the start, but he wanted to be friends. How I forced my feelings down so I wouldn't lose him or get hurt, but then I got my heart broken anyway when I saw him kiss another girl at that party. How that night was the reason I finally said yes to a date with Derrick.

Then I tell her about the wedding day–things I never even told Rhodes–like how Derrick got a mysterious text, left, and then showed back up to our honeymoon suite at two a.m. smelling like perfume. How I ignored every red flag because all I wanted was to be loved by somebody who wouldn't leave me.

Kaci's eyes mist over as I tell my story, but the dam finally breaks when I say that, and she starts to cry. "Wren, why didn't you come to me? I understand not wanting to go to Archie or Rhodes, but you can *always* come to me."

I inhale her sweet lilac scent and focus on my breaths, calming myself down so I don't get sick. It doesn't happen often anymore but crying too hard can trigger my gag reflex, and for somebody with a serious fear of throwing up, it's a nightmare.

"I didn't want y'all to know what I was putting up with. Daddy would have made a fuss and sat me down for one of his talks and Rho would've started a fight. Rhodes already hated Derrick but if he knew the things my husband was doing it would've landed him in jail. Plus, by that point, it just felt like it was too late. I didn't want to end up like my mom and run out on a marriage just because things got hard."

She lets out a sound that's a half sigh, half groan and

kisses the top of my head. "Sweetie, I didn't even meet the woman, but I know for a fact you're *nothing* like her. Your mama ran out on a great man and her *infant daughter* because she was overwhelmed and refused to get help. You were in a toxic, borderline-dangerous marriage and not a single person would have faulted you for leaving."

I wipe my nose on my sleeve with a sniffle and a sad laugh escapes. "I guess it doesn't matter now. He decided to show the league who he is so I didn't have to. And now I'm here and my best friend is my boyfriend because apparently, he's been in love with me for years, and I was too blind to see it."

A snort filters through the kitchen, and I spin around so fast I nearly fall off my seat. "Daddy!" I gasp, running straight into his open arms. His chest shakes with suppressed laughter, likely at my expense, but I don't care. I'm sure he heard most of that, but I kind of hope he did so I don't have to repeat it.

"Hey there, Starshine. I heard a little rumor that my baby girl got a new beau and a new baby all in one week, and I thought I'd come straight to the source and see if it's true." His voice is filled with barely disguised mirth, and I choose to ignore it, releasing him to plop back in my seat just as Dom joins us again.

I take an obnoxiously long sip of my tea and hold eye contact with the three adults staring at me like I'm the second coming of Jesus. "Y'all are worse gossips than ladies at the hair salon the day after church. Do you have nothing better to do than obsess over your children's love lives?"

They share a glance, but it's Dominic who shrugs. "Nope. So, tell us, is it official?"

I can't stop my smile, but I bite down on my lip anyway. "It might be."

Cheers erupt, and then I'm crushed in a very enthusiastic group hug. Kaci strokes my hair and sniffs. She glances up at her husband, the excitement clear on her face. "You hear that, honey? Wren's about to *legally* be our daughter!"

I choke on my own spit and push them off me. "Whoa there." I gulp some tea. "You're moving this relationship faster than a knife fight in a phone booth. I'd like to give it more than half a day and be *legally* divorced before you start to ring wedding bells."

The dads snicker but Mama Gray just shakes her head and wanders to her office, muttering about bridal magazines.

"Since you mentioned divorce." My dad sits down beside me. Dominic leans over on the opposite side of the island with a concerned look on his face. "How is that situation? You said Jeremy put you in contact with his lawyer, right?"

I nod, pull up the lawyer's email on my phone and slide it in front of them. I planned to tell Rho this morning when he got home but...yeah. "Derrick contested the divorce and has threatened to sue."

I was so angry when I found out and that same anger is reflected on their faces now. "Sue over what?! That son of a bitch cheated on you publicly, and there's video evidence."

I grimace and take my phone back so I can put it away. "That's the problem. He's claiming defamation of character, specifically libel since the video was emailed to the entire organization yesterday by an unknown source. His agent has somehow twisted it to make it seem like I'm the one who sent it since the video was originally sent to my work email. But Jeremy's lawyer says he doesn't have any ground to stand on since the person who sent the video to me in the first place could have easily forwarded it. I'll likely need to fly back so they can go through my laptop and phone." I heave a sigh and drop my face into my hands. "And on top of all that, I still have to figure out how Rhodes and I will make things work. My job is in Seattle and his is here. I still have another year in my contract with the team before I can even think about resigning." My words are mumbled, and I rub my temples. I've got a migraine just thinking about all the things I have to do in the coming weeks.

Dad rubs my back like he used to when I was a kid, and my stress ebbs away slowly. "We're right here with you, Starshine. You have a whole team of people at your back."

Appreciation washes over me in waves. I don't know what I did to earn such loyal family and friends, but I'll do whatever it takes to keep them. Which also means finding a way to successfully live my life between Charleston and Seattle without giving up my family or my career.

CHAPTER 25
RHODES

"HOW ARE YOU, STARLING?" I ask Wren when she walks into my bedroom. Her four weeks here flew by and technically end tomorrow, but she's planned a video conference with her team to decide her next steps rather than fly back to do it in person.

I'd be lying if I said I wasn't grateful for the extra time with her, but anxiety has been making me nauseous for days as I wonder how we'll handle a long-distance relationship on top of our hectic work schedules.

Wren dives onto my bed and attaches herself to my side, placing kisses on my bare chest. She relaxes and melts into me and my heart threatens to beat right out of my chest. I spent so long thinking I'd never have her, it's kind of hard to believe she's really mine.

"I'm tired," she sighs. "On top of contesting the divorce and trying to sue me, Derrick's been texting me nonstop, and they alternate between frantic, mean, and downright gross. I took screenshots and sent them all to the lawyer, but I wish I didn't have to see it."

My heart hurts for her. I'm so happy she's with me

now, but I'm sad that she's going through a situation she fought so hard to avoid. "What kind of things did he send you?" I'm not sure I want to know, but it also kills me that I don't. I hate that I can't protect her from this—*from him*.

With a groan, she pulls her phone from her pocket and gently drops it on my chest. Then she buries her face in my ribs. Her breath tickles, but I try not to squirm. "Feel free to look, but don't say I didn't warn you when you have to bleach your eyes later."

Picking up her phone, I realize I don't know her password. "Uh, Starling?"

She snorts. "one-one-one-five."

Something about that sticks in my brain, and send a questioning look her way.

Peeking one eye up at me, she raises a brow. "Your jersey number and the year we met."

My heart cracks wide open, and I brush the hair back from her forehead with a smile. "Fuck, I love you."

She sighs happily and cuddles closer to my side in answer.

When I open up her texts, the first thing I see is an image I wish I could burn from my retinas. "Jesus *Christ*, Wren! A little warning would have been nice!" I know I'm yelling but I can't help it.

I wonder if Wren's therapist is accepting new clients.

She giggles into my side while I fight the urge to gag. "I did warn you that you'd need eye bleach, to be fair. I have to wait for the lawyer to email me confirmation that he got the screenshots so I can delete them."

I don't *want* to look, but it's like a car crash. You can't help but stare. "Why does it look like a yam?"

Wren is silent for a few seconds before absolutely

screeching with laughter, and that triggers my own. If we weren't on the bed already, we'd both be on the floor.

"You...said...it looks like...a YAM!" She barely manages to gasp the words out. "Holy shit, that's the best thing I've ever heard. I can't wait to tell Ella."

I don't love seeing Monroe's dick, but I do love her laugh. It always makes her sound so free and happy and with all the stress she's got on her shoulders, she deserves every moment of happiness.

While she's distracted, I read through the rest of the texts, getting angrier the more I read. But I do huff when I see his name in her phone. I bet one of the guys did that. The texts start the day she left and from the looks of it, he sends a few every week.

This guy is fucking unhinged.

DICK

Sugar, I'm sorry. It was just a one-time thing. Please come home.

Come on, Wren. I apologized. What more do you want? She didn't mean anything.

Your little attitude is fucking ridiculous. It's time for you to come home and act like my fucking wife again.

Divorce papers?! Are you fucking SERIOUS? I'm not signing these. Knock off the tantrum and come home now, Wren.

image

Don't you miss me, Sugar? I miss you.

It's been three weeks. Get your ass home or I swear you'll regret it.

> Fine, you asked for it. Your little "friend" won't want anything to do with your slutty ass when I'm through with you.
>
> I hope you like being sued. I figured it was about time you contributed something since I gave you a place to live and did pretty much everything else for you too.
>
> *image*
>
> *image*
>
> *video*
>
> I spent some quality time with a few of my own "best friends" last night. Good fucking luck ever finding somebody as good as me, whore.

The last message has me *furious*. Who does he think he is? And what exactly does he hope to accomplish by sending her a video of his dick in yet another woman's mouth? I know Wren would never stoop so low as to leak these, but he's pretty fucking stupid to assume she wouldn't. Or maybe he hopes she will?

"Hey, Starling?"

She lifts her head with a small smile, her laughter having finally subsided. "Yeah, Rho?"

I brush some of her soft hair back again and tuck it behind her ear, leaning down to drop a kiss on her forehead. "I just want you to know that I'm proud of you for not responding, but you're also willingly taking his abuse, and it kind of seems like you don't care."

Her expression shutters. "Well, responding would just provoke him, and I'm not stupid enough to give him ammunition for his lawsuit. Not to mention all the evidence this gives me for our divorce proceedings. If he keeps this up I don't see any judge in the world granting him more than what he's legally owed. Initially I was worried he would get a high amount of alimony because I make more than he does, but my lawyer is positive his behavior will negate that. He can't be sure though because Washington is a no-fault state. If we had gotten married here, it would be different."

I don't really understand legalese outside of baseball contracts, so I raise an eyebrow at her.

"Sorry," she continues, "that means that even though he cheated and there's evidence, neither of us is at fault for the divorce, and I could still owe him money every month so he can maintain his lifestyle. Normally, a couple would split the assets evenly, which means we would sell the apartment and split the profit, but I was adamant all I want is a clean break."

Shaking my head, I set her phone on the nightstand and pull her back into my arms. "God, you're incredible. The fact that you're even able to function right now is a testament to your strength, Starling. I'm truly in awe of you."

I can just make out the blush on her cheeks, but when I move in for a kiss, her phone rings. She sits up and leans over me to grab it, her eyes widening as she quickly answers. I can only hear her side of the conversation, but the longer the call goes on, the more nervous she gets.

Ten minutes pass before she hangs up and my worry is through the roof. Whoever that was, it doesn't seem like good news based on the way she curls into herself with her arms around her knees.

"Wren? Who was that?" I rub my hand across her

back in slow circles to help keep her calm, but it's hard when I can barely keep myself in check.

Clearing her throat, she turns fear-filled eyes my way. "That was my lawyer. They moved up the divorce proceedings."

She looks terrified, but shouldn't she be happy? It's not like they're going to deny the divorce or grant the crazy fucker alimony. "Okay...that's a good thing, right? Why do you look like you're headed for a guillotine?"

She takes a shaky breath and finally looks me in the eyes. "Rhodes, the hearing is *tomorrow* in Seattle."

Her whole body trembles, so I pick her up and plant her sideways in my lap, replacing her arms with mine where they rest around her knees. "I know, love. But why do you look so scared?" She just stares at me blankly for several seconds until it clicks, and I instantly feel like a jerk. "Because he'll be there, and you'll have to see him."

"Bingo," she whispers.

"Baby," I sigh, resting my head on the top of hers. The scent of apples and honey and *home* wash over me, and I take a deep breath and let it center me. The last thing she needs right now is another pissed-off man scaring her. "I know you'll have Archie and your lawyer, but do you want me there? Or do you think that would make things worse? My only priority is you."

A sniffle is the only answer I get for a few minutes, and I give her space to think it through. Obviously, I would give anything to be there, but I mean it when I say she's my only priority. Her safety and comfort will always come first, and if she doesn't think rubbing our relationship in his face is the right move, then I'll stay home and trust that Archie will take care of her.

"I think...you should be there," she says hesitantly.

"Worst-case scenario, he loses it in front of the judge and proves my point—that he's too unstable to be married. Best case, he's on his best behavior and we get through the day without any metaphorical bloodshed. I do worry he'll bring up our relationship as evidence of infidelity on my side..."

"So, we don't say a word about it. I'll talk to our parents, and if they flat-out ask you can be honest, but you did say it's a no-fault thing right? I bet it wouldn't matter either way since we can prove nothing happened before you got here."

She sighs but nods. "Thank you so much, Rho. I'll feel a million times better with you at my back for this."

I keep my face impassive but on the inside I'm melting with relief. "Anything for you, Starling."

CHAPTER 26
WREN

WE'VE BEEN WAITING for the better part of an hour as the judge reviews our case, and I feel like I'm about to throw up. Rhodes, his parents, my dad, and I flew in late last night, so I didn't get much sleep, and it has me on edge. I only saw Derrick for a moment when we came into the courthouse and he looked awful. His cheeks are sunken, and his hair is longer than I've ever seen it. His game day suit that used to fit impeccably now hangs at awkward angles on his too-thin body.

Did he really fall this far in four weeks, or have I just been oblivious to his appearance?

No. No way. Because the first video was from the same week, and he looked the same as always, so why does he look so terrible now? It can't just be because I left. I barely saw him when we lived together. And based on the string of partners he's been trying to throw in my face, he's not hard up for company.

"You alright, baby girl?" My dad's voice startles me out of my daze, and I turn to look at him guiltily.

"I'm okay. I was just thinking about Derrick," I

whisper to him. Rhodes is on the other side of me, but he's on the phone with his agent talking about a brand deal he just landed with a major sportswear company. I'm so dang proud of him.

My dad's eyebrows rise in shock, and he stares at me. "Not like that!" I hiss, glancing at Rho. He blows me a kiss, and I wink before I return my gaze to my father. "I just mean, he looks...different. And I was wondering if he really changed that much in a month or if I was a worse wife than I realized by not noticing."

He shakes his head and tosses an arm over my shoulder. "Let's call a spade a spade here, Starshine. The boy looks like shit."

I snort and quickly cover my mouth. "*Daddy*."

Shrugging, he glances around the room. "Sorry, Wren, but I can't find it in me to say a single nice word about the man who disrespected my daughter. Honestly, he's lucky he can still walk. The guy is as worthless as gum on a boot heel when it comes to basic human decency."

I sigh because he's not wrong. "I know that, but I was with him for over five years if you count college, and it wasn't all bad. Just...most of it." I grimace and then it's his turn to sigh.

"I'm sorry I wasn't there, Starshine. If I had known—"

"You would be in jail, and I would be a widow," I interrupt him with a knowing look. "And for what it's worth, I didn't want anyone to know. It was easier to stay than it would have been to rock the boat by leaving."

He goes to respond when we're called into the courtroom, and my nerves resurface with a vengeance. Before I can make it through the door, Rhodes yanks me sideways into a semi-hidden alcove. Without a word, he grips the back of my neck and pulls my mouth to his for a kiss that is definitely not appropriate for a public setting.

Our breaths are loud in the small space when he pulls away and runs his thumb under the side of my lip, probably fixing a smudge. "I just needed to remind you that I'm here. Whatever they say in there doesn't change anything between us, you hear me?" His voice is barely more than a whisper, but it's still firm.

"I hear you, Rho." I whisper back.

He smirks and looks around to make sure nobody can hear us. "Great. Then let's go so my girlfriend can get divorced." He leads me into the room with a hand hovering over my back, and thankfully, the judge isn't here yet, so he didn't see me come in late.

My eyes water when I see not only my and Rho's family, but also Jeremy, Jamie, Wesley, and Asher. I suck back the tears as best I can and walk to the front of the courtroom where my lawyer, William, sits, ignoring the murmured jabs from my ex and his lawyer.

Wes blows me an exaggerated kiss, and Asher smacks him on the back of the head while Jamie snickers. Jeremy rolls his eyes, used to their antics, and mouths, "Good luck, Cupcake."

I smile at him just as the judge enters, and we all take a seat.

"This judge is notoriously even-keeled but brutally honest," William whispers. "Don't be surprised if he asks some pretty invasive questions."

My body feels like it weighs a thousand pounds, and my anxiety makes it hard to breathe. I breathe in for a count of five, hold it, and then breathe out for the same. After a few breaths I can focus on the judge.

"Good morning, everybody. My name is Judge

Collins, and I will be presiding over this hearing today. Now, both parties have submitted written and video statements with their respective reasons for wanting," he glances to Derrick "and *not* wanting this divorce, and I've seen ample evidence to support the claims, but I do have one question before I make my ruling." His voice is deep and stern as he addresses the room.

I feel myself start to panic but one glance back at Rhodes calms me; no matter what happens, he won't run. I've always been lucky to have such a phenomenal support system, but Derrick isolated me from most of it. Even after getting so close with the guys in Seattle, I couldn't help but feel like a part of my soul was missing. It became this constant chasm of sadness in my chest that I tried to fill with work. And sure, that worked for a little while, but ultimately, being home has shown me how much more at peace I am here. The thought of going back to Washington and finding a new place to live so I can continue my work shouldn't fill me with dread, but it does, and I know I need to find some time to talk to Jeremy alone.

"I see here we have ample reasons for Mrs. Reid to be granted this divorce, the most relevant at this time being irreconcilable differences. Is that still the case?" the judge asks. His focus is mostly on Derrick's lawyer, but he does glance at mine as well.

Derrick's voice rings out around the silent room, and it sends a spear of anxiety through my system. "That bitch —" his lawyer elbows him, forcing a grunt from Derrick.

"Yes, your honor," Derrick's lawyer says. "Mrs. Reid has made her requests clear, and her only wish is to be granted the divorce. The jointly-owned property and bank accounts will be allotted to my client with no contest from the filing party." I could be wrong, but it seems like he's annoyed with Derrick, likely because of his outburst.

Judge Collins clears his throat with a nod, pulls out a thick folder, and holds it up for the court to see. "I've read through all thirty police reports that span the course of your forty-eight months of residence at the Concourse Apartment Complex, and I have to say I'm severely disappointed with the lack of professionalism and follow through on behalf of the precinct. *Ms.* Reid was seen in visible distress multiple times with many domestic disturbances reported, and yet charges were never filed beyond written warnings, nor was either party interviewed."

My heart lodges in my throat, and I keep my eyes trained forward so I don't have to see the look on my family's faces when they put the pieces together and figure out I lied to them about how bad it was before I left.

"It is because of everything I've seen today that I have no hesitation in granting Ms. Reid the divorce and forgoing alimony from either party, as well as tossing out the concurrent legal suit filed by Mr. Monroe. I will also grant Ms. Reid's request to allot any property and joint account holdings to Mr. Monroe."

The room erupts into chaos, but Derrick is the loudest and most aggressive, forcing the court officers to physically restrain him as Judge Collins bangs his gavel. "And furthermore, it is because of the evidence presented I *strongly* suggest you keep your threats to yourself Mr. Monroe, lest you find yourself in contempt of court."

The judge continues to glare at my ex-husband "I am extremely disheartened by the lack of justice before now, and if I see you in this courtroom again because of a domestic violence charge, I will not hesitate to toss you behind bars."

Derrick continues to mouth off until eventually the judge orders him to be detained until he calms down. His lawyer makes a frantic phone call and glances back at my ex every few seconds with panicked eyes.

I ignore it all, too stricken by the knowledge that I'm free. There's no sadness or hurt like I expected, only a sense of calm that's so potent it's practically tangible. When I look back at Rhodes and see his breathtaking smile, I know, without a doubt, this is exactly how it had to happen. My marriage to Derrick wasn't good, and I didn't go through with it for the right reasons, but I truly believe it led me to where I was meant to be all along.

CHAPTER 27
WREN

"HOW ARE YOU HANDLING EVERYTHING, Cupcake? I expected at least a few tears or even some wallowing. You just went through a traumatic divorce after your ex publicly cheated on you. I know how hard you fought to make it work and watching him throw it away must have hurt even if you weren't in love with him anymore."

After the trial earlier this week, Jeremy, Jamie, Asher, and Wes flew back to South Carolina with us, and I invited Jeremy to join me for lunch at Lotus to catch up since I've only seen him virtually this past month. He and the guys have been staying with my dad, but today they have to fly back to Seattle for training.

Taking a bite of my food, I ponder his question. "I'm way better than I thought I would be." In any other situation that might have been something I said just to placate him so he wouldn't worry, but this time it's true. The whole thing could have been a bigger deal, but our marriage was already so strained, it feels like a weight was lifted off my shoulders.

"This all almost feels like a natural conclusion, which

probably sounds weird," I say through a laugh. "But a part of me always knew there was something seriously wrong, so even though it was a shock, I'm relieved. I did cry for a bit, but it was my way of coming to terms with the knowledge that four years of my life were wasted on someone who was only out for himself. It sounds terrible, but I don't think I was actually sad about our marriage ending."

Jeremy grabs my hand and squeezes it gently. "Cupcake, it doesn't sound like anything more than you finally getting what you deserve. Derrick was, and is, fucking terrible. He never deserved you, and your relief doesn't make you a bad person."

Logically, I know that's true, but hearing it out loud helps alleviate some of my guilt. I smile at him in appreciation as we both tuck into our dumplings for a few minutes in comfortable silence.

"How is it that you have better dumplings in a *South Carolina strip mall* than we do in all of Seattle, where we have dozens of authentic Chinese restaurants?" Jeremy asks in amazement.

I snicker, because I have no idea why the owners decided to open up in this spot, but I'm damn glad they did. "I don't know, but everybody I've ever brought here says the same thing. These little pillows of heaven are a Godsend."

"So." I clear my throat. "Have you heard anything more from the owners about Derrick's contract?" I hadn't originally planned on asking, but after Derrick's texts, Dominic convinced me I needed to bring it to the team's management. He said he didn't want me in an unsafe environment when I returned to work.

Jeremy frowns, pushing food around his plate. "I had a meeting with the owners to discuss his future with the

Sirens and...let's just say it didn't swing in my favor." He sighs, his expression sad. "Turns out the morality clause is more of a formality than anything else. In their eyes, cheating is a normal and expected part of professional sports, and the fact that you're both still under your respective Siren's contracts basically means they plan to sweep it under the rug."

I nod, having expected as much. Jeremy watches me with his giant arms crossed over his chest. The way his eyes roam over my face makes me shuffle down into my seat nervously. "Now that we have the basics covered..." He raises a thick eyebrow. "You ready to talk about the real reason you invited me here without the guys?"

My earlier guilt comes back full force at the look on his face, and I wince.

With a sigh, he squeezes my hand again. "You're leaving us, aren't you?" Tears fill my eyes when I shrug and Jeremy nods in understanding. "I could see it on your face the day of the trial and again just now. You're so happy here, Cupcake. I'm not saying you weren't happy in Seattle, but you practically *glow* here."

I can't help but smile at that. So much has changed over the last month, but I wouldn't have it any other way. "Part of it is that Rhodes and I are finally together, and I hate that I would be away from him so much," I say quietly. Jeremy met Rho the day of the trial and the two have gotten along like peas and carrots. "But I feel at home here in a way I never did there. I'm so grateful for my four years with the Sirens and to you most of all. You took a chance on me when I was just a kid, and I'll always love you for that, but I think it's time for me to make a change."

Grinning, he shakes his head. "Well, you'll need to

come back at least one more time to get your stuff and sign some paperwork if you're gonna quit on me. There is an escape clause in your contract and that includes not being forced to work in a hostile environment. Monroe definitely qualifies." I swallow nervously and he lets go of my hand to tap the table with his knuckles. "Really though, I'm incredibly proud of you Wren. I know you've had to make a lot of hard decisions lately, but you've handled it with grace and maturity far beyond your years. I'm honored to be your friend, and I expect multiple visits a year."

"Damn it, Jer," I sniffle. "Of course, I'll come back to visit. I'm going to hate not seeing you every day."

His smile softens and he places money down on the bill. "Alright, Cupcake. I've gotta head to the airport and you need to tell your new bodyguard about your trip to Seattle."

I'll miss my job and my friends, and I might even miss the Washington rain a little bit, but I can't wait to start the rest of my life here in Charleston.

Rhodes is at practice with Finn when I get back, so I quickly change and pack a bag. The sooner I handle everything in Washington, the sooner I can get back to Rhodes and Finn. I've just packed the last few things I'll need from the guest bathroom when my phone starts vibrating on the nightstand, and the steady buzz of nonstop notifications nearly sends it tumbling onto the floor.

My eyes widen. There are more than a hundred notifications, but Asher's name pops up on the screen before I can read any of them, and I hurry to answer the call. My nerves are too shot to even appreciate the irony of someone changing his ringtone to "Hot Mess" by Zoe Clark (Ash is the most put-together guy I know).

"Wren, I need you to do me a favor and *do not* look at your phone. I'll be there in two minutes." His voice is frantic as several other voices shout in the background.

My stomach drops at the urgency in his tone. Asher isn't one to lose his cool, and he should be headed to the airport, so my own panic immediately spikes in response. I pull the phone from my ear and scroll through my notifications, clicking on a video link against my better judgment. What I see on the screen has me running back into the bathroom to empty the contents of my stomach.

"Wren!" Three voices shout from downstairs. I must have forgotten to lock the door when I got home, but a wash of relief runs through me because they're here.

Jamie is the first to make it into the bathroom, and his face crumbles when he sees me on my knees, hugging the toilet. "Baby Reid," he gasps as he sits down next to me. He grabs my hair, holds it back, and whispers assurances while I heave.

"Jamie," I groan. My voice echoes off the porcelain, but I don't feel like I'm going to be sick again, so I flush and put the lid down, resting my sweaty face on the cold seat. "Please don't tell me everything will be okay when it probably won't."

Wes walks over and gently picks up my head so he can sit on the toilet lid. When he's settled, he sets my head against his knees and runs a cold washcloth over my face and neck to cool me down. "People have sex tapes leak all the time, Wren. It's not like you're with some random guy, he was your husband. It'll blow over fast and in a month we'll laugh about it."

My eyes burn as I start to cry, and I can barely get the words out between heaves for air. "I didn't know I was being filmed."

They freeze in sync, but it's Asher who growls, "What did you just say?"

I clear my throat and wince—the amount of tears I've shed this week has it all swollen and irritated. Ash grabs me the water from my nightstand, and I take a sip, letting the cool liquid soothe my raw throat. "That was the only time I ever got blackout drunk after we moved to Seattle," I whisper. "The night I told y'all about my feelings for Rhodes? I went home and tried to go to bed but Derrick was all over me for the first time in months. Had I been more sober, I would have been suspicious at how insistent he was, but I was drunk and exhausted and too emotionally wrung out to fight him on it."

Another round of nausea overwhelms me, but I swallow down the bile. "I never would have...I didn't consent to that. I was barely even conscious, for fuck's sake! I trusted my *husband* to take care of me. Not film me at my most vulnerable." My chest heaves, and sobs wrack my body.

"What do you want to do, Wren? We need to report this to the police and to the team," Jamie says softly, rubbing my back.

Thoughts fly through my mind too fast, and my panic continues to rise. All I know is that I need to get out of here *now*.

"I can't let any of this affect Rhodes or his career. I mean, God, I didn't even think about that. We got together before my divorce was even final, what if our relationship had gotten out to the press? He's a public figure, they could have torn him apart. I was going to move back to Charleston to be with him and now I can't even..." I trail off guiltily, realizing my slip too late.

Three sets of wide eyes find mine, and I can see the hurt on Wes and Jamie's faces, but Ash keeps his expression neutral. "You were going to leave without telling us?" Wes asks frustratedly.

"*No!*" I shout. "Of course not. I was literally packing a bag to fly to Seattle right now. I want to see if I can even get out of the last year of my contract, and I was going to tell y'all when I knew for sure. I promise, I never would have left without saying goodbye."

Asher sits down next to me, wraps an arm around my back, and rests his head on top of mine. "We know that, Wren. It was just a shock to hear, especially when we're already dealing with a crisis right now."

I take in a deep breath and hold it until the tears stop. I can't afford to break down right now. "I'm so sorry. I didn't think before I spoke, and I shouldn't have told you like that. When does your flight leave?"

They look at each other in silent communication but, again, it's Asher who answers. "We were on our way to the jet when the news broke, actually."

I nod, standing on shaky legs. "Great, then let's go. I need to get out of here. I'll just stay in Seattle longer than I planned and grab a hotel while I figure things out."

They roll their eyes at me, and Jamie grabs my bag, leading me down the stairs. "You know I have a guest room, and I'm not gonna let our favorite PR badass stay in a hotel. But do we need to swing by the stadium so you can talk to Rhodes before we leave?"

I shake my head slowly even though guilt swamps me as we leave the house. My therapist would tell me I'm undoing years of progress by running away but I can't help it. I'm terrified of the disappointment and hurt I'll see on Rhode's face right now, and it's making me feel sick again. Jamie's brows shoot up in disbelief, so I blurt out the first thing that pops into my head. "No, uh...he's at a brand shoot all day, so I'll just call him when we land."

Jamie looks like he doesn't believe me, but I make my way to the car and pray he doesn't push it. I can't see Rhodes right now. Not when I'm so embarrassed and ashamed that I didn't consider his career before dragging him into my mess. Rhodes was a virgin until three weeks ago, and even though he knows I'm not, I know the video will probably hurt him. Plus, I'm terrified that his entire opinion of me will change now that the entire world has seen me naked, drunk, and having sex.

My stomach ties in knots the whole drive to the airport, and texts and calls from my family come in rapid-fire. The only person I answer is my dad before I turn off my phone. I feel like a coward running because of this, but I'm overwhelmed and scared of what this will do to my personal life and my career.

Logically, I know it's not a huge deal. I mean, people have sex with their spouses literally every day. But it's not every day that your spouse films you having sex without your knowledge and then shares it with the world. It's true, I don't know for sure that Derrick leaked the video, but I can't think of anybody else who would have access to a personal video like that.

After we're in the air, I finally let myself start to think. The sooner I can come up with a solution, the sooner I can fix the mess I just made. Jeremy hugs me to his side as

I stare out the window silently, listening to him mutter death threats the entire five-hour flight to Seattle. Once we land, Jeremy, Wes, and Asher head to the stadium to do damage control with Sirens management, while Jamie and I make the short trip to his apartment.

I don't say a word the entire time, and only turn my phone back on once I make it to Jamie's spare bedroom. I scroll through the myriad of missed messages. Now that I'm away from South Carolina, the guilt of leaving how I did threatens to choke me and sends tears down my cheeks.

I spend the next several hours ignoring every knock on the door and every attempt at conversation. Instead, I lie in the dark room with my tired eyes trained on the blank wall opposite the bed as I pretend the whole world hasn't seen me naked. Why the hell did Derrick record that video? The fact that I was so drunk I barely remember the sex makes me feel kind of gross. But he was my husband, not a stranger or some one-night-stand—I trusted him.

I know I should call Rhodes and deal with the fallout of running away, but as my body warms under the blankets, my eyes slide shut. My tired mind goes blissfully blank for the first time all day, and I let sleep claim me.

Angry boyfriends and police reports are tomorrow's problem.

CHAPTER 28
RHODES

I CAN'T WAIT *to get home and see my girl.*

Practice was brutal today, and my whole body aches as I walk into the locker room. Conversation comes to a complete halt when I round the corner, and several of my teammates send sympathetic glances my way. I chalk up the weirdness to Coach calling me out halfway through practice for being distracted. Which I was.

I hurry through a shower and am halfway dressed when Aidan and Copeland corner me by my locker, looks of confusion, fury, and sadness on their faces.

"Have you checked your phone yet?" Aidan asks softly. They're freaking me the hell out, and when I shake my head Cope hands me his. Nothing could have prepared me for what I see on the screen.

"What the *fuck* is this?" I hiss, grabbing my own phone out of my locker in a panic. I have dozens of calls and texts from my parents, Archie, and the guys in Seattle, but not a single one from Wren. "Where did you get that?" I ask them. My voice is frenzied, but I can't fucking help it.

Cope winces, and Aid looks miserable. "It's everywhere, Rho. An anonymous Twitter account leaked it this morning, and it spread like wildfire. They're more focused on him because he's a pro athlete, but Wren isn't exactly anonymous. There's chatter that the Sirens might fire her over this, and the media is going insane over the double standard. Especially given her ex literally *just* had his own video leaked last month. There's a hashtag and everything."

Slamming my locker shut, I grab my bag and barely stop long enough to appreciate the supportive words from the girls upstairs as I grab Finn from them, then stomp out to my SUV. Apparently, literally everybody has seen the goddamn video before me, and they're all as angry about it as I am. I gently buckle Finn into his harness and toss my bag in the back, hitting the button to dial Jamie from my Bluetooth.

"I guess you saw the video." Jamie says when he answers. "We're already working to get it removed, but since the account that released it is a dummy account, the platform is being a pain in the ass about it.

"We know it was Derrick, so why the fuck isn't he in handcuffs? Isn't this considered revenge porn?" I growl.

The line goes quiet long enough that I check to make sure I didn't drop the call. Then a gust of air crackles through the speakers. "We can't prove it was him," he murmurs angrily. "The bastard is MIA, and until we can convince Wren to go to the police with his threatening texts, they won't even look into it."

His words register, and I nearly slam on the breaks. "Wait, why would *you* have to get her to go to the police? Isn't that something Archie and I should do since she's here?"

"Oh... so, there's probably something you should know." His tone tells me I won't like what he has to say. "Wren is here...in Seattle."

I jerk the wheel in shock and when another car honks at me, I pull off the road. "She's in Seattle?!" I practically shout. "Why? I can be there in six hours. I'm gonna miss some practice, but I'll figure it out because—"

"Rhodes, man, I don't think you should come." He says it gently, but that doesn't stop white hot anger from searing my veins and turning my vision red.

"You can't keep me from my girl when she's dealing with something like this!" I yell as I slam my hand down on the steering wheel. I like Jamie, but if he thinks he can tell me what to do when it comes to *my* girlfriend, he's in for a rude awakening.

"Will you drop your fucking ego and just *think* for a second, Gray?" he says in admonishment. "Consider what's going through her head right now and ask yourself if your presence would help or hurt that?"

I take a second to seriously consider his words. Wren and I have been best friends for nearly eight years, and she knows I wouldn't leave her over something like this, so why didn't she call me?

I consider everything that's happened over the last week and realize that even though her divorce is finalized, it hasn't gone public yet. To the public, this will look like a husband and wife having sex, so their outrage on her behalf makes sense. But if details about *our* relationship come out before their divorce news drops, the media will crucify both of us and paint Derrick as the victim. Add on how mortified she probably is, and damn it all to hell, Jamie's right. If I know one thing about Wren Reid, it's that she's a runner when she's overwhelmed. And I'd bet my last dollar she's trying to protect our careers, and she's probably worried my feelings are hurt by the stupid video even though I don't give a fuck.

Should I give her space to deal with it on her own, or would that dig our relationship's grave before it even has a chance?

I heave a deep sigh and rest my head on the steering wheel. I just want her to be happy, but that's not going to happen unless we figure this out. "Okay," I concede. "How long do I give her before I hop on a plane? Because I can't just sit here and do nothing while Wren deals with this on her own, Jamie. It's not gonna happen."

He snorts. "I wouldn't expect you to just sit there and twiddle your damn thumbs, Rhodes. Why don't you go see Archie and get his opinion. Part of her concern is her career, so you could try and help her find a new job. Because Jeremy just called me and her chances of getting out of her contract early are looking pretty good after all this." His voice goes somber at the end, but something he said snags my attention.

"Wait... what do you mean, getting out of her contract early? She didn't mention that." Hope blooms in my chest. She was already trying to quit her job? An idea forms in my head.

Jamie clears his throat awkwardly. "Oops? I don't think I was supposed to say anything."

I chuckle, tapping my fingers on the steering wheel. "I won't say a word unless she tells me first. Call me if anything changes, yeah?"

We say our goodbyes and hang up, and I feel better with a plan of action and turn on my blinker to head back to the stadium, dialing Archie on my way. I'm pretty sure he's got a class today, so I know he won't be home. I don't care what I have to do, I'll do everything in my power to make sure Wren has something good to come back to.

"And have the police been notified?" Sarah asks. She's been gunning to hire Wren since the day they met, so I'm glad she's here.

I'm in a meeting with the Raptors' manager and senior PR staff, trying to secure Wren a backup plan if she's able to get out of her contract. I'm also trying not to snap every time someone asks another question about the video.

I'm flushed with anger, so I take off my hoodie, hoping to cool down before the heat makes me even more irritable. Sarah notices and tosses me a bottle of water, and I smile gratefully.

"This morning was a pretty big shock for Wren, so she hasn't gone to the police yet." I grimace, raking a hand through my hair. "To be frank, she's not taking it well. Her divorce from the player in the video was only finalized last week, and now her privacy has been violated, and she's embarrassed. Add in the rumors flying about her termination and not his," pausing, I sigh and scrub my hands down my face. "It's not good."

Anna, our head of non-roster staff, has been quietly absorbing all the information along with everything Sarah has said. Anna handles every person in the building that isn't a player or someone in management. She scoffs, and my mouth parts slightly in surprise at the look of annoyance on her face, but she waves me off.

"Sorry, that was uncouth of me. I find it absolutely abhorrent that her employers are protecting a now two-time media fuck-up over their prized employee. That woman has grown their socials by a margin of nearly two-hundred percent since joining the staff four years ago, so for them to even consider throwing that away over one maliciously-leaked video and the word of a player with obviously hostile motives and *multiple* accusations of harassment? It's a tragic double-standard."

"Accusations of harassment? I didn't know there were any." Surprise coats my words, but I really should have seen it coming. To do something like this isn't the work of a stable person.

She nods, her brows pinched in anger. "He's had two women come forward in the last two days with evidence that he was harassing them when they ended their respective sexual relationships. It seems both women chose to come forward only *after* they found out he had a sexually transmitted illness and didn't disclose prior to said relations."

My stomach sinks, and I'm so fucking thankful Wren got out of her marriage when she did.

The team's general manager, Jack, finally speaks from the head of the table with thinly-veiled disgust in his tone. "If they would rather keep a media disaster like that on their roster than someone as useful as Wren Reid, then we won't hesitate to scoop her up and make it worth her while, provided she interviews well."

He glances at Anna. "Get a hold of legal and have a preemptive contract drawn up, and whatever her previous salary, we'll match it with a fifteen percent increase and benefits. I would say that's more than fair given her talent and track record."

My eyes widen in shock, and I nearly choke. I don't know how much she's been making, but I do know it was more than Derrick, and his base salary isn't anything to scoff at despite his bench-player status.

Even Anna looks surprised, but her smirk is telling. Wren is getting a hell of a deal, and she's earned every bit of it with her talent and kindness.

"I already liked Wren when I met her last month, so I made some calls after you scheduled this meeting and from everyone I've talked to in the league, she's a dream to work with. Her direct supervisor Jeremy was highly complimentary of her and her skills. Not a single person on the Sirens team or ours has a negative word to say about her aside from our intern Whitney, but I'll let y'all puzzle that one out on your own," Sarah says with a flat look. I try really hard not to laugh, covering my mouth to hide a grin.

Jack nods and a small smile pulls at the corners of his lips when he turns to me. He shakes my hand as he stands. "Give my regards to Miss Reid, and feel free to make her aware of our intentions at your discretion. I would love to have her in for an interview in the next two weeks, but from what I'm hearing, it sounds like we would be honored to welcome her to the Raptors family."

I may not be able to exact revenge on Derrick for what he's done, but at least I could help set Wren up for success despite this minor setback. Right now, my job is to make her see that this is just a blip on the radar, and I'll be by her side no matter what.

CHAPTER 29
WREN

THE GUYS LET me wallow for two days before they interrupt my self-imposed isolation. On the third day, I'm woken up rather abruptly when Wesley unlocks the door and rips open the curtains, nearly blinding me.

"Gah! What'd you have to go and do that for?" I grumble, tossing the blankets over my head so I can burrow further into my cave of fabric.

"Alright, Wren. I know you're embarrassed, and I know you're hurt, but it's time to get up and rejoin the rest of us in the real world. You need to turn your phone back on and communicate with the people who love you because you left them with no explanation, and they're worried sick. This isn't the girl I know and love." Wes sits on the edge of the bed and gently pulls down the covers, brushing my tangled, greasy hair back so he can look in my eyes.

I sigh because I know he's right. "I can't face the world when I know they've literally seen me naked, Wes. This is like the dream where you stand up in front of the class and realize you forgot to wear pants, but, ya know, real." My words barely come out as more than a croak, and I have to clear my throat several times. Apparently not speaking for two days steals your voice.

He kisses my forehead and grabs my hands until I'm standing. Then he pulls me into a hard hug. "I know, honey. And that's why I'm here. That's also why I brought reinforcements." The last part is whispered into my hair as he rests his head on mine. I cringe thinking about what I probably smell like right now.

Then his words register, and I blink owlishly at him. "Reinforcements?"

"Oh, my sweet girl."

Moisture springs to my eyes when I hear her voice, but a fresh rush of embarrassment follows quickly on its heels. Dropping back down to the bed, I hide my face in my hands and cry as Mama Gray wraps me in her arms. Her familiar scent soothes my frayed edges as she pats my hair.

"It's alright, sweetie, just let it all out." Her voice strips the cover of numbness I've hidden under the last few days and sobs explode out of my throat in a sound so mournful, it startles even me. It feels like a pressure valve is released on my soul, and I'm finally able to grieve the things I've ignored for too long.

I relive feelings of abandonment toward my mother and the guilt I feel that my dad traded his own happiness for mine for so long. I'm glad he found Caroline, and I can't wait to meet her, but I'm terrified to have another mother figure in my life. Even if she hates me, I would never ask my dad to break up with her when he's finally happy, especially knowing he delayed that happiness for twenty-four years.

I cry from the unresolved trauma associated with

Derrick's verbal abuse. I endured it for four years only to be cheated on and publicly humiliated. I grieve my traumatic divorce. It was so hard to watch the person I thought I knew become unstable. Derrick's threatening texts have stopped, but I remember the way he looked at the trial and the way he blew up when the judge finalized our divorce. Even though I'm angry with him, I still care about him as a man I once loved.

I mourn the lost time that I'll never get back with Rhodes because we were both too afraid to admit our feelings, but at the same time, I know this is exactly how things were supposed to happen.

And finally, I struggle to cope with the aftermath of my leaked sex tape and how violated I feel.

I let out every bit of pain while the closest person I've ever had to a mother rocks me like a child. It's cathartic and everything I tried to tell myself I didn't need. I have no idea how long we sit there, but the sun is high in the sky and casts a blinding light through the room when I finally lift my head off her soaked shirt and wipe my tender eyes.

Cupping my cheeks in her soft hands, Kaci lifts up my head and uses a tissue from the nightstand to wipe my face. I'm sure I look a mess with snot and tears all over, but for once, I can't bring myself to care. The color of her eyes reminds me of Rhodes, and the tears threaten to start all over again. If she's here, that means he probably is too, right?

She smiles sadly at the look on my face and shakes her head. "He's not here, Wren."

My hope is stomped into the dirt with her admission, but she's quick to correct herself.

"He's not here because he knew you wanted space to

process this yourself without your boyfriend coming to the rescue. Jamie called him and told him you were safe but needed time. When a few days went by with no word from you, we were all worried, so it was easy for me to hop on a plane when Wesley called." She pauses to snicker. "Plus, it's been years since I had a cute boy come calling, and it was fun to rile up Dominic a little bit on the way here."

That pulls a small huff of laughter from me, and I'm sure that was her goal. But my insecurities still roar full force in my head and heart, along with the heavy weight of all the things I need to do.

I try to talk again but a tickle in my throat sends me into a coughing fit, so I take several long sips of water before I'm able to rasp out, "I think I need to call my therapist."

Kaci nods, but we're interrupted by a knock on the door. It opens only a few inches, revealing a face so much like Rhodes's, it makes my stomach twist with guilt at the reminder that I ran away.

"Hey there, Wren," his deep voice soothes me just as much as his wife's...until he opens his mouth. "I hate to be the one to tell you this, kid, because you're still very cute, but you need a shower."

Kaci and I scoff at the same time and say, "Rude." We turn to each other with crazy smiles and shout, "Jinx! You owe me a Coke." We burst into giggles, but I catch a whiff of my own breath and cringe. Dominic is right, I desperately need to take a shower and brush my teeth before I do anything else.

"Alright." Resignation drips from my words. "I need to get ready and then I should probably head to the stadium to get a fix on where my career stands and if this will make it easier to circumvent my contract."

Mama Gray kisses my head one more time before she leaves, dragging her husband out with her as she chastises him for his insensitive comment. Then I'm alone for the first time all morning, so I finally make my way into the bathroom.

I go through my routine on autopilot. The numbness is gone after the ridiculous amount of crying I just did, so I'm hopeful the calm I feel is acceptance. From all the murmured arguments I've heard through the walls, it's safe to assume I'll be losing my job today, and while the thought makes me sad, I had planned to leave anyway. I can't help but wonder if Derrick will have any consequences.

I think what scares me more is that this scandal could impact my ability to get a PR job anywhere else. After all, who wants a public relations manager who can't even manage her own public image? As I step into a shower that's hotter than the sixth circle of hell, I brainstorm ways to handle the fallout from all of this.

The reminder of the video sends a shudder through my body despite the scalding water beating down my back. I still feel violated, but I also understand it wasn't my fault. I couldn't have stopped something out of my control. This is all on Derrick. He might've released the tape as payback for the divorce if his last texts are anything to go by, but I wish I knew for sure.

He barely showed any interest in me after the first months of our marriage and it only got worse over the last four years. So why would he be so angry about a divorce? Is it just because it made him look bad? He has always been concerned with his image, which is part of why getting the video that started all this was so shocking.

As I dry off, I realize something just doesn't add up with this whole situation. The more I think about it, the more confused I get. If I'm fired and he gets off scot-free *again, it* doesn't look good for his public image. I mean, Derrick isn't a complete idiot, but I also don't think he's smart enough to release a tape and then cover his tracks.

Unless... he had help from someone who's really good with social media.

Trying to puzzle it out is giving me a migraine, so I drop it for now and focus on doing my makeup to perfection. If I'm about to walk into my job only to quit or be fired, then I want to look damned good doing it. I refuse to let them make me feel bad for something that wasn't my fault.

Everybody except for my dad and Rhodes are there to greet me with hugs and supportive words when I emerge from Jamie's guest room, but Rhodes's absence sends a shooting pain to my heart. I have no one to blame but myself. As soon as I handle everything here, I need to apologize for the way I ran and make sure he knows it will never happen again.

CHAPTER 30
WREN

"MISS REID, thank you for coming; it's always a pleasure."

Like I expected, I was pulled into a meeting with the board of directors the moment I entered the building. The team's owner Alexander "Big Al" Scott does a terrible job disguising his distaste for me with his welcoming words.

I've met the man a total of four times in four years and not one of those was a positive interaction. He stands at five feet, six inches, and seems to struggle with a Napoleon complex, often using his brutish personality to intimidate anyone taller than him.

Nodding in respect, I take my seat at the large conference table where several other staff members are already seated. Ella is the only other woman here, and my brows furrow. Normally I wouldn't think anything of it, but a subordinate shouldn't be included in something like this unless they were directly involved.

Al doesn't hesitate to jump right in, which thankfully doesn't give my nerves a chance to break past the stone façade plastered on my face. "It's been brought to our attention that this past week you were involved in an extremely public display of lewdness," he says haughtily. "Do you deny this?"

My nostrils flare as I breathe out angrily. He's making it out to seem like I *caused it*. "Last week an inappropriate tape was released of me and my now ex-husband. I was not aware the encounter was filmed, nor was I made aware such a video existed. I take my career and professionalism very seriously and unlike my ex-husband, I've never once put myself in a position to damage the Siren's reputation."

His face gets redder as I continue, and by the end of my explanation, he slams his palms down on the wood table hard enough to rattle the water glasses scattered across it. *"ENOUGH!"* He roars. "I will not allow you to waltz in here and slander one of my players like this!"

My jaw drops at his words. "Slandering? How in the world could I slander someone who was just divorced for infidelity and has had not one, but *two* lewd videos leaked in the last month?" I do my best to keep my tone relatively respectful, but it's damn hard when all I want to do is rage at how unbelievable this conversation has been from the second I walked in here.

He waves me off with a cruel smirk, bringing my attention to a shiny white scar that runs through his upper lip. "It's a classic he-said-she-said, and unfortunately since you're in breach of the morality clause in your contract, you're relieved of your position, effective immediately. Security will escort you to collect your belongings and you'll surrender all your passwords and access codes to Miss Reyes," he says gleefully, pointing at Ella.

I raise an eyebrow and glance around the room. "And Derrick? Will he be released for his part in the 'public display of lewdness' as well? Or am I the only one being vilified here?" I let some of the anger I've repressed slip into my tone, and I see pride reflected in the eyes of a couple of the board members. It's nice to know not every person here thinks ill of me.

Al doesn't say anything, he just crosses his arms with that infuriating smirk still firmly planted on his pudgy face.

I don't say a word either as I stand to leave the room, opting for a silent nod instead. I don't trust myself not to say something that might come back to bite me later. I guess now I know why Ella's here. She's been given my job. When Ella didn't try to contact me before I came in, I had assumed it was because my phone had been shut off for days, but the look on her face as she watches me leave the room is almost...*giddy*.

It takes less than fifteen minutes to pack up four years of accomplishments and memories, and instead of feeling devastated, my departure is almost bittersweet. I always assumed I'd be leaving the Sirens at some point in my career, but to be dismissed so suddenly, and for something that was out of my control, is hard. It doesn't matter that I was about to quit anyway.

"Hey, you doing okay?" Ella's quiet voice reaches my ears, and I nearly flinch before reminding myself she's been my friend for years. It's not her fault management chose to handle it this way. Despite the weird smile she had as I left the conference room, surely she's not happy about my termination.

I brush off the suspicion in my gut and give her a small smile. "I'm alright. It's crazy because I was actually planning to resign this week before shit hit the fan so I could move back to South Carolina and be with Rhodes."

Her jaw drops, and I stifle a laugh.

"Oh, surprise! Apparently he's been in love with me since freshman year of college and just never told me. God, so much has happened in the last month, and I haven't had a chance to tell you any of it! I texted you a few times but never heard back," I trail off quietly. I had forgotten with everything that was going on, but honestly, my feelings are hurt that she never once checked in on me or replied to any of my texts while my world was falling apart.

She waves her hand in the air dismissively. "It's been crazy busy here; I must have forgotten."

Okay then...maybe she just feels awkward because of the whole being fired thing. Does she think I'd be upset with her? Jeremy walks in before I can ask. His face is a mask of fury until he sees me, and his expression softens. Pulling me into a hug, he kisses the top of my head and groans.

"God, I am so sorry this is what you had to walk into, Cupcake. I had an inkling, but I should've fucking guessed Alexander would say some heinous shit like that. Misogynistic ass pig," he murmurs under his breath.

I crack up, my shoulders shaking under the weight of his beefy arms. "Ass pig?" I ask through my giggles.

I swear to God, the big guy actually *blushes*. "It's nothing," he grumbles, the deep timbre of his words makes his chest rumble under my cheek. "Just something in a book series I read."

I don't want to embarrass him when he's being so sweet, but I vow to scour his house at a later date and find those books. We hear a quiet scoff behind us, and I turn in shock to see Ella with a stormy look on her face. Her pretty brown eyes are dark with anger, but the expression drops the minute she sees us staring.

Pulling from Jeremy's hold, I grab my lone box of possessions and take a final glance around one of my favorite places in the world. I don't want to show my sadness here, so I do my best to keep my emotions in check, but it's hard. I first set foot in this office when I was barely out of college and didn't know a single person aside from Derrick.

Seattle is where I found the guys that became my family, where I started my career, and where I finally realized my worth as a person and a romantic partner. The Wren standing here today would never settle for less when it comes to the people in her life—whether that's a romantic partner, a friend, or a family member.

I turn to smile at Ella, but she returns it with a grimace. My stomach drops, and I'm worried our friendship won't survive this.

I bring her in for a tight hug, frowning when she leaves her arms by her sides, refusing to return the embrace. "You'll come to visit sometime, won't you? I'll be here as much as I can to see you and the guys. Though I have to say it'll be weird when I have to get a visitor's pass to come up here."

"You can't be up here even with a visitor's pass. It's employees only." Her words come out quick and harsh. I step back in shock at her tone, but she has that weird grimace-smile cemented in place again. Offering her a brittle smile of my own, I nod slowly and exchange a concerned look with Jeremy.

"Right, of course. Um...I guess I'll see you around then? Text me if you're ever in Charleston and wanna grab lunch or something."

As I talk, I notice her expression shift into her usual bright, happy one as she looks behind me. I turn around and see a small group of players just outside the door in what looks to be a heated discussion. Ella backs up and fluffs her hair, barely sparing me a glance. "Wonderful to catch up, but some of us actually have to work," she snarks on her way out of the glass-walled office.

I follow her out, more confused than ever, but I'm distracted by the group of men who nearly tackle me in their haste to get in a hug. Several deep voices speak at the same time and too fast for me to really make out what any of them are saying, but Jeremy shouts and they all quiet down.

"This is bullshit, Baby Reid," Wes says angrily. There's a murmur of agreement among the players and it brings a smile to my face.

"I don't disagree with you, but we can't change their decision, so I'll make the best of it. And you know I'll still watch all of your games and root for you from my couch."

That spurs a round of excited chatter about the upcoming season, and while they're distracted, I scan the small room, my eyes catching on Jamie near the back. He raises an eyebrow in question, and I scratch the back of my neck, flicking my eyes to the door. He nods in understanding and tells the crowd that we need to go. I'm so thankful he can read me so well.

Seeing so many people go to bat for me has been eye-opening, but also incredibly overwhelming. I'm anxious and emotionally drained and just so *tired*. I need to crash at Jamie's for a few hours and then get my butt on a plane back home. It feels like it's been weeks since I was home with Rhodes and Finn.

It's time I go see my boys.

CHAPTER 31
RHODES

WREN HAS BEEN GONE for three days, and if it weren't for the constant updates from my parents and the guys, I would be chomping at the bit to get on a plane and haul her cute ass back home. I've taken Finn for long walks on the beach every day after practice, and it's given me a lot of time to think about everything that's happened.

My initial anger and frustration have withered away the more I consider why she ran. I thought this video might be the final straw that broke her composure, and based on what my mom said, it looks like I was right.

Wren is, and always has been, olympic-level good at running from her emotions. In college when life got messy, she'd run to the nearest bar and drown her sorrows in vanilla vodka and cream soda and then call me in tears to pick her up.

Unfortunately, she's now an adult with access to private planes, so she can run much farther than the local college bar. From my talk with Jamie, I know she probably ran because she was scared our relationship would change after that stupid, goddamned video was leaked, but I need her to know that she couldn't be more wrong.

Yeah, seeing the video sucked. I still feel sick about it, but I feel sick *for* her. Not because of her. I never expected Wren to remain abstinent but knowing about something and seeing it are two entirely different things. I want to work through my own emotions before she gets home, so I can support her, one-hundred percent.

Today is my first appointment with a psychologist Coach Benny recommended to me, and I'm nervous. I haven't seen a mental health professional since college when my anxiety was at its worst, and I've never met this woman before. We're starting with a virtual appointment, so I won't have the added discomfort of a new environment.

It feels kind of stupid to go to therapy for someone else's problem, especially since the tape being leaked didn't impact my life as much as hers. But it hurt the woman I love, and it's probably affecting her mental health. So I want every tool available to help her feel secure.

My laptop pings, which alerts me to an incoming video call, and my muscles tense. I walk to the couch like I'm prepared for battle, every nerve ending on edge and ready to take me down in a synchronized onslaught of panic. I settle into my preferred spot in the corner of the couch and accept the call, doing my best to smile.

The woman on the other end of the metaphorical couch is older with gray hair and a kind smile that immediately puts me at ease. "Hello, Rhodes, my name is Doctor Constance Whitlock, but you can call me Connie or Doc. Whatever you're most comfortable with is fine with me," she grins. "I know we talked on the phone about your reasons for starting therapy again, but why don't you go over it one more time in a little more detail so I have a better idea why you're here."

My brows furrow and my head tilts as I stare at her through the screen. "You're not going to tell me what I need based on what I told you over the phone?" That's been my experience with psychologists.

She laughs softly. "No, Rhodes, that isn't how I run my practice. My goal isn't to diagnose you in an hour or numb your feelings with medication. You already told me you don't think medication is necessary, so we'll treat this as maintenance unless you tell me otherwise. Let's start with the reason you decided to come back to therapy."

Taking a deep breath, I nod, unsure where to start, but it's like she reads my mind when her face softens. "If you don't know where to start, let's start at the beginning."

That brings a smile to my face because the beginning of me and Wren is my favorite part.

"Alright, well, eight years ago I met this girl..."

Just shy of an hour later, I have a pint of ice cream in my hand with Finn cuddled up to my side, and Doc is on her second box of tissues.

"And so you see, she's my angel come to earth, and it kills me that I can't take away her stress. Add that to the jealousy I feel about the video, and it's like I'm on a hair trigger, ready to blow at the slightest irritation."

Wiping under her eyes, Doc takes a minute before she speaks, which I really appreciate. It feels like she cares enough to give me thoughtful advice and not just some generic breathing techniques to regulate my anger or a pill to chill me out.

"I think what you're feeling is completely normal and even expected after an experience like this," she says at last. "And Wren being the only one of you *in* the video doesn't negate the fact that it made you uncomfortable as well."

Doc's unbiased validation of my feelings makes me feel one-hundred pounds lighter. I smile gratefully and rub a hand over the left side of my chest to try and will away the emotional ache. "Thanks for that, Doc. I feel less like a selfish asshole, excuse my language, after getting that all off my chest to someone who isn't part of this mess."

She nods sympathetically. "Wren will always be your best friend, and that's fine! It's healthy, even. Especially in a relationship like yours that requires more trust than the average relationship with you on the road so much. But you shouldn't *only* rely on each other either. It's important to have unbiased, third-party advice sometimes. That's why I advocate for therapy even for "healthy" people." She puts the word healthy in air quotes, making me snort.

A smirk crosses her face, and I'm hit with so much gratitude—to Benny, for recommending Connie, and to the woman herself who is, hands down, the best therapist I've ever had.

"You know, Doc, I think you were born to shrink people's brains. You're pretty good at it."

She lets out an infectious, full-bellied laugh, and I laugh with her. But the joy of the moment reminds me that my girl isn't here, and my heart plummets. *She would love Doc.* In fact...

"Hey Doc?"

She's still chuckling lightly when she answers. "Yes, Rhodes?"

I rub my sweaty palms together, more nervous now than I was before the session began. "Could I maybe... bring Wren to an appointment sometime? Or even recommend you to her for her own therapy if she moves here? I don't know if that's like...a no-no or some ethical issue, but I think she would love you."

A bright smile crosses her face, and she taps her pen against the notepad on her knee. "There's no legal reason I can't see both of you individually, but there would need to be firm boundaries in place. I won't discuss the details from our sessions with her, and the same would go for the opposite if I were to treat Wren."

Nodding emphatically, I give her a cheeky grin and wink. "You got it, Doc. Secret squirrel meetings. I hear you loud and clear," I say with a salute.

She shakes her head with a laugh and checks her watch. "It looks like that's our time for today. Did you have any questions before I go?"

I shake my head, already feeling much better. Plus, talking about college gave me an idea. Hopefully, my surprise for Wren will help with any big feelings she's got right now. I'll give her three more days of space before I track her down, but for now, I have an errand to run.

Signing off from my session with Dr. Connie, I grab my keys, Google the nearest apparel printing shop, and text Aidan to invite him along. Copeland is out of town for a few days dealing with some family stuff, otherwise I'd invite him, too.

> **ME**
> I'm gonna make something to cheer Wren up. Wanna come?

> **PREACHER**
> Crew is with my mom, so as long as there's food involved, hell yeah.

> **ME**
> Sweet. Pick you up in five?

> **PREACHER**
> See you soon, Streaks.

He lives just down the road, so it's only a couple of minutes before he's yanking open my passenger door and dropping his happy ass into the seat. Aidan buckles his seatbelt, slaps his hands on his knees and beams at me. "So what are we doing for my new bestie?"

It's nice to finally see him so excited about something. The guy has gone through so much in the last five years since Crew's mom left, so he's earned some happiness that doesn't come from his kid or baseball.

I smile at him out of the corner of my eye and grab a bundle of fabric out of the backseat. "Here's what I'm thinking..."

CHAPTER 32
WREN

AFTER AN OBSESSIVE NUMBER of hugs from Jamie, Wes, Asher, and Jeremy, I hopped on a plane back to Charleston with Kaci and Dom and had them drop me off at Rhodes's house to surprise him. I'm nauseous with nerves the entire ride there, and by the time I unlock the front door, my heart is beating so fast, I feel faint.

"Hello?" I call out into the quiet house. The only answer is Finn's enthusiastic yip from the mudroom. It's the middle of the afternoon, but Rhodes shouldn't have practice today. Oh well. Now I have time to start dinner. I'm mostly useless in the kitchen, but surely I can't mess up fried chicken and mac 'n' cheese if I follow the recipes Mama Gray gave me.

When I enter the mudroom, Finn wriggles excitedly and whines when he sees me. I drop to my knees in front of his kennel and let him out, overwhelmed by how much bigger he looks after being away for a week. "Hi baby boy!" I coo. "Did you miss me while I was gone?" He licks my face as if in answer, and I laugh loudly.

Holding him under his furry front legs, I lift him up

and look into his soulful blue eyes. "I missed you so much, big guy. I promise to never leave like that again, okay? I missed you and your daddy too much." I let Finn outside to potty and put some fresh food and water on the patio so he can play while I cook.

An hour later, I throw the pan into the sink with a crash as frustrated tears spring to my eyes. I take in the smoke coming off the ruined chicken and huff a sigh through my nose.

"Dude, I think your house is on...fire." Aidan's worried voice catches my attention and I turn off the stove, forgetting all about my tears as I spin around to face the two men who I didn't hear walk in.

My cheeks burn so hot I swear I hear a sizzle before I hurriedly wipe the tears away. "Uhm... hi," I choke out.

Aidan looks like he's fighting a laugh, but Rhodes just stands awkwardly in the kitchen doorway with his eyes wide and mouth ajar as he takes in the disaster.

Following his line of sight, I grimace and hold out my hands. "I'm so sorry. I just wanted to surprise you with dinner, but then the oil got too hot, and the chicken started burnin', and then the water boiled over. It just... went to hell in a hand basket from there," I say sheepishly.

His eyes shoot to mine as I ramble and he snaps, taking three large strides across the room and hugging me so tightly, I feel my ribs creak in protest. Rho buries his nose in my hair and takes a deep breath, letting out a shaky sigh as he holds me to his chest. "You're here," he whispers. "You came home."

I nod into his chest and inhale the scent of cypress and vetiver that always reminds me of him.

A big hand lands on my shoulder, and I glance up to find Aidan's bright smile on me. "Welcome back, Wren."

He claps Rho on the back and smirks at him over my head. "I'll text you later, but for now, I'll get out of your hair."

The front door bangs shut a few seconds later, but Rhodes and I stay locked in our embrace as we savor the moment.

I pull back first and take a few steps away to clear my head. Being around Rhodes Gray is overwhelming in all the best ways, but it also makes it hard to think rationally, and I owe him an apology.

"Rho... I'm so sorry."

His eyes widen again, and he takes a step forward before he catches himself and leans on the island instead. He drops to his elbows and gives me his full attention. "You have no reason to apologize, Starling."

"I do though." Stepping forward, I grip the other side of the island with both hands, squeezing to distract myself from the dread that threatens to steal my words. "I got scared. Scared that once you saw that video you'd realize we didn't think our relationship through, and I was scared of how that could impact our careers. I know now that something like that wouldn't change things between us, but at the time I panicked and the only thing I could think to do was—"

"Run." He finishes for me, nodding like he already knew. "You didn't trust me enough to stay, Wren. And yeah, I get why. Your mom left, which was unfair, and I'm sure the video brought up a lot of hard feelings. But instead of coming to me, you fell back on old habits and took off without a word."

His words are true, but that doesn't take away the sting from the disappointment in his tone. Growing up, I was always the good girl, the girl who never rocked the boat with anybody, even at the expense of myself. But I feel like the last six weeks all I've done is rock the boat, and I wonder if this time I've capsized it.

Rhodes runs a hand through his curly brown hair, tugging on the locks in frustration. "I can't do this if you're always going to have one foot out the door, Wren. I've been in love with you for my entire adult life, but that alone isn't enough to make this work. I won't give you an ultimatum, but if you need some time..." he sighs heavily. "We jumped into this really fast because I was so ready to be with you, but I let outside opinions sway me and never really considered if you were ready to be with me."

A thick layer of despair settles over my soul at his words. "You... want to break up?"

He rounds the counter with wide eyes, cupping my face in his warm hands. "Baby, no," he breathes, placing a soft kiss on my forehead.

Rho moves to hug me and his lips move against my skin as he speaks. "I would wait forever and a day for you, Starling. All I mean is if you need time alone to find yourself and heal after everything, I understand, and I'll still be here when you're ready."

My immediate reaction is to refuse, but when I take a minute to really consider what he's saying, he might be right. I wasn't in love with Derrick, and I wasn't happy, and that was a *four-year marriage*. I jumped right into this relationship with Rhodes less than a month after it ended.

"I think I need to find a new therapist now that I'm here," I whisper, loving how safe I feel with his strong arms wrapped around me. "And I think maybe I should go stay with my dad for a while. Not forever, but just until I have a few sessions under my belt and feel ready to share more of myself with you. I hate the idea of not being with you all the time, but I hate the thought of hurting you even more."

When I tilt my head up, Rhodes's sad, hazel eyes stare back, but he doesn't look upset. "Whatever you need, Starling." His lips purse as he pulls a card from his pocket and steps back, putting some distance between us. "I don't want to overstep, but I actually started seeing someone while you were gone, and I think you might really like her."

My jaw nearly hits the floor and my stomach drops. *What the hell does he mean he's seeing someone?!*

Rhodes must see the look on my face, and he visibly pales even as my cheeks heat. "Jesus, I'm sorry. That's not what I meant at all. I started seeing a *psychologist*. I had my first session with her while you were in Seattle, and I think she could be really good for you, too. But like I said, if I'm overstepping, tell me to fuck off."

Relief crashes through me, and I have to grip the counter again for balance so I don't fall to my knees. When he said he started seeing someone I almost vomited all over the kitchen floor.

Way to assume the worst, Wren. This is why you need therapy.

Taking the card, I glance down at it with a smile. "You know what's funny?"

He starts to clean up the mess I made with my attempt at cooking, but glances at me from the corner of his eye with a questioning look.

"Benny actually recommended her to me back in college. Just after you were drafted, he pulled me aside and said I should call her if I ever needed to talk." A small laugh escapes. "I'm pretty sure he's sweet on her. The man was grinnin' like a possum eating fire ants every time he said her name."

He snorts and pauses his pan-scrubbing to glance back at me. "Why would a possum—you know what? Never mind. I could totally see them together. I'm pretty sure Doc isn't married and neither is Benny. I wonder..." he trails off, absentmindedly washing the pan again.

"Anyhow," I start, returning to my original train of thought. "I'll give her a call, but I think you're right. It never felt like we rushed in because we have so much history between us. And even if I wasn't in love with Derrick anymore, it was still a marriage. I think I need time to grieve the change properly and sort through some of these complicated emotions before we go any further."

I feel like I might cry, but I do my best to choke back the tears. "This isn't goodbye, and it isn't the end of us. This is me knowing you're right and taking care of my mental health so I can be fair to you. I was in a one-sided relationship, and I'll never do that to you, Rho. I respect you too much."

Rhodes wipes his hands dry on a dishtowel and pulls me into his arms, holding me like I'm precious. "I'll be here, baby. The moment you decide you're ready. Just..." he trails off, clearing his throat. "Just please come back to me, okay?" Finn's tiny nails clack against the floor as he pads into the kitchen and whines until Rho picks him up.

Rhodes smiles, squishing his face up against Finn's, and I take my phone out to snap a picture. Snatching it out of my hands, he presses buttons until he can set the photo of him and Finnegan as my lock screen. He hands it back to me with a sad smile. "I love you, Starling, and I'm so damn proud to call you mine."

CHAPTER 33
WREN

TWO DAYS after my talk with Rhodes, I find myself on a surprisingly comfortable purple couch in Dr. Connie Whitlock's office, spilling my guts to the kind woman.

"I just wanted somebody to love me unconditionally, you know? And that's what marriage is supposed to be: loving your partner in sickness and in health, for richer or poorer, till death do you part. That's all I wanted." I sniffle.

My words are barely more than a whisper, but she hears them and hands me a box of tissues. I take it gratefully, blowing my nose in a very unladylike way. I stare at her pitifully. It feels weird to discuss something so heavy in a room that's this bright and happy.

She nods sagely and clasps her hands together. "Wren, it's not unreasonable for you to expect a basic level of common decency from your partner. Marriage vows are supposed to be a sacred thing, but they're not the be-all-end-all of relationships. Your mother walked out on her marriage and that could have deterred you from commitment, but instead, it had the opposite effect. You were driven from a young age to seek that commitment and stability no matter the cost to yourself."

I go to speak, but she holds her hand up. "Not that you're to blame for your ex-husband's actions. His choices are his alone and never your fault or burden to carry. I simply mean I believe your path to healing may very well involve learning that you don't *need* to rely on someone else for stability. You're incredibly successful on your own merit, Wren, and you have a solid support system."

Kind eyes hold my gaze as I hand her back the tissue box. "But should you choose to pursue a romantic relationship any time soon, I think your top priorities should be complete transparency and asking for help from your partner when necessary. Don't cast your needs aside for anyone, Wren."

She glances at her watch and closes her notebook after making a few final notes. "Your homework for this week is to find a new hobby. Something you can comfortably do alone that makes you happy. Does that sound doable?"

My mind is already spinning with ideas, and each one fans the flames of excitement in my chest. "It does. Thanks Dr. Whitlock."

She sends me a pointed look. "I told you, it's Doc or Connie. Dr. Whitlock makes me feel old."

I laugh and give her a thumbs up as I stand and gather my belongings. "You got it, Connie. See you next week?"

Smiling, she waves me on. "Same time, same place. Call the number I gave you if you need me before then."

I took Connie's homework seriously, which is how I wind up alone at a pottery painting studio in Mount Pleasant on a Friday night. *Color Me Crazy* is a cute little shop tucked away off a main road only a couple of shops down from the Italian restaurant my dad and I went to a few weeks ago. The scent of paint and clay accosts my nose when I walk in, but it's oddly enjoyable.

"Hello, and welcome to Color Me Crazy. What can I help you with today?" A quiet voice greets me. Turning to the front counter, I see a woman around my age, if not a little younger. I walk over to the counter with a bright smile.

"Hi, I was hoping to paint...something today." She giggles at my hesitation, and her demeanor puts me instantly at ease.

"Well, you can definitely do that. Come on, I'll show you all the pieces we have to pick from and get you set up at a table. My name is Lyla, by the way." She switches between anxiously fiddling with her sleeves and her left ring finger as we walk. There's a thin tan line on her finger she keeps touching and I wonder if she's married.

Something about Lyla reminds me of myself, and I make a silent vow to make friends with her if she's open to it. "My name is Wren. So, how long have you worked here?"

She seems genuinely surprised I asked, and it takes her a minute to answer. "I, um, I just started here maybe a month ago? I'm double majoring in childhood education and psychology, so I took a job here to try and offset some of the student loans."

My eyes widen. "That's incredible, Lyla! God, you must be crazy busy. I can't even imagine. How much longer do you have before you graduate?"

Her smile changes her whole face, making her mossy green eyes light up. "I only have two months left, and I'm so ready to be done."

Lyla shows me all the pottery options, and I pick out a cute mug covered in lemons. She leads me to a table and helps me set up the paints while I debate whether I should ask her to sit with me. I don't want her to think I'm hitting on her or being creepy, but I haven't made a female friend since Ella, so I have no idea what I'm doing.

Deciding to go for it, I clear my throat awkwardly. "Hey, I hope this isn't weird, and if I'm distracting you from your job, feel free to tell me no. But would you maybe wanna sit with me and hang out for a bit?"

Her face lights up again, but she looks stunned too. "You want to hang out with me?" She asks quietly, a bit of suspicion lacing her tone.

I smile and give her an honest answer. "I just recently moved back here after living in Washington state for four years, and even before I left, I didn't really have any female friends. You seem so nice, and I plan on spending a lot of time here, so I figured I might as well try to make a friend too."

I panic when her eyes water, terrified I've upset her. "I'm so sorry, you can absolutely tell me no! I didn't mean to make you uncomfortable at your job—"

Lyla gasps. "NO!" She shouts. Flinching, she slaps

her hands over her mouth and stares around the shop in horror with a grimace, sitting down in the chair across from me. "Sorry, I just mean, I would love to be friends with you. I don't have any friends, really," she frowns. "That makes me sound like a loser, but it's true. I moved here recently, too, and don't really have any family or know anyone. It's been pretty lonely."

She looks so sad, and her whispered words make me want to be her friend even more. I pull my phone out, so I can make a new contact, and hand it to her. "If we're gonna be friends, we should probably exchange numbers. But be warned, I talk a lot, and sometimes I geek out over baseball. I also have a bunch of nosy family members who will probably try and adopt you if you ever meet them, and a baseball-player boyfriend who's normally attached to my hip."

A loud laugh escapes her, but she gets that same panicked look and dials it down to a quiet giggle. "That's okay. Like I said, I don't really have anyone, so I'm kind of jealous you have so many people around you."

I'm determined to pull Lyla out of her shell one laugh at a time. Smirking at her, I put my number in her tiny flip phone. "Stick with me, babe. Soon enough you'll have more people in your life than you know what to do with."

A faraway look crosses her face, her lips curling up slightly in the corners, and she sighs wistfully. "I think I'd like that, Wren."

Grinning at her, I start to paint my lemon mug. "Excellent. Friends it is, then. Why don't you grab that cherry mug I saw you staring at and join me if you don't have anything else to do. My treat."

She checks the time on her phone just as a door opens

to the back of the shop. "My shift just ended, actually, so let me clock out, and I'll be right back."

As she walks away, I decide right then I'll do whatever I can to bring some happiness to Lyla's life.

Maybe finding a hobby was a good idea for more than just therapy after all.

CHAPTER 34
RHODES

WE HAVE our first away series of the season this week, and ironically it's against the Sirens. We're staying in a hotel near the stadium, but we got here a day early, so a lot of the guys are going out tonight since tomorrow is a night game and we can sleep in.

I'm on the hotel bed, scrolling through pictures of Wren, when a knock on the door pulls me out of an inevitable anxiety spiral. I haven't talked to her beyond a few texts and not being able to see her before our first game of the season has me in a worse headspace than I'd like to admit.

I open the door to my room and stop short when I see a petite blonde with a notebook and a bright smile. "Um, hi?" I don't mean to sound rude, but nobody should be able to get on this floor but the team and their guests.

"Hi!" She says in a cheery voice. "My name is Ella Barnes. I'm here from the Sirens PR team to do some pregame interviews. I thought maybe we could go down to the hotel bar and grab a drink while we chat?" The last part is said in a flirty question, but neither my agent nor coach said anything about interviews. And all I want to do is lock myself in my room and work up the nerve to call Wren.

"Oh, uh. Andrews and Ryan are just a few doors down if you want to interview them. I don't mean to be rude, but I was just about to call my girlfriend, so..." Something clicks in my brain, and I look at her again with fresh eyes. "Oh, hey! You said your name is Ella? You worked with Wren Reid, right?"

A scowl takes over her heart shaped face. "She was fired last week for leaking a sex tape. Honestly, though, Derrick could do so much better anyway." She flips her hair, scanning my body in a way that makes me feel gross. "I'm the new head of PR, so trust me, I'm more than qualified to take care of you. Your interview, that is." She says this with a smirk that I'm sure she thinks is alluring as she trails her finger down my hand, which is still gripping the door handle.

Ripping my hand away from her, I cradle it to my chest like I've been burned. "That's great, but like I said, I think Andrews or Ryan will be your best bet. They're just down there," I say, pointing to their shared room. "It's Ryan's first game in the majors, so that would make for a great interview, I bet."

Anger flashes across her face, but just as quickly as it came, the emotion disappears, leaving a bright smile. "You got it, Mr. Gray. I'll come back later to see if you've changed your mind. And trust me when I say you wouldn't ask for Wren after you worked with me." She winks and saunters off down the hall.

I shiver. I wonder if telling her Wren is my girlfriend would've helped. Based on the way she reacted when I brought Wren up the first time, I don't think it would have. Didn't Wren say she and Ella are friends? That seems like a weird way to talk about your friend.

Another knock startles me, but this time it's just Aidan and Copeland. Cope has a six-pack of beer, so I invite them in to hang out. We don't like going out if we don't have to, especially because we've seen how some of the team likes to party. It's easier to stay in and chill, just the three of us.

"Did you guys see the blonde chick with a notebook out there?" I ask them, wondering if the weird vibe I got was just me.

They both nod, but Copeland shoots me a look. "You and Wren are still together right? You wouldn't think about doing anything?"

I rear back, hurt by his suggestion. "What the fuck, Cope? Of course I wouldn't. You know we're just taking a step back right now. I would never fuck around on Wren."

He nods with his hands up in apology. "You're right, sorry. I got a text from Carly today, and it messed with my head. I know you'd never do anything to jeopardize your relationship or hurt Wren."

I look at Aidan and grimace, reaching out to clap Copeland on the shoulder. "Sorry man. Is there anything you need from us?"

He scrubs his heavily tattooed hands down his face with a sigh. "No, but thanks for the offer. I blocked her again, but she seems to get a new number every year just to bother me. It's been five goddamned years; why can't she just move the fuck on and leave me alone?" He groans, pinches the bridge of his nose, and takes a deep breath. "Whatever. Enough about my shit. Who was the blonde chick? She had crazy eyes."

"Like, legit crazy eyes? Are you sure?" I ask him

worriedly. Cope has an uncanny ability to spot problematic people before they say a word and had suspected Carly of cheating on him long before he caught them in the act.

Nodding, he and Aid glance at me with concern. "Why do you look freaked out?" Aidan asks. "Do you know her or something?"

I shake my head slowly. "No...but Wren does."

They glance at each other. "Tell us everything."

"Let me do some digging, and I'll talk to you if I find anything, okay?" Copeland says. I nod in agreement, and they head back to their rooms, leaving me alone with my thoughts.

I told the guys everything Wren said about Ella, and then about the way Ella reacted when I mentioned Wren. And then I brought up my suspicions about the sex tape and how I wasn't sure Derrick had actually leaked it. The guy just doesn't seem smart enough to successfully cover his tracks.

I strip off my shirt and get comfortable in the bed. I'm dying to see my girl, so I grab my laptop and hit the button to video-chat and wait as it rings. Just when I think she won't answer, the call connects and I get an eyeful of long, tan legs.

"Sorry! Sorry, I was just getting out of the shower when I heard the call come through and I didn't want to miss you," she says in a rush, setting the phone on her nightstand while she moves to grab clothes from the dresser.

"Wren." My voice comes out in a croak. Clearing my throat, I try again. "Starling...you're naked. And back in our house."

She spins around, cheeks flushed as she covers as much of herself as she can. Biting back a groan because it's the first time I've seen her naked in weeks, I push a hand down on my rapidly swelling erection. She must see the heat in my eyes because she drops her arm from her breasts and sits down on the bed.

She tilts the phone up so all I can see is the top swells of her breasts and her gorgeous face, still pink either from the shower or embarrassment. "Is that a problem for you, Roly-Coly?" She asks. Her voice is low and husky and doing absolutely nothing to curb the flow of blood to my dick.

I take a deep breath and try to focus on literally *anything* else, but she's naked in *our* house, *in our bed*. "I thought we were taking a step back?" The words pain me to say, but I don't ever want her to regret anything that happens between us.

"We are," she says slowly. "But I also miss you so much. And being here, surrounded by your smell..." she moans, and it's the sexiest thing I've ever heard. "You smell so freaking good, Rho."

I smirk at her through the screen, leaning forward in a fruitless attempt to get a closer look at her perfect tits. "Do you miss me so much that just smelling my cologne turns you on, baby?"

Her pupils dilate and she nods frantically. I palm my cock again, grunting quietly. She freezes, eyes wide and locked on the bottom of the screen where just the top of my V muscles are visible. I flex just a little bit for her benefit. A quiet whimper slips from her lips, and I lick mine, desperately wishing I could taste her sweet mouth right now. "Are you good with this, Starling?" She nods again, but I shake my head. "Words, Wren. I need to know you won't regret this later."

She snaps out of her lustful fog, and her eyes meet mine. "I could never regret anything we do, Rho. I really, *really* want this."

"Good," I say with a dark chuckle. "Then set the phone back on the nightstand so I can see all of you while you touch yourself for me."

She gasps, but does as I say, and it turns me on that much more. I move the laptop back and push my sweats below my ass, exposing my hard-as-steel cock. Her pussy is already wet, making me moan as I slide my hand down to grip my erection, giving it a few firm strokes.

"Fuck, baby. Show me how you play with that pretty pink cunt when you're alone and needy."

Whimpering, she slides two fingers into herself, wetting them and rubbing circles over her swollen clit. "I want to see you too," she begs.

"You beg so sweet, Starling. I can't wait to get my mouth back on you," I groan and my mouth waters as I imagine her taste on my tongue. Gripping my cock again, I stroke it slowly, making sure the angle is just right so she can see the precum on my tip.

She speeds up as she fingers herself, using her other hand to pinch and twist her rosy nipples until they're hard points on her chest.

"That's it, baby, add another finger," I pant out, my own release dangerously close already. I'm so pent up seeing her like this–knowing she trusts me.

She moans even louder. "I'm so close, Rho."

"I'm almost there, Starling. Come for me, baby," I say with a groan, using my other hand to massage my balls.

"Ohhh God, yes! I'm coming!" She yells.

Her fingers work her clit in rapid circles, dragging her release out, and it sets mine off, my hand works over my length as ropes of come shoot onto my stomach and neck. "Fuck, that's my girl," I breathe.

We're both breathing heavily with satisfied smiles on our faces until hers drops suddenly, and she grabs a blanket to cover herself. I sit up, alarmed at the sudden shift in her demeanor.

"Wren! Starling, what's wrong? What just happened?" I panic as my mind runs through every worst-case scenario.

"You didn't record that, did you?" She asks in a whisper.

My heart stops. "Of course not! You know I would never, *ever* do that to you. I swear, baby. You can check everything when I get back if you want to."

Her eyes shut tight, crinkling in the corners. "No, I'm sorry. I shouldn't have even asked. I know you wouldn't do that. It's just, something weird happened today, and my emotions are all over the place because of it."

I'm immediately on high alert. "What happened, Wren?"

She looks at me guiltily and shrugs. "My Instagram account was hacked, and somebody posted some old pictures from college. Nothing terrible, but things like me passed out drunk in the bed of a truck with my clothes out of sorts, me dancing on the table at that bar we used to go to, me on our Spring break trip to Cannon Beach with a joint in my hand; stuff like that."

My ears ring, and I see red, but I know I need to keep my temper in check in front of her. "I'm so sorry, Starling. Were you able to get it taken down? And do you think it was Derrick again?"

"I'm working on it, but since cannabis is legal in Oregon, none of the pictures are technically incriminating. I'm gonna try not to panic if it takes a few days like it did with the video." She cringes. "They managed to change the email and everything, so I have to contact Instagram to change my password and regain access to my account. And I guess it could have been Derrick, but I don't know..."

"You don't know?" I ask gently.

Nodding with a sigh, Wren locks eyes with me. "He's not some hacker, Rho. I just can't see how he could this. Add in the video and anonymous texts, and it just seems too sophisticated for someone like him. I mean for God's sake; it took him a year to learn how to work the security system at his apartment."

It's like a record scratch when my thoughts pause on what she said. "Hang on a second. *What* anonymous texts, Wren?"

She shoots me an apologetic grimace. "Oops?" I level her with a glare, and she groans. "I'm sorry! We've just had so much going on I honestly forgot to mention it. I've gotten some nasty texts from an unknown number. The person calls me a slut, untalented, a gold digger, etcetera. You name it, they've said it."

I rake my hands through my hair in exasperation. "Wren Andromeda," I say sternly. "What did we agree on just last week?"

She whines, standing up to slip into one of my old

practice shirts. "I know, babe. I'm sorry. I promise I'll tell you everything from now on."

My frustration melts away when she calls me babe. I think that's the first time she's used a pet name for me that wasn't a nickname she gave me before we got together. I look at my beautiful girl who's currently across the country and sigh. "I miss you, Starling. I wish you were here."

Her smile lights up the room, bringing a smile to my own face. "I miss you too, Rho. But I'll be in your jersey and watching the game from the comfort of your living room." She giggles at my raised brow. "Sorry, *our* living room."

Seeing her in my practice shirt reminds me what I had made for her. "Oh! Baby, go in our bedroom and look on the left side of the bed. There should be a wrapped box with your name on it."

Wren squeals and runs to our room while I grab a washcloth and clean myself up.

God, I hope she likes it.

CHAPTER 35
WREN

MY PHONE DINGS when I get back to the guest room with the box, so I pick it up and grimace when I see another text from Derrick and two from the anonymous number. I intentionally ignore the anonymous weirdo, but a very small part of me wants to hear Derrick out because at the very least, it might give me some closure.

DICK

> Wren, please, you have to know I had nothing to do with that video!

> I swear, I was angry but I wouldn't have done something so stupid. I'm being investigated by the police for fuck's sake. The team temporarily suspended me because of the investigation.

> I came to Charleston to see you. Is there any way you would be willing to meet and talk? Bring whoever you want. I'll be at Hotel Indigo in room 210 until Wednesday.

After clicking out of Derrick's messages with an

annoyed grunt, I see the new unread messages from the anonymous sender. I know I shouldn't look, but curiosity gets the best of me and I open them.

> UNKNOWN
>
> Having some trouble getting into your Instagram account, whore?
>
> It's about time people finally see you for the fake you are.

"Starling, you okay? You spaced out on me." Rhodes's voice startles me, almost making me drop my phone. I promised him no more lies, so with a sigh, I tell him about all the texts I've gotten over the last week, both from the random number and from Derrick.

He smiles at me through the screen, which is not the reaction I expected. "Thank you for telling me, baby. I'm really proud of you for being honest."

His praise lights me up inside, and I realize choosing to be honest rather than bottling up my problems feels really good. The crushing weight of panic I feel when I have to make big decisions alone isn't as heavy as usual.

Maybe Connie had a point.

"You get back on Monday, right?" I ask him nervously. I'm worried he won't react well to my plans, but I'm going with or without him. If he says no, I'll just ask my dad or Dominic.

A resigned sigh is my answer, and he gives me a critical look. "You want to meet with Derrick?"

I offer a small nod, fully prepared for his refusal. But I should know better by now: Rho is Derrick's opposite in every way. Instead of saying no, he asks me why I want to go.

"Maybe it's naïve of me, but I believe him when he

says he didn't do it. I mean, it's obvious he took the video, but I really don't think he leaked it. He could get kicked off the team, or worse, arrested. Baseball is the only thing he cares about and without me babysitting him, nobody's around to prevent his bad behavior from turning into PR nightmares. Like all the times I had to pick him up from a bar when he tried to drive home drunk. The Sirens suspended him because he's being investigated by the police over the leaked video."

His head tilts to the side in contemplation, and he nods once slowly. "Yesterday, I would have said you were letting your heart get in the way of logic, but honestly, I think you might be right." He goes quiet and looks like he wants to say something. I wait him out, as he decides what he wants to share.

His lips pull into a grimace. "I met Ella today."

I'm confused and borderline concerned by the look on his face. "Okayyy?" I say, dragging it out. "And? Did you like her?" She hasn't responded to anything I've sent her since I left Seattle, but I just assumed she was busy with her new position.

"Starling..." he says nervously. "She hit on me multiple times and said some not great things about you."

Everything in me goes cold at his words as her behavior from the last few weeks runs through my mind on a loop. "Why would she do that?" I pause as something occurs to me. I don't think I ever showed her a picture of you..." I whisper.

"What?"

I minimize the video window and look through all the pictures I've sent Ella since we started working together, but I don't find any of Rhodes. "She has no idea that you're *my* Rhodes. I talked about you all the time, but now that I think about it, whenever I brought up you or my life before Seattle, she'd change the subject. Honestly, most of what we talked about was work and Derrick. But even then, I can't imagine why she would say anything bad about me."

He looks unsure but waves me off. "Maybe I misinterpreted what she said." A huge yawn overtakes him and as soon as I glance at the time I feel guilty. It's almost one in the morning, and he has a game tomorrow.

"Rho," I groan. "You should have gone to bed hours ago. You need a full night's rest before the game."

He looks at me with sleepy eyes that make my heart melt. When his hair is all wild, and he's half asleep like this, it reminds me of when we'd pull all-nighters to cram for exams. Or the times we'd have movie marathons where we both inevitably crashed during the third installment of whatever series we chose for that week.

"I'll go to sleep as soon as you open your gift, Starling. I want to see your face."

I gasp dramatically. I can't believe I forgot! I tear into the pretty blue wrapping paper and find a plain white box. Rhodes looks so adorably eager that his expression amps up my own excitement. Lifting the lid, a Carolina blue sweatshirt greets me.

"Thanks Rho," I say with a grin. He always says I look best in blue, so the fact that he picked this out for me is sweet.

He chuckles. "Open it up and look at it, baby."

Confused, I pull it out and inspect it. "Oh my God," I whisper. The back looks like one of his jerseys with his last name and his number, eleven, embroidered in a brilliant white, and the same number but smaller is embroidered on the bottom of the right sleeve. On the front is a printed four-leaf clover with "Rhodes's Good Luck Charm" embroidered over it, also in white. It looks almost exactly like the one I gave him, only his is white with blue embroidery.

"Rhodes..."

His smile is blinding, even from three thousand miles away. "Do you like it? I figured now we can be that sickeningly cute couple that matches, and this way you have part of me with you whenever I'm away, like I have from you. My forever Good Luck Charm deserves a little luck of her own."

Stick a fork in me because I. Am. Done. A melted, mystified, puddle of goo on the rug. If I wasn't already in love with Rhodes, this would have sealed the deal, and I wonder if this is how he felt when I gave him his hoodie all those years ago.

Eight years earlier

"Roly-Coly-Oly," I sing as I barge into Rhodes's dorm room after my impromptu skip day. I'm sure Daddy will lecture me later, but once I show him why I skipped, I know he'll understand. Rhodes's breakdown last night scared me. He's as unflappable as they come, and even though I've only known him a little less than a year, I've never seen him upset like that.

Rho was lucky enough to get a single room this year after he and Derrick got into it over Derrick hitting on me repeatedly, so I don't feel bad barging in. He made me an illegal copy of his key and told me to use it whenever I want. I do always knock first anyway, but this time I knew he'd likely be taking his pre-game nap and figured it was safe.

A large lump on the bed is my only hint that he's actually here, so instead of calling his name again, I set the bag on his desk and lie next to him, pulling the blanket down so I can see his stupidly perfect face.

Butterflies assault my stomach with shocking intensity, but I take a metaphorical bug zapper to them and shove down the pesky feelings that always threaten spill out of my mouth when I spend too much time focused on how handsome my best friend is.

After spending what probably amounted to a creepy number of minutes admiring how the stubble on his jaw turns him from boy-next-door to rugged player, I run my finger gently down his nose. The sleepy smile he gives me attempts to revive the butterflies I just obliterated. "Hey, Starling," he yawns, tossing an arm over my side. "Did you come to wish me luck before I leave?"

My face gets warm when I glance at the bag on his desk, so I'm sure my cheeks are pink with embarrassment. His eyebrows go up and something like heat flashes in his eyes, but it's gone so fast I'm pretty sure I imagined it. "I, uh." I clear my suddenly dry throat. "I actually brought you something...for luck. You can open it now if you want."

He shoots up to a seated position, nearly head butting me in the process. "You got me a present? What is it?"

With shaky hands I give him the bag and watch him tear into it. You would think he'd been deprived of kindness his whole life with the level of enthusiasm he shows opening the gift, but that's just Rhodes Gray for you. The boy gives one hundred and ten percent on and off the field.

Pulling out the sweatshirt, he gapes at it silently for several minutes—long enough that I start to ramble nervously. "You sounded so scared last night, Rho, and I hate that I can't be with you at every game to alleviate some of that worry. You've always called me your 'Wren

Luck Charm', and I thought maybe having a physical symbol of that luck might help keep the anxiety at bay. If you take this with you, you'll always have a piece of home to keep you grounded in case everything gets to be too much."

His warm hazel eyes mist over, which brings out the green and makes me wonder if I just screwed up. "Wren," he chokes. A single tear rolls down his cheek and then he shifts me to sit on his lap, yanking me into a bone-crushing hug so fast I don't even have a chance to process it. "You have no idea how much this means to me."

Relief has me relaxing in his arms while I also try not to fixate on the fact that I'm in his lap. We've always been pretty affectionate, but this feels different somehow. "It's not too cheesy?" I ask quietly.

He sniffles, shaking his head. "It's perfect, Starling. Now I always have the best part of home with me," he murmurs as he runs his fingers over my name embroidered on the front of the four-leaf clover.

I didn't know it at the time, but the very next night would change the course of our lives. That was the night I saw him kissing some random girl at a party and finally gave in to Derrick's incessant flirting just to numb some of the hurt.

Choking back tears at my boyfriend's ability to always know what I need; I hug the sweatshirt to my chest. "I love it, babe. I love *you*." I glance at the clock and cringe. We lost track of time again. "I'll be cheering you on from the couch for every game, and on Monday, I'll be at the airport to pick you up."

He sighs happily, his eyes barely more than slits. "I love you, Starling. Get some sleep, and I'll see you soon."

I make my way into Rhodes's bed a few minutes later

and breathe in the scent of cypress and vetiver, letting the gentle spice of his cologne lull me to sleep. My career and things with this cyber stalker feel kind of up in the air right now, but as long as I have Rho on my side, I know everything will be okay.

CHAPTER 36
WREN

THIS WEEKEND without Rhodes has been so much more fun than I expected. Friday night, I met up with all the parents for dinner at a food truck festival and since it was outdoors, I was able to bring Finnegan along, much to Mama Gray's delight. I even invited Lyla, and everybody loved her.

Then today, Lyla and I spent the whole day together. It's been a while since I've had this much fun with a girl-friend. She and Finn are thick as thieves, and she's taken to calling herself his 'Auntie Lyla.'

We're in my dad's kitchen debating on what to do tonight when Lyla's phone starts to ring incessantly from an unknown number. She blanches and drops her glass to the tile floor where it shatters.

"Oh my God," she gasps. Her eyes gloss over as her breaths quicken. "Wren, I-I-I'm so s-sorry. If you c-can point me to the broom, I'll clean it up!"

I've noticed that Lyla can be a little flighty and nervous, but this is the first time I've seen her freak out like this. Gently grabbing her hands with mine, I stop her before she can step on the glass. "Lyla," I say softly. "It was an accident. I promise everything is okay, and nobody is upset."

Her face turns fire-engine-red, and she quickly averts her gaze. "Can I help you clean it up?"

The more time I spend with her, the more I wonder if she's running from something or someone. She's always anxious and on high alert, and her classes are online, so she could live anywhere if she needed to hide. Plus, the ring tan line that's now starting to fade. I'm not going to pry though. I have a feeling that would ruin our budding friendship.

"Tell you what," I say with a small smile. "I'm gonna clean this up really quick, and you're gonna go home and pack a bag to come spend the night at Rhodes's house with me. Bring your comfiest pajamas and your favorite blanket, and we'll make it a sleepover. He's not home, so we'll have the place to ourselves."

That gets a quiet laugh out of her. "A sleepover? Aren't those for little kids and like...middle school girls?"

I snicker. "They are, but we're adult women, so who's going to tell us we can't have a sleepover? Rho's pantry is stocked with snacks; his couch feels like a freaking cloud, and we can order takeout and get ice cream. Let's stay up all night, watch movies, and then get a late brunch tomorrow. Seems like the perfect bonding opportunity, if you ask me."

She seems skeptical until a wide smile breaks out over her usually solemn face. "Can we get Chinese food?"

Grinning, I pull up the number on my phone for Lotus. "I'll do you one better."

"I know you wanted to get brunch, but what if we went and got more of those life-changing dumplings instead?"

Lyla's whines have me cackling in the driver's seat of Rhodes's SUV. We had the best night and did everything we talked about, like ordering and eating *way* too much food. "Lyla, we had four orders of dumplings. I'm pretty sure if we have any more, we'll *turn into dumplings*," I say between heavy breaths. "Quit makin' me laugh, or I'm liable to crash the dang car."

She chuckles in the seat beside me as she fiddles with something in her bag.

Glancing at her out of the corner of my eye, I see the flash of an orange cap and feel my eyes widen. "Lyla, do you have allergies?"

A startled look crosses her face until she realizes she's been playing with her epi-pen. "Umm yeah, I do. It's kinda weird though." Her nose scrunches up as the apples of her cheeks turn pink. I wait her out curiously. "I'm allergic to artificial cinnamon. So things like flavored alcohol, gum, candy, certain snacks and foods."

"Wow, that is weird."

Lyla leans across the console to gently smack my arm as I snicker. "Hey!"

It's really nice to see her joking around with me so freely after the glass incident, and I tell her as much.

Her face goes a bit pale as she heaves a deep sigh. "I left a really bad situation back home in Maryland." She shudders. "My family, my friends, my ex. I couldn't trust anyone, so I ran. My job is cash-only, under the table and so is my apartment. Nobody can know I'm here, Wren. Please, don't tell anyone," her voice is barely audible.

The day I met Rhodes comes back to me like no time has passed, bringing a smile to my face as I hold out a pinky. "Did you ever make pinky promises as a kid?"

She nods warily. "Yeah as a *kid*."

I nod back but keep my expression serious. "Excellent. So in our family, we take these very seriously. You make a pinky promise, and you're takin' that promise to the grave. Make sense?"

"That's kinda cute," she says with a small smile.

"I think so too," I grin. "I promise I won't say a word about anything you tell me. I'd never put the safety of my new future bestie at risk." Lyla looks like she's about to cry but luckily I'm turning into the parking lot of my favorite brunch spot so I'm able to distract her.

"Okay," I say, turning off the car. "How do you feel about some classic southern biscuits and gravy and maybe a pastry or two?"

She groans and I smother a laugh. "If you keep feeding me like this, you'll never get rid of me."

Walking into the cozy restaurant is like I've stepped into a time machine in the best way. Rho and I used to make the two-hour drive here nearly every single weekend in college and the owners always fawned all over us. I'm pretty sure we even brought Derrick here a few times when they were still rooming together.

"Is that our little sunny girl?" Ma's exuberant voice rings out through the dining room, and it brings a wide smile to my face. Tara "Ma" and Thaddeus "Pa" Taylor have been running this restaurant for thirty years and always say they plan to die here.

"Ma," I smile brightly.

The boisterous woman pulls me into a hug. "My girl, it sure is good to see you again. I can't believe I missed you last week when you picked up your to-go order! You know that boy of yours still comes in here nearly every Sunday with two very hunky friends. I swear I don't know how anyone keeps those bottomless pits fed," she gripes as she leads us over to a table. "Who's this pretty little thing?" She asks when she notices Lyla behind me.

Lyla has a faraway look in her eyes, so I grip her hand and give it a gentle squeeze, pulling her into the booth next to me. "This is my new friend, Lyla. She doesn't have any family here, so we've adopted her."

Ma smiles, patting Lyla gently on the hand. "Well then, welcome to the family, honey. You ladies want anything to drink?"

"Can I have a vanilla cranberry mimosa, please?" I ask, putting my hands in the prayer position under my chin.

She rolls her eyes. "I guess since you're legal now I can't tell you no." she chuckles. Turning to Lyla, she raises an eyebrow. "Anything for you, darlin'?

Lyla's wide eyes peruse the menu. "I don't really drink..." she whispers.

"That's okay! You can get anything here without alcohol, or if you want to try a drink, you can. Whatever sounds best to you."

"Can I do the prickly pear mimosa but as a lemonade instead?" She asks quietly.

Ma puts her pad away and waves us off with a grin. "'Course you can. I'll be right back out with those. Y'all just give me a holler if you need anything at all."

As soon as she walks away, I turn to ask Lyla what she

wants to eat but a throat clearing next to us startles me. A gaze I didn't expect to see until Monday meets mine, and I suck in a sharp breath.

Derrick's red-rimmed brown eyes peer down at me. "Hey, Wren."

CHAPTER 37
WREN

"DERRICK," I breathe. My voice is barely more than a nervous rasp as I take in the disheveled man standing in front of our booth. His normally perfect blond hair is messy like he's been running his fingers through it, and he's got dark circles under his eyes.

"Can we talk?" He asks hoarsely.

Lyla looks between us with raised eyebrows, and I give her the barest shake of my head. I told her all about Derrick last night, so I'm sure she'll follow my lead.

Clearing my throat, I keep my head high as I address him. "I'm having brunch with a friend right now, so I can't. But didn't we already agree to meet on Monday?"

"We did, but it's really important. I think the sooner we talk, the better. If you have the time, would you *please* consider meeting with me today?"

The sorrow on his face surprises me, but he does seem more alert and healthier than when I last saw him in court. I consider him for a moment and finally nod. "I can meet you at your hotel after I make sure my friend gets home safe."

He nods and leaves us be. Turning to my friend, I let out a long breath. "Shit. I didn't think he could still make me that nervous."

She grips my hand tightly under the table. "Are you sure you should meet him, Wren? Is it even safe to be alone with him?"

I shake my head just as Pa shows up with our drinks. He slides into the booth across from us and squeezes my free hand. "Hey sunny girl. I saw that lad botherin' you lasses. Need me ta beat anyone up fer ya?" He asks gruffly in his thick brogue, flexing his pale arm. Pa is just about six feet tall with an average build, wild red hair, and blue eyes. The man is as Irish as they come.

With a loud laugh, I hug him back. "That's my ex-husband, Derrick. And unfortunately, I need to meet with him to clear the air before we part ways for good. I'll let you know about the beating though."

He chuckles and squeezes my hand one final time as he gets up. "You do that, sunny. You lasses have an idea of what ye want?"

"Can we get two of your biscuit plates and an... actually, your pastries aren't made with artificial cinnamon are they? My friend here has a severe allergy."

Pa scoffs. "There's nothing artificial in this restaurant, sunny. Ma would wreck the gaff."

I grin and turn to see my friend with a touched look on her face. "Apple pie or gingerbread?" I ask Lyla.

Her eyes widen, and she nearly drools. "Yes."

Giggling, I turn back to Pa. "And one each of your apple pie and gingerbread pop tarts, please."

Pa salutes us with a tap of his pen on my nose. "Yer wish is my command, sunny girl."

"Wren," Lyla sniffs, a glassy sheen covering her green eyes. "Thank you for considering my allergy."

I give her a confused look. "That's what friends do, Ly."

"So," she leans in again. "What do you think Derrick wants?"

Sighing, I watch him amble down the sidewalk through the large windows and notice him shoot a sidelong glance at the restaurant as he leaves. "Honestly, Lyla? I think he just wants to clear his name. But either way, I'll find out today and then say goodbye once and for all."

I take out my phone and send two texts, hoping at least one of them answers so I can feel safe and get this meeting with Derrick over and done.

She squeezes my hand softly, offering a reassuring smile. "Everything will work out how it's supposed to, Wren."

I only hope it works out in my favor, and without any drama.

"You sure you wanna do this, Starshine? You don't owe that bastard another minute of your time," my dad murmurs as we sit in my parked car. I'm psyching myself up to meet Derrick at a small coffee shop next to his hotel and thanking my lucky stars Dad could come with me. I know I told Rhodes I would wait for him, but I feel like bringing Dad along is the next best thing.

"I'm sure, Dad. I have questions that only Derrick can answer, and I think I deserve some closure."

He nods as we exit the car, and I'm immensely grateful that he trusts me to make my own decisions. A small bell above the door chimes when we walk in, and even though I'm anxious to meet with my ex, I'm happy he chose this place. It's not too busy, and the colorful, cozy armchairs and picture windows make for a relaxed atmosphere.

Derrick is already perched in a corner chair on his phone, so I grab my iced chocolate chai and a black coffee for my dad before cautiously lowering myself into the seat opposite him. Dad takes a seat close enough to make me feel safe, but far enough away that we have the illusion of privacy. Derrick noticed my arrival at some point because his phone is face down on the table in front of him, and he's nervously playing with the corner of a manila folder I didn't notice he had.

As soon as I'm settled, Derrick clears his throat softly. "Wren, before I say anything else, I owe you an apology," he pauses, grimacing. "Truthfully, I owe you a hell of a lot more than an apology, but for now it's about all I have to give that's worth your time."

I barely manage to hold back my snort of derision. "Sorry ain't worth nothin' when you stooped so low you'd have to look up to see Hell, Derrick. I gave you six years of my life, and what you did was downright cruel."

His eyes fill with tears, shocking me enough that I pause my tirade.

"I checked myself into rehab the day we had our court hearing," he murmurs quietly as he wipes away a tear that slipped free. "I passed out in the holding cell, and when I woke up, I was in the hospital. They found…a lot of drugs in my system."

My eyes fly open and my mind freezes. "Derrick, you were using?"

He sighs wearily, back hunched like he's got the weight of the world on his shoulders. It looks like he's gained a bit of weight since I saw him last, but again, I wonder how I didn't notice something so serious.

"You remember a few years ago when I stumbled home drunk with those scratches on my back?"

I nod, the memory coming back with sharp clarity. "You lied to me, but you left to sleep in the guest room before I could ask any more questions."

Shame tightens his features as he nods. "I did lie. That night was the first time I got high, and I was so out of it I don't even remember sleeping with someone." He pauses, lowering his voice. "It wasn't the first time I'd cheated, just the first time I forgot to try and hide it."

Three months ago that confession would have sent a hot poker straight through my heart, but now, it just makes me sad. I take my hand off of the arm of the chair and tentatively reach out to put it on Derrick's forearm.

His eyes lock on my hand and stay there as he continues speaking. "I was at a party and someone brought coke, and I was so amped up from our win that I didn't even hesitate before trying it."

I sputter. "I'm sorry," I cough out. "Just to clarify, you cheated on me with God knows how many women *before* you were using, correct? I hate to break it to you, Derrick, but you can't use being on drugs as an excuse for something you did before you were even on them."

He nods, cheeks flushing brighter by the minute. "I know, and I'm not trying to excuse any of it. I was fucking terrible to you. But compared to the rest of the team, I'm a shit player, and you were so damn successful and happy, not to mention made more than me. I was jealous and insecure, and before I knew it, I had spiraled. I drank, partied, smoked, and slept my way through as many girls as possible until that didn't work anymore," he trails off, lost in thought.

"That's when I started using—when alcohol stopped giving me confidence, I turned to harder stuff. You leaving was a wake-up call for me. I know I might never earn your forgiveness, especially after all the things I did, but I wanted you to know that nothing I did was ever your fault. It was something I should've talked to you about and dealt with years ago, and I didn't."

Little things I ignored over the years start to click into place. Times he would come home smelling like perfume or I'd find glitter on his clothes. All the forgotten dates and "late practices." And while his confessions don't erase all the hurt he caused; they do finally shed some light on *why*.

He sniffs hard, blowing his nose in a napkin. "Anyway," he waves a hand in the air, "I didn't drag you and your pops out to talk about my sob story. I just couldn't stand the thought of you believing anything I ever did was somehow your fault."

I quirk a small smile. "Thanks. I never really blamed myself for your actions, but I did blame myself for choosing to stay so long. If I'm honest, I probably was at least a tiny bit to blame. I thought I could use you for the emotional security I should have had in myself."

The corners of Derrick's mouth turn down slightly, but in lieu of a reply he grabs the manila folder off the table. "This is the other reason I asked you here. It's proof that I didn't leak the tape, and evidence of who really did. I can't lay all the blame elsewhere though. I knew you wouldn't like it, took the video anyway, *and* I was irresponsible enough to keep it on my phone. I thought you deserved to know who leaked it before the police make the arrest tonight."

Raising an eyebrow, I take the folder and flip it open to look over the report. "Did you hire a private investigator?"

"I did. I was angry with you for leaving, but after the trial, I started my program and got clean. It only took me ten days of misery in detox to realize I was actually angry with myself for turning into my dad. He may not have been an addict, but he did cheat on my mom a lot. And when that video of us was leaked? That made me realize just how stupid I'd been. I put you and your career in a terrible position, and I'll never be able to make that up to you, but hopefully this is a start."

There are dozens of pages of information here on Ella Barnes—texts, phone calls, login information for various fake accounts, including the one that leaked the sex tape and the one that hacked my Instagram. But what shocks me the most is how far back some of this goes.

"She went to college at Ridgeview, too?" I gasp.

"I'm pretty sure you've been her target for longer than any of us knew. And then you showed up in Seattle and took the job she wanted *after* she had already been working with the Sirens for a year. I have a feeling that just made it all worse. You're sweet, brilliant, and so talented, and people like her are envious of that."

A sick feeling turns in my stomach knowing Rhodes is in Seattle right now and that Jamie, Wes, and Asher still have to work with her every day. Worry starts to bog down my mind until something Derrick said earlier catches my attention. "Wait, did you say arrested?"

He smirks but goes to stand after checking his watch. "I did, but would you mind if we walk back to my hotel while I explain? One of the stipulations for my outpatient treatment program is a super-early curfew, and I don't really want to break it the first day I spend outside of my room."

I nod and stop to let my dad know what's going on, and he offers to follow me and Derrick to the hotel but hangs back so we can still talk.

During the short walk to the Indigo, Derrick explains what happened when he took everything to the police, how he hired a PI to clear his name, and once he figured out who did it, how he took everything to the police. He also tells me more about his time in treatment and his plans moving forward.

I follow him to his first floor room but look around in confusion as something dawns on me. "Wait, you said you're suspended from the team, right? How did that happen? And how did that lead to you being in a hotel in Charleston."

He runs a hand through his hair. "I went to management, came clean about my drug problem and told them I was checking myself into rehab. Obviously, I broke the morality clause when I cheated on you, but they also have a seriously strict drug policy. Big Al fought the board on it, but ultimately I was suspended pending contract review. As for why I'm in Charleston? The minute I was free to leave the rehab center I hopped on a plane here. You deserved the truth and mailing all this would have taken too long."

That makes me snort. "We have this crazy thing called email now. It's almost instantaneous."

He just shrugs. "I didn't think of that. So," he asks when we stop in front of his hotel room door. "What's next for the great Wren Reid?"

I laugh lightly, thinking about my answer. "Honestly, I don't really know. I'll look for a job, I guess."

He stares at me with a question in his eyes. "And Rhodes? I saw him at the trial with you." A blush heats my cheeks. Definitely not a topic I thought he'd willingly bring up, but I can't stop my lovesick smile. He smiles in return, shaking his head. "He always was better for you than me. I was so jealous of y'all's relationship for the longest time, but now I think it was just because I knew you would be happier without me. It was just another shortcoming to add to the extensive list."

My guilt must show on my face because he pulls me in for a tentative hug. I barely manage not to stiffen up, my nerves around him triggering my flight response. "I was the one who pushed you away, Wren. I didn't let you in, and that's on me. You deserve every single bit of happiness you can find after all that I put you through, and from the way your face just lit up, I'd guess that's him."

Checking to make sure I consent, he leans in and places a light kiss on my cheek. "You're gonna do great things, Wren. And I'll always cheer you on from afar. But if you're ever back in Seattle…"

A relieved breath leaves my mouth in a huff, and I squeeze his hand once. "Maybe someday I'll come say hi."

CHAPTER 38
RHODES

COMING off of an away series with nothing but wins under our belt is always a rush, and things have been so incredible with Wren this weekend that I can't even be bothered to say no when the guys drag me out to celebrate on Sunday night. We head to a club in downtown Seattle, and I share my location with my girl, so she has it just in case.

Better safe than sorry. This place looks seedy as hell.

Our rented party bus pulls up outside of a suspiciously empty-looking warehouse, making Aidan and I glance at each other warily. Cope may be a wild card, but me and Aid would actually like to survive long enough to see our loved ones again.

Copeland shakes his head and shoves us unceremoniously off the bus. "I've been here a dozen times," he murmurs so only we can hear. "It's perfectly safe. Do you really think I'd risk the wrath of Wren *or* Crew if one of y'all didn't come home?" He shivers in mock fear.

Aidan and I crack up at the obvious distress on his face, but I concede. I trust my friend not to lead me into a murder den. Now that I'm on the sidewalk, I can feel the deep bass vibrating the air around us. Inside the club is worse, and we're greeted with a thick layer of fog that smells of sweat and sex.

I grimace and stop near the entrance so I can shoot one last text to Wren, waving the guys on to the table.

> **ME**
> Wish you were here, Starling. This is so not my scene.

> **STARLING**
> Didn't you just get there? It can't be that bad already.

> **ME**
> Trust me, it is. It smells worse in here than our locker room after a summer of brutal practices.

> **STARLING**
> Oh so you're used to it then lol. Go have some fun, babe. You've earned it.

> **ME**
> Fine, but can we have a different kind of fun when I get home tomorrow?

> **STARLING**
> Be a good boy and let loose tonight, and I promise to do something extra fun when you get home.

> **ME**
> You don't play fair, but I love you anyway, my little tease. 😏

> **STARLING**
> Love you too 🥺 Oh and hey I need to catch you up on the Derrick thing when you get home. Nothing bad, but I saw him today and wanted you to hear it from me.

> **ME**
> Okay, baby. Are you safe?

> **STARLING**
> Perfectly safe and settled at Dad's.
>
> *image*

> **ME**
> Goddamn, Starling. You look better in my number than I do. I expect to see you in that and nothing else on Monday night.

> **STARLING**
> Already on it. 😉

I'm really glad I wore my Wren Luck Charm hoodie tonight because her text about Derrick has my anxiety ready to spiral. I know she's home safe, and she wouldn't see him alone after promising me she'd have backup, So I need to trust that she knew what she was doing. I slide my phone into my jeans pocket with a sigh and glance up, stumbling back in shock to find three smirking men inches from my face.

"Hey!" I shout with a laugh. "What are you guys doing here?"

Jamie, Wes, and Asher look happy to see me, and it feels really good to know they like me, especially given how they felt about Derrick. Wes even pulls me into a hug, surprising the hell out of me.

It's nearly impossible to hear their responses on the dance floor, so we make our way to one of the roped-off booths to a chorus of friendly boos from my teammates. They all know who the guys are in some capacity and like to give me shit for "fraternizing with the enemy." I don't see Copeland or Aidan, so I'm guessing they're dancing or at the bar.

Jamie claps me on the back with a smirk as we sit down. "You're looking a little distracted there, Gray. Got something better to do than celebrate your big wins?"

I flip him off as a goofy smile curves my lips. "Absolutely. I'm ready to get home to my girl."

Even Asher smiles a little at my words, and I feel like I've just won a small victory, but then his expression turns serious. "How is she? We haven't heard much since she went home."

"Honestly, she's great, man. She went back to therapy, found a hobby she can do alone, and she even made a girlfriend." My chest swells with pride for Wren. She's doing so well, and I couldn't be more proud if I tried.

They look impressed but it's Wesley who shoots me a grateful look. "You're really good for her, Rhodes. But don't think that just because we like you means we won't kick your ass if you do anything to hurt her." Vehemence laces his voice, and I'm suddenly really glad Wren has them in her corner.

Just then, Copeland and Aidan find us. "Hey! Long time no see, little brother," Aidan says, punching Wesley on the arm.

Wes glares at his brother and hits him back. "You just saw me last week, you asshole."

Aidan smirks as he and Cope slide in the booth. "I know, I just assume you've done something worth a punch since you left."

Jamie cracks up and agrees, and Wes turns a dirty glare on his friend.

"Hello, boys," a silky voice says from behind us. I turn in my seat to see Ella standing at the end of our both and nearly do a double take at how different she looks from Thursday afternoon when she tried to interview me. Gone is the professional updo and business-casual pantsuit. She's wearing a scrap of material I'm not sure can be called a dress and a pair of heels so high, I'm surprised she can walk.

A quick glance around the table shows I'm not the only one confused by her presence, but Jamie politely greets her anyway. "Hey, Ella. Didn't know you'd be here tonight. I don't think anybody else from the Sirens came but us," he says skeptically.

I texted all three of them with my suspicions about Ella after she came to my room on Thursday night, so I'm interested to see how this plays out.

She bats her eyelashes at him and turns to me, squeezing herself into the five-inch gap between me and the end of the booth. I scoot as far away as I can without putting myself in Jamie's lap. "Um, do you mind?" I ask her when she continues to scoot closer. Asher, who's directly across from me, looks pissed, but that also seems to be his default expression so I'm not sure what he's really thinking.

"I just wanted to apologize," she purrs, placing her hand on my thigh. I push it off as the others make sounds of incredulity. "I didn't realize your girlfriend was *Wren* when I stopped by your room a few days ago." She hisses

Wren's name in disgust, and it has me seconds away from losing my cool.

I give her a terse nod and scoot the barest inch farther away, so she isn't breathing on my neck when she speaks. "She is, so would you mind not sitting so close?"

Ella scoffs, examining her nails. "What?" She asks sarcastically. "Can poor little Princess Wren not handle some competition?"

I'm pretty sure the sound that comes out of my mouth at her words can only be classified as a growl. "First of all, there is no fucking *competition* where my girlfriend is involved." My voice is deadly calm. "Nobody else ever had a chance."

Her lip pokes out in a poor excuse for a pout that makes one of the guys snort. The longer she's in my space, the more irritated I get. I would never hurt a woman, but if she touches me again, I may call security.

Her voice is full of fake sympathy as she pulls out her phone, setting it face up on the table, so we can all see the picture on the screen. "I hate to be the one to tell you this, but your precious girlfriend is really just a pathetic cleat chaser. She tricked Derrick into marriage and then when he finally got sick of her, she ran to her backup—you. And now she's back with him again."

On the screen in front of us is a picture of Wren at a hotel in downtown Charleston. "Okay?" I raise an eyebrow at the woman next to me. "I fail to see the problem here."

She uses a long, red nail to swipe to the next picture, which is vastly more incriminating than the first. I hear Jamie suck in a shocked breath next to me, but I refuse to react. Wren told me she saw Derrick today, and I know she'll fill me in tomorrow when I get home.

Any picture can be taken out of context, but even I have to admit the picture of them hugging in front of an open hotel room door as Derrick kisses her cheek would make her look guilty as hell if I didn't know any better.

A single quirked eyebrow is my only reaction, and Ella's confidence falters. But she recovers quickly, turning her icy glare to the other men in the booth. "Guess you can finally see that your perfect *Baby Reid*," she spits the words out, her tone laced with malice, "really is the leech Derrick always said she was."

My hands shake with anger under the table, and I know if we weren't in public right now, I'd have some choice words for this chick. I have no idea what my face looks like right now, but it must be what Ella wanted to see because she looks thrilled.

Wes startles me out of my pissed-off haze when he slams his hands down on the table hard enough to rattle all the glasses. "The fuck did you just say about my best friend?" he growls. "Wren has more talent, kindness, and class in her little finger than you have in your entire body, Ella."

She gasps and brings one hand to rest on the table, pointing a finger at Wesley. "You can't talk to me like that! I control your careers now." The words are a hiss, and even though she's still only a few inches away, I can barely hear her.

I thought Asher looked pissed off earlier, but right now, he looks downright murderous. Turning cold eyes to their PR manager, we watch Asher's eyes scan her slowly before he sneers. "So that's the real reason behind all of this, is it? You're jealous."

Jamie slides something into my hand under the table without taking his eyes off Ash, and a quick look down shows me his phone is set to record. I glance up in surprise and he winks.

Asher doubles down as Ella sputters and tries to defend herself, but he just talks over her. "You're so painfully jealous of Wren Reid that you somehow got a hold of and leaked her sex tape, stole her job, and now you're trying to steal her boyfriend. You wanna call someone pathetic? Pot meet fucking kettle."

Her mouth starts to gape open, but she catches herself and twists it into a smug smirk. "You have no proof that I leaked that tape."

Ash keeps pushing which makes me think he knows about the phone somehow. "But you did..." he leans in like he's sharing a secret with her and flips his expression to a flirty smile I didn't know he was capable of. It would be convincing if it weren't for the fury in his eyes. "Leak the tape, I mean. Who else would have the audacity and brilliance to do that? How *did* you pull it off?"

Hook, line, and sinker, she falls for his act. Flipping her hair behind her shoulder, she gloats freely about her fucked up long-game plan. "No, you don't even understand how easy it was to earn myself a place in Derrick's bed his first year on the team. From there, getting his iCloud login was a piece of cake. I did have to befriend innocent little Wren after he changed his password since he wouldn't give me a second night, but she's so oblivious she never even noticed me sneaking in and out of their room."

Holy hell. He really didn't do it.

"We thought you girls were friends," Jamie chimes in.

Ella scoffs. "As if. Everybody was so quick to fawn all over the pretty blonde with abandonment issues as if she didn't just follow Derrick here like a desperate little girl."

She waves a hand in the air as if dismissing the idea. "I saw through it from day one. I'm telling you, she's a snake in the grass."

"And the social media posts?" I ask quietly, barely able to mask the rage that colors my words. "The anonymous texts?"

She fucking *preens* at my questions. "All me. Guess sleeping with that hacker nerd finally paid off after all," she says with a breathy laugh.

Huffing out a humorless chuckle, Wes lands the fatal blow to her ego. "Well bless your heart. I honestly can't tell if you thought you could weasel your way into wife and girlfriend status or if you're just a sociopath who has a creepy, unhealthy obsession with a girl who thought was her friend."

Asher speaks over her outraged gasps to twist the knife further. "Well said, Wes. It's pretty sad you had to work *this hard* just to get a fraction of the attention Wren gets just by being herself. Did you ever stop to consider that not acting like a conniving bitch might help you more than this crazy-ass plan you just confessed to?"

Before she has a chance to respond, the biggest man I've ever seen in real life stalks up behind Ella, clamps a meaty paw down on her shoulder and follows it with a silver cuff on her wrist. "Ella Barnes?" He asks in a gravelly voice.

"What the hell are you doing, you psycho?!" She screeches. "Let me go!"

Wild eyes frantically search our booth, but if she thinks anyone here will help her, she's more delusional than I thought.

"Somebody help!" She shouts. "Call 9-1-1!"

The big guy currently hauling her out of her seat

offers a cold smile. "No need. We're already here," he holds a small bifold out to me, showing his credentials. "Detective Wright. You're close with Wren Reid, correct?"

We all nod, but I shake his hand. "Boyfriend," I say, pointing to myself. "Best friends." I hook my thumb in the guy's direction. The detective passes Ella off to the nearest uniformed officer and takes a seat in the booth with us, setting a card on the table.

"I'll be in contact with her soon, but in the meantime, please offer her my sincerest apologies for how her case was handled by this department. We've worked overtime to clean house the last several months. We didn't have enough evidence to arrest Ms. Barnes until this morning when we received credible information from a Mr... Monroe," he says, glancing at his phone.

The guys and I exchange looks of concern and surprise, wondering what Wren's ex gave them. Detective Wright excuses himself, and I let out a sigh of relief.

Ella's arrest lifts a weight off my chest. For better or worse, I'll make sure nobody hurts my girl again.

CHAPTER 39
RHODES

"YOU ARE in so much trouble, Starling," I whisper into Wren's ear as I wrap her in my arms. We're at my parents' house for a family barbecue to celebrate the Raptor's win this morning, and my little tease is in one of my jerseys and shorts that make her legs look ten miles long.

It's been a little over a month since Ella was arrested, and Wren is so much lighter now that we know who was behind all of the virtual attacks, especially after Detective Wright contacted her to apologize for the department's negligence. She still goes to therapy every week and keeps her stuff at Archie's, though we both sleep at our house most nights. I think it makes her feel better to say she's "living" with her dad for now. She also nailed her interview with the Raptors just like we expected, and her contract should be here any day now.

She finally had a chance to fill us in about her conversation with Derrick, and to say we were stunned is an understatement. I don't think I'll ever forgive him for the things he did to her, but Wren has always had a bigger heart than me, and I know she doesn't hold it against him because of everything he was going through.

We also finally met Archie's girlfriend, the infamous Caroline, last weekend, and the women hit it off right away. I know Wren was worried about their dynamic, but I honestly think when Caroline moves in with Archie next month, she and Wren will be spending a lot of time together.

"Mmm," she purrs, rubbing her tight ass against my half-hard cock. "You gonna punish me later, Roly-Coly?"

Gripping her hips firmly, I move her away from my pelvis before things get awkward in front of the family. "Starling," I tug slightly on one of her cute braids, which earns me a heated look. "Behave, and I'll reward you in the shower when we get home." I murmur the words against her neck and nip under her ear.

"Hey there, lovebirds! No necking in the kitchen. That's how we start fires." My dad's voice interrupts our moment when he and Walter step into the room, both holding plates piled precariously high with different cuts of meat. I snicker hearing him use that phrase. Archie used to say that when we were in college and fucking around in his kitchen. Nine times out of ten we were trashed and foraging for drunk snacks, but I digress.

Dominic Gray never met a grill he couldn't master, and Walt loves to hang out and micromanage him while he cooks. Even though we've turned this week's family barbecue into a celebration, it doesn't feel much different than usual. Now that Walter doesn't have any puppies to take care of, he joins us a few times a month. I'm pretty sure it's just so he can see Finn and Wren, but we all enjoy the time with him, nonetheless.

Finnegan comes trotting in closely followed by my

mom and Archie, and I drop to my knees to cuddle my baby. Although at just shy of six months old and almost sixty pounds, calling him a baby is laughable. The dude is huge. Wren still lets him sleep on her lap, and I love watching them snuggle together.

"Wren, honey, something was just delivered for you," mom says as she hands over a large, certified envelope. I keep myself busy playing with Finn so that my smile doesn't give anything away.

When I hear her whisper "Oh my God." I figure it's safe to stand. She squeals, dropping the papers onto the island as she does a little happy dance that involves a lot of bouncing. I bite my fist to hold back a groan.

For the love of God do not get hard in front of your parents.

I'm so busy distracting my thoughts that I miss Wren saying my name until my dad lightly smacks me upside the head. "Sorry, what?" I ask with a blush.

She smiles affectionately, used to my daydreaming. "Did you know about the changes they made?" She asks, thrusting the contract into my face.

I smirk and shrug as I read over the details laid out in the document. The pay has me raising an eyebrow, but I guess I shouldn't be surprised. It's a little more than they originally discussed, which makes me wonder what exactly happened during her interview.

"You've earned it, baby. I'm so proud of you!" I give her a sloppy kiss on the cheek, and she screeches with laughter.

Archie's reading over the contract now too, and he lets out a low whistle. "So now you get to live by your family, follow your boyfriend around all season, *and* get paid to make him look good? You got yourself a sweet deal there, kiddo." He chuckles and continues to tease his daughter, but the warmth in his eyes is impossible to miss.

He pulls me aside while Wren chats with my parents and hugs me hard, patting my back a few times. His voice is choked when he finally speaks. "Thank you for helping my Starshine get her shine back, Rhodes. I couldn't imagine anyone better for our girl than you. Thank you for giving Wren the family she needs."

My heart swells with his whispered words. "You did that, Arch. Wren is who she is today because you raised her so well. Sure, her family is bigger now, but she never *needed* anyone but you. If we ever have kids one day, I hope to be half the father to them as you are to her."

Mom's voice startles us when she appears next to us with tears in her eyes. "We're so lucky to have met you and your sweet girl, Archie. Thank *you* for always treating my boy like your own."

I pull away from Archie and laugh as I wave them off. "Okay, enough sappy shit. We have a new job to celebrate!"

The rest of the night is spent talking logistics about who will watch Finn when we're gone, which really means Wren and I just listened to all the parents argue about who got him during which games, and watching Wren show off all her art from Color Me Crazy. After making sure Finn can stay with my parents, we say our goodbyes and hightail it to my SUV, laughing like a pair of trouble-making kids.

It's time to take my girl home.

"You're such a little tease, Starling. Do you get off on making me nearly embarrass myself in public?" I groan once we make it into the house. Our hands are everywhere, touching whatever skin we can reach in a desperate race to get the other naked first.

I drop to my knees to pull off her shorts and lace thong, stopping to place open-mouthed kisses on each of her hips. I slide my hands up her torso and drag my jersey up, nearly growling when I see she's braless. Dragging my tongue over her nipple, I suck it into my mouth and give it a gentle nip.

Her gasp spurs me on as I move to the other side, but she digs her fingers into my hair and pulls me up before I can take it into my mouth. Wren kisses me intensely, massaging my tongue with hers and forcing a moan out of me as the jersey falls from my hands to cover her again. My cock has been like granite since we left dinner, and I'm dying to get inside my girl.

I pull back and slap her ass with a smirk as I lead her up the stairs. "I'm pretty sure I promised you a punishment, baby. Go bend over the bed for me."

She pouts but does as I say, and it sends a little thrill up my spine. We still experiment and try new things together all the time, but there's something about this strong, independent woman letting me take control that turns me on more than anything else.

I follow her to the bedroom, only to stop short in the doorway with a growl when I see her bent over, tying her hair up into a messy bun. Her dripping pussy peeks out just beneath the hem of my blue jersey. "Starling, are you trying to kill me?"

She stands up with a breathy giggle and walks towards the bed, swinging her hips a little more than necessary, intentionally driving me crazy. I prowl her way and bend her back into a deep kiss. Circling a gentle hand around her neck, I break the kiss and turn her so her back is pressed to my chest.

Keeping my hands soft, I massage her shoulders to working out the knots. Her quiet sighs of pleasure do nothing to lessen the erection pressed against her lower back. We're only separated by two thin layers of clothing, but it's two too many.

Wren grinds her ass back against me again, so I reach down and smack the outside of her thigh. "You're a little needy today, aren't you, baby?

She moans quietly in response, and I chuckle darkly. Placing a line of kisses down her throat, I move us forward until her chest is pressed against the wall. Landing another slap against her thigh, I force her hips back into mine. A quiet whimper falls from her lips as I cup her sex, just barely pressing the heel of my palm against her clit.

"Have I told you lately how much I love your sweet pussy?"

She turns so her cheek rests against the wall and arches a sassy eyebrow. "This morning over coffee when I came down in nothing but your shirt."

That makes me laugh. "Good point," I say with a nod. Lowering my mouth to her ear I whisper, "Now be a good girl and go put your hands on the bed so I can punish your pretty ass."

I step back so she can move, but Wren takes my

instructions one step farther and drops so her shoulders touch the bed. I take the opportunity to step back and enjoy the view of my dream girl bent over for me, my number plastered to her back, her needy pussy dripping down her thighs *for me*.

I step forward and glide my hand over her smooth ass cheek. Without warning, I bring my hand down in a hard smack that makes her whimper. Her cries and pleas for more spur me on and I land five more on each cheek in quick succession.

"Rhodes," she begs.

That one breathless word is my undoing. I flip Wren over and move her to the head of the bed as I push my boxer briefs off. "I can't think straight when you say my name like that, Starling—all breathless and sexy and begging to be fucked. You know I can't resist you when you sound like that."

The little brat winks and pulls my hips forward so the tip of my cock brushes her wet heat. "I know."

Slowly sheathing myself inside of her, I curse. It doesn't matter how many times we do this; every time feels like the first time all over again.

Small fingers run through my hair and tug, making me speed up my thrusts. "Oh, fuck!" Wren cries out. I pull out, and she whines, but I slap her ass again and turn her over so she's on her knees. I take a second to admire the handprints from her punishment before plunging back in and angling my hips so the tip of my cock drags along her sweet spot with every pump.

Her cries echo around the room as she clamps down on me, and the noises send fire licking down my spine. With my tattooed hand wrapped around her throat, I haul her upright. Thrusting faster, I bring one hand down to circle her clit, and she's so wet my finger nearly slips off.

"You gonna be a good girl come for me, baby?"

A harsh cry escapes her as she nods. "Don't stop!"

"I couldn't if I tried, Starling, but I need you to get there. Come for me now," I growl. I'm so close to an orgasm, but I need her to get there first, so I drop my hand from her throat and pinch her nipple while still rubbing her clit. She screams out her release, dragging me with her into ecstasy. I thrust one, two, three more times and empty myself as far inside her as I can with a hoarse shout.

Wren collapses beneath me as I sit back on my heels to catch my breath, and I can barely see the wide smile that bunches her flushed cheeks. I tilt her face to the side and kiss her swollen lips, resting my forehead against her cheek. That sweet apple and honey scent I know and love wraps around me. "Let me grab a washcloth and clean us up."

Wren is almost asleep by the time I get back from the bathroom. She startles a bit when I swipe the warm cloth between her legs. Tossing it into the laundry, I slide us under the covers and wrap my girl in my arms, our foreheads pressed together on one pillow.

I think she's asleep until her murmured voice breaks the silence around us. "I know we've been focused on me pretty much the entire last few months, and I'm so grateful you've given me the space to grieve and grow and heal. But how are *you* feeling after everything that's happened?"

Sighing, I kiss the top of her head as love for this woman washes over me in a wave. "Like I'm finally home."

EPILOGUE

Rhodes
Six Months Later

"SO WHEN ARE you gonna marry that sweet girl of yours, boy? It's been a decade, quit draggin' your damned feet." Walter's gruff voice is the first thing I hear when I let Finn out of the SUV to explore Mr. Hendrick's farm.

Snickering, I level him with an amused look. "As soon as I find the perfect ring. I already have it planned out. She only goes to therapy once a month now, and all the dust has settled from earlier this year. I think it's about time I locked her down for good."

He nods but stays silent while we watch Finn chase ducks down by the pond. Wren and I try to bring Finn out to see Walter and the farm at least once a month, but she had a huge meeting today with the owner of the Raptors, so I decided to come alone.

"You could always knock her up," he murmurs, making me choke on my own laughter.

"Walt!"

He chuckles with a shrug. "Didn't work for me, obviously. But I sure did have fun tryin'," the old man says with a smirk.

I snort and shake my head. "Wren doesn't want biological kids. And honestly, I don't think I do either," I say quietly. I'm sure he won't judge us, but knowing he and Elizabeth couldn't have kids of their own might be a sore spot when he hears that news. But apparently, I underestimated him because he agrees with me.

"Ain't nothin' wrong with that. Y'all just enjoy your time together while you can. Lord knows we don't get enough of it." His eyes gloss over for a minute, but he quickly shakes it off with a smile. "Here, this is for you."

He hands me a small blue box and motions for me to open it. My lips part in shock when I do. Nestled inside is a stunning ring that *screams* Wren. "It's a two-point-five carat emerald cut center stone with a tapered baguette stone on either side. This was the ring I gave to my Lizzie nearly forty years ago," Walter says quietly. "Spent damn near every penny I had on it just praying she'd say yes. Little did I know she'd kick me to the couch for a week for spendin' so much money on a ring."

I laugh but my heart races so fast I'm worried I might actually have a heart attack. He grabs my shoulders with weathered hands, bringing my attention back to him. "Lizzie and I didn't have any kids, Rhodes. You've always humored me with visits, especially since she passed on, but the last eight months of seeing y'all and the family all the time has made me feel less lonely. And that's priceless to me."

His voice shakes the more he talks about Lizzie, but he charges on. "Take her ring and give it a new love to represent. Wren reminds me so much of my wife. I can't think of another person that deserves it more."

I carefully close the ring box and tuck it into my pocket. "I don't know that I'll ever be able to thank you enough for this, Walt. Wren adores you and I know this will mean so much more to her than anything I could buy."

He pats me on the back. "Just promise me you'll cherish every day you get to spend with her."

Taking a deep breath, I pull him in for a hard hug. "You have my word."

Wren

"Are we there yet?" I whine.

Rhodes snorts, lacing our fingers together on the center console. "We've been in the car for two minutes, Starling."

I huff out a breath and pout for good measure. "The longest two minutes of my *life*. You blindfolded me, babe. You could be leading me to my death for all I know."

The anticipation is killing me. Rhodes had a post-season workout this morning at the stadium after a well-earned two weeks off. The Raptors lost in the second round of the playoffs this year, so Benny gave them all some mandatory rest days before workouts started up again.

Finn is in the backseat because his giant one-hundred-and-fifteen-pound butt is officially too big to be a lap dog, but that sure as heck doesn't stop me from trying to hold him whenever we cuddle.

Only a few short minutes later, Rhodes puts the SUV in park and silently guides me across what feels like gravel, the only sound I can make out is Finn's huge paws crunching along behind us.

He specifically asked me to wear the sweatshirt he had made for me, so I wore that with shorts and white high-top sneakers since it's still pretty warm during late October in South Carolina.

Wherever we are, I can tell it's outside because the breeze feels amazing as it blows across the slight sunburn on the bridge of my nose. I've taken up running over the last several months to keep in shape when we travel—which is a lot. I love it, but last week I forgot sunscreen

EPILOGUE CONT.

and got a bright red burn over my cheeks and nose. Since then it's just turned into more freckles for Rho to kiss.

I don't even realize my attention has strayed until Rhodes pulls me to a stop and kisses me senseless with my eyes still covered. He kisses me every day, but there's a reverence in this one that isn't usually there. When he backs away, there's a rustling sound and then in a hushed tone, he tells me to pull off the blindfold.

The second my eyes adjust to the bright sun, I gasp, and my hands fly up to cover my mouth. "Rho..."

His eyes are shiny with unshed tears as he kneels in front of me, a little blue box held in his outstretched hand. "I fell in love with you hard and fast the day we met. You looked like an angel come to earth, and I was so desperate to have you in my life that even having you as a friend felt like more than I deserved."

I sniffle, dangerously close to crying myself. I glance around and see we're standing on home plate at Rebel Park and Finn is laying off to the side, chewing on a baseball.

"I had no idea back then that you would become my everything, but I wouldn't do a single thing differently. Over the last nine years you've been my best friend, my soulmate, my home. Hell, you're the very reason I remember to *breathe* when life becomes too much."

With a visible breath, he opens the box and reveals my dream ring. Tears spring to my eyes, his emotion triggering mine.

"I don't know how I got lucky enough for you to be all of those, but right now I'd like to ask you to be one more thing for me. Wren Andromeda Reid, will you be my wife?"

I don't even have to think about my answer, shouting

an enthusiastic "Yes!" I jump into his outstretched arms, knocking us to the dirt. We're both laughing and crying as Rhodes takes multiple tries to get the ring on my finger with shaky hands.

The field around us erupts in chaos as all of our family and friends rush us from the dugouts, showering us with congratulations and love.

I spent so many years desperate for a place to belong, but as I look around and see everyone we love here to witness this moment that's been years in the making, I realize I had one all along. It took me a long time, but I know now.

I'm finally home.

The End

ACKNOWLEDGMENTS

This book is arguably the one that means the most to me, and I have so many people I want to thank for helping me breathe life into this story and these characters.

First and foremost, my Alpha team. Kennedy, Sierra, Devin, Amber, Sarah, Vilija, and Kayla, thank you for keeping me sane and working through logistics with me. I adore you all.

To my editors, Sara and Laura, thank you for kicking my ass with rewrites and helping me give this story the attention to detail it deserved. I can honestly say this book wouldn't be half as good as it is without the two of you.

I want to thank my family, for supporting me on my author journey and reading my books even when I beg them not to. It makes our check-in calls so much more fun.

Sabrina, my soulmate. I love you endlessly. Thank you for supporting my book baby while you cooked an *actual* baby. (And thank you S & S, for being so dang cute and brightening my screen with your perfect little faces.)

My PS fam, for supporting me and every book I write unconditionally. I wouldn't have half my readers if it weren't for y'all.

And last but not least, my readers. Thank you for taking a chance on Rhodes and Wren, I hope you loved them as much as I do.

CHARACTER GUIDE

Main Characters:
Rhodes Gray - #11, First Baseman for the Charleston Raptors, hopelessly obsessed with Wren Reid
Wren Reid - Former PR for the Seattle Sirens, Current head of PR for the Charleston Raptors, madly in love with Rhodes Gray

Charleston Crew:
Archie Reid - Wren's dad, Professor of Astronomy at Ridgeview University
Kaci Gray - Rhodes's Mom, Lawyer
Dominic Gray - Rhodes's Dad, Lawyer
Aidan Black - #23, Catcher for the Charleston Raptors, Wesley's older brother
Crew Black - Aidan's son
Copeland Hawthorne - #13, Pitcher for the Charleston Raptors
Lyla Taylor - Wren's friend

CHARACTER GUIDE

Seattle Crew:

Wesley Black - #32, Catcher for the Seattle Sirens, Wren's friend

Jamison Reid - #9, Pitcher for the Seattle Sirens, Wren's friend

Asher Linwood - #2, Shortstop for the Seattle Sirens, Wren's friend

Jeremy Cross - General Manager for the Seattle Sirens

Derrick Monroe - Wren's ex-husband, former Third Baseman for the Seattle Sirens

ABOUT THE AUTHOR

Holly Crawford is a self-published author who primarily writes sports romance where the pants are tight and the men are head over heels for their partners. She lives in Washington state with her husband, son, dog, and cats.

She started writing in 2023 and made the leap into publishing not long after. When Holly isn't writing, she's answering emails at her day job and watching whatever movie her ADHD is hyper-fixated on that week.

Finally Home is her second published book, with many more to come.

Join Holly's reader group

Printed in Great Britain
by Amazon